WEDDING BRIDE AND DOOM

WEDDING BRIDE AND DOOM

A WEDDING PLANNER MYSTERY

MARY KARNES

LEVEL BEST BOOKS

First published by Level Best Books 2023

Author Photo Credit: Sara McIngvale

First edition

ISBN: 978-1-68512-403-8

Cover art by Level Best Designs

This book was professionally typeset on Reedsy.
Find out more at reedsy.com

To my immediate family, too many to name individually...lucky me.

Praise for Wedding Bride and Doom

"Witty and entertaining— and a terrific mystery. With style and skill and a true ear for dialogue, Karnes captures the constant juggling of a smart and relatable single mom struggling to regain her power in a world where weddings, high school romances, dark secrets, and murder combine to threaten all she holds dear. A page-turner of a story, and a wonderful debut!"—Hank Phillippi Ryan, *USA Today* bestselling author of *The House Guest*

Chapter One

Wedding Tips by Kate: Do the Math. Nail down the wedding budget and guest list ASAP because they affect the rest of your planning.

"Planning a wedding is a simple process," said no bride ever. I knew this to be true. I'd helped many plan their "special day," from the oddest, a couple who wanted a *Star Trek-themed* wedding...yes, the ring bearer was Mr. Spock...to my favorite, a wedding at the bride's parents' country farm. No matter how simple or extravagant, there was always the 180-degree event that turned my sweet bride into bridezilla. My newest client would likely be no exception.

"Kate, do you think I should put 'Black Tie Mandatory' on the invitations? It's so, so, so important to me." Marcy Simpson was Hartford's debutant of the year. She was marrying the son of Rolf Wilson, uber-wealthy landowner of the largest tobacco farm in southern New England.

I was negotiating a contract to help plan the 'over-the-top wedding' Marcy's family expected. The excitement was wearing off, and thc cold reality was hitting that this was a make-or-break wedding for me. I had a very successful business in Orange County, California, but I left it lock, stock, and barrel when my marriage broke up a year ago. Here, in New England, I was trading on my good name and reputation from California, but I had to prove myself. Ellis, my daughter, and I had moved back home after the divorce. Well, back to *my* home. Having friends and family close by made the transition easier, but I constantly worried about the health of my business. It had been a fun hobby when I was married, but now I depended on it to support Ellis and myself. Starting over wasn't easy.

This was my highest-profile wedding in my new geography so far, with an outrageous budget and a guest list of over three hundred.

I smiled at the petite, honey-blond Marcy and attempted to exude an air of calm and competency. I had to set my nerves aside and be a professional. *You can do this, Kate.* Did I believe that?

We were lunching at my favorite seafood restaurant, Harry's Fish, in my charming village of Eastbury, Connecticut. The restaurant was cozy, and a fire blazed in the building's 1700 hearth. It had formally been the renovated home's heat source and cooking place, the true heart of the home, where the family gathered to share a meal, warm themselves from the harsh New England winter, and discuss their day. It was used for much the same purpose as a restaurant now. The main dining room was furnished with excellent reproductions of 1700 furnishings—broad, long tables and sturdy chairs. The floor's finish was scarred, the polish shiny with use.

I signaled to our server. Booking this wedding was cause for celebration, and I could think of no better way to do so than order Harry's signature double chocolate cake. I had already enjoyed the special of the day, a yummy squash-filled ravioli with a delicate cream sauce, and indulged in Harry's plentiful breadbasket and sage butter.

"Will that be one or two slices?" Our server politely asked.

"Two," I said.

"One," Marcy said at exactly the same moment.

We both giggled. She smiled sweetly. I felt tender toward Marcy. And, by the way, her restraint, and my lack thereof, was perhaps the reason for the differences in our figures. I was still trying to lose the last ten pounds I gained after a bike accident right before my divorce. Well, it was more than a small accident. I had broken my tibia and had endured months of physical therapy. I was still self-conscious about wearing dresses and skirts; I hated the scar on my leg. But right now, I wasn't going to worry about my weight *or* my scar. I was going to enjoy the cake.

"Smile!"

As I savored the last bite of chocolate cake, my mind was already whirling with selecting the best vendors for Marcy's wedding. A flash popped in my face.

"Smile!" Marcy leaned into me again, snapping a photo of us with her iPhone.

I felt certain the first pic had me wrapping my mouth around my chocolate-covered fork, eyes closed in ecstasy. I didn't have a chance to "smile." I hoped the second photo turned out better.

"Here," she held up the phone for me to look at her handiwork.

I tried not to grimace as I looked at the photo of me, in portrait mode no less. I saw a middle-aged woman with shiny brown hair, thanks to my standing six-week appointment with Lydia at the Beauty Barn. My blue eyes were my favorite feature, or was it my smile? My ex, Grant, had always said it was my smile, and his words had pleased me. Yep, the photo wasn't a great one. I needed to invest in some new business clothes.

"I plan to document my wedding planning process with pictures and get one of those companies to make a photo book out of it," Marcy said. Brilliant idea. I'd pass that on to other brides, but I was going to be prepared next time and smile. Never too early to start.

"Hey, Marcy. Will you take another?" If anyone understood the value of photo approval, it had to be Marcy. This time I smiled as she clicked away.

"I want those cute as a button. Waterford Crystal Christmas ornaments as the guest favors," Marcy gushed. "Do you think they should be all the same, or should we have some sort of theme, like 'The Twelve Days of Christmas?' And we'll have them engraved with our wedding date, of course."

I tried not to cringe. Marcy surprised me. I thought she'd exercise better restraint with flashing her family's wealth. No one wanted to hang someone else's wedding ornament on their Christmas tree, even if it *was* Waterford. Brides who went down this path were trying to impress. I didn't think that was Marcy's or her family's style. I'd have to squelch this idea and fast. Part of my duty of being a wedding planner was to encourage discerning taste. Okay, the taste was mine, but some things were black and white.

"And my sorority sister Kaleen had the most *gorgeous* artificial flower trees...all white! I want that, but in my wedding colors, rose and gold,"

Marcy continued.

Obviously, this hadn't been run by her mother. I highly doubted the Grand Dame Simpson would give the green light to such a sight. Yikes!

Marcy wanted to hold her wedding at the Wadsworth Mansion in Middletown, a family tradition. As well as boasting breathtaking gardens, perfect for formal photos, the venue allowed the bride to choose her own caterer. I had the perfect one in mind, but I needed to book her before she was grabbed up by another aggressive bride and planner.

Now, the part I hated: the contract signing. I don't know why it made me so uncomfortable. I'd flagged all the spots Marcy was supposed to sign and initial my contract. I handed Marcy the flagged contract. There was an awkward moment when I handed her a pen.

She took both, a slight tremor in her hand. Huh…this was new. "I thought my mom was going to sign."

That was fine with me. Her mom would be paying the bills anyway.

"No worries. Would you like to take it home for your mom to sign, and I can get it tomorrow when we tour the reception venue?"

"Oh, Kate, I might as well be open about it. I'm severely dyslexic, and I have to take a bit to read anything over carefully." She looked so embarrassed.

I was surprised, but we all had some issue, right?

"Oh, gosh, Marcy. Don't give it another thought. You can take the contract home and go over it, and either you or your mom can sign." I placed my hand over hers. "It's ok."

She took a breath and exhaled slowly. "Thanks, Kate. It's worse when I try to hide it and rush." She still wasn't meeting my gaze. Her eyes filled with tears. "It was hard growing up. Kids weren't always nice. And reading aloud in the classroom, you know, how everyone takes a turn. I thought I'd die. People look at me, realize who my family is, and think my life is perfect. If they only knew. Thank goodness I was a math whiz. At least I didn't feel completely stupid."

This was one of the few times I didn't know what to say. So, I just squeezed her hand a little tighter.

It was time to wrap things up. I was ready to pay the bill and get to my next appointment when Marcy abruptly stunned me again.

"Kate, I'm so excited about this wedding and your role in it. But there's something that's putting a damper on everything."

Oh, boy, here we go. I knew this was too good to be true. Now the silliness began. But Marcy's next words surprised me.

"There's a family ring that has been missing since my grandmother's day. The firstborn daughter of each new generation inherits it on her wedding day, and I so want to wear that ring."

Whaaaat? Did I hear correctly? Marcy wanted me to find a ring that had been missing for seventy-five-plus years? I didn't respond at first. I had to be delicate about this. I couldn't say, "Are you crazy? What makes you think I can find a ring that has been lost since perhaps World War II? I'm a wedding planner, not a private investigator!" I needed to keep this particular bride happy, so she'd refer me to all her society friends. It was vital to my fledgling business's survival.

So, instead of saying what I wanted to, I said, "Wow, Marcy! That's quite a story. But what makes you think I can find the ring when your family hasn't been able to for so many years?"

Marcy quirked a brow at me. I really liked that expression and wished I could replicate it. "Well, because you can do anything, Kate Ludlow. Everyone knows that. I know you're new to the business here, but I read all your California reviews. You don't really think my mom would hire just anyone for my wedding, do you? And you do realize she chose you over Ivy Jackman." She smiled rather ruefully again.

Oh, yes, the dreaded Ivy Jackman, my biggest and nastiest competitor. So, wow, just wow. As ridiculous as it sounded, I had to give this ring hunt a shot. Planned or not, Marcy knew how to sweet-talk me into agreement, or should I say threaten me, and I was in no position to say no.

"I'm flattered, Marcy," and I was. "I'll give it a shot. Maybe your mom has a photo of the ring and additional details?"

"We have a couple photos. I'll ask Mom about them."

I smiled, trying not to telegraph my anxiety at this daunting task.

Time to continue my day, so I quickly said goodbye to Marcy, this time with a warm hug. We confirmed our meeting time the next morning to go see the Wadsworth Mansion.

Chapter Two

When it comes to your wedding pictures, two perspectives are better than one. Consider a second photographer...one for you and one for your fiancé.

The next morning, I met with Marcy and the formidable mother of the bride, Joyce Simpson, at the Wadsworth Mansion in Middletown. Joyce was an older version of her daughter: petite, fine-boned, and impeccably dressed. This morning she sported a gray-blue St. John knit suit with nude heels. Her silver-blond hair was fashioned in a neat French twist, nary a hair out of place.

The Wadsworth was closed in the mornings, but, of course, an exception was made for the Simpson family.

The mansion's website provided some history of the site. *"In 1900, three years after his marriage to Katharine Fearing Hubbard, Colonel Clarence S. Wadsworth began preparing plans for the site of their future country summer residence, 'Long Hill,' in the rolling hills of western Middletown. An authority on the emerging science of forestry and conservation, Colonel Wadsworth had a concern for the environment far ahead of his time. Working with the nationally renowned landscape architectural firm, the Olmsted Brothers, 500 acres of Long Hill were designed in the tradition of a working landscape. They created an estate that evolved from the formal and classical near the Mansion to varied, well-managed forests and pastures. The New York architecture firm of Hoppin and Koen designed a domain on par with the estates of Lenox, Massachusetts, and the 'cottages' of Newport, Rhode Island. For over 30 years, Long Hill was the center of ceremonial life for the Wadsworth and Hubbard families. In 1934, a thousand guests, escorted by the Governor's Foot Guard, celebrated the wedding of the Wadsworths' son Julius and his wife, Cleome, at Long Hill."*

It was a beautiful stately town-owned building that was available for events. The grounds boasted gorgeous flowers and a romantic wooded area. Even if there was a light rain, common in New England, the woods were so heavy, they acted as a natural umbrella. Perfect for wedding photos. I'd viewed several wedding pictures from the Wadsworth on photographers' Instagram pages, and they all had a fairy-tale vibe; the gardens were that lush. Two-hundred-year-old trees gave that effect.

We walked in and were greeted by the lovely caretaker Dina.

She came and shook our hands, her matronly appearance oozing warmth. She absolutely wanted to be on the right side of Joyce Simpson. "Welcome, ladies. I'm so glad you've decided to choose us for your venue. You won't be disappointed. Come on into my office, and we'll sign the paperwork."

"I'd like to look around some first, if you don't mind." Joyce gave Dina the stink-eye, as if she should have anticipated this request.

Dina sucked in her breath; pink tinged her cheeks. "Of course! Would you like a cup of tea first? I know there are some things in the kitchen." Dina was scrambling now.

Joyce was silent, letting the fact that refreshments had *not* been offered before the pedestrian task of money changing hands was suggested. Yikes. Heaven help me if she ever came to *my* office.

"I think not now." Joyce proceeded into ballroom A.

In my opinion, the Wadsworth was perfect, well, almost. I loved the warm environment created because there wasn't just one large ballroom but two, with a large foyer area in between. This was also a drawback, as one had to work hard at making the party inclusive. In warm weather, the bride could make use of the massive brick-covered patio that doubled as a dance floor. This helped unite the two rooms. Smaller weddings would use just one of the formal areas, but Marcy's wedding would need every bit of spare space. I was still nervous that we had picked a venue that might not meet our needs, but Marcy had her heart set on the Wadsworth Mansion, and Marcy got what Marcy wanted.

Joyce walked straight to a framed black-and-white photograph prominently hanging on the far wall. We followed like chastised puppy dogs. I could tell Dina was afraid to make another faux pas.

"There she is, Marcy." Joyce's Botoxed face broke into an almost smile.

We were looking at a photograph of a remarkably beautiful woman. Joyce favored her, but her resemblance to Marcy was uncanny. She had the same straight short nose, high cheekbones, big eyes, and glossy blond hair. If she hadn't been dressed in '30s-era clothing, I'd have thought it was Marcy.

"She's beautiful," Marcy whispered.

"Yes, Marcy, one of our special brides, your grandmother." Dina seemed to still be trying to redeem herself. "While she was married at home in a small ceremony, an elderly Colonel Wadsworth and his wife, Katherine, hosted a ball in her honor a couple of weeks later. It was the social event of the year." Dina beamed, gesturing with her right hand toward the photo, much like a game show host.

"My grandmother, Eveline," Marcy said reverently, by way of introduction, not taking her gaze off the beautiful woman. "She's the main reason I want to hold my wedding here. I never met her, but I feel like I can share my special day with her in a small way." Marcy's eyes filled.

We were all quiet for a moment, soaking in the purity of Eveline's beauty.

"Mama!" Marcy broke the spell. "Look! Grandma Ev doesn't have the ring on. I thought you said she lost it around twenty years into her marriage. Wouldn't you think she'd have it on for her wedding portrait?"

While I wouldn't call this photo a *wedding portrait*—she wasn't wearing what looked to be a wedding dress or a veil, but it was obviously a formal portrait commemorating her marriage. So, I'd have to agree with Marcy. I'd think Eveline would have worn the family bridal ring for this photo.

Joyce's mouth dropped open and then shut. "Well, I wouldn't know about that." She turned on her heel and made her way to Dina's office.

That was...weird but, then again, this was Joyce Simpson we were talking about, and it seemed now was the appropriate time to sign that paperwork and draft a check for the deposit.

Joyce's eagerness to sign the venue contract reminded me of my own.

We all followed her into the office.

"Mrs. Simpson," Joyce had still not invited me to call her Joyce, "did you happen to bring my contract today? Marcy said you wished to look it over."

Joyce raised her head from looking over the Wadsworth contract. She looked honestly chagrinned. "Oh, Kate. I do apologize. I'll bring it to the dress fitting tomorrow. You will be there, correct?" She had the same eyebrow quirk as her daughter.

"Of course," I smiled demurely.

And then, with a few strokes of Joyce's pen—she was a lefty—and a $5,000 deposit, we had our venue.

Chapter Three

Would you consider e-invitations?

After the Wadsworth and a stop at the bakery, I headed back to Main Street and parked in front of my favorite flower shop, The Flower Basket. I wanted to send flowers to Marcy and Joyce as a "thank you for your business" gift.

The day was beautiful. Historically, April in New England was either cold, or it was warm. That was to say, there was no guessing what April in New England would feel like. Most of the trees had budded early, their delicate, light-green leaves sending springtime hope to Eastbury residents. The tulips planted around the town green were in full bloom. I loved them and had missed their brilliant colors when I lived in California.

I was persnickety about the flowers I sent to clients. I wanted to select the blooms I wished to be delivered to the Simpsons, and, unfortunately, that meant a visit with Lori-Sue. Lori-Sue and I had history. And while she wasn't my favorite person, no one could dispute her creativity. Given our *history*, old and recent, I came bearing gifts, a coffee in each hand and a couple of jelly-filled donuts. Hopefully, this peace offering would smooth over our little tiff yesterday. Our latest dust-up had occurred when I had offered to bring to her shop the wooden rounds my most recent bride had rented from Lori-Sue to use as centerpieces. In my mind, why should Lori-Sue make the trip out to the venue to collect the centerpieces after the wedding when I was there and could return them for her post-wedding? But Lori-Sue didn't like how I stored them in the cartons she had provided. Some nasty texts were exchanged. She was being a bit of a brat, and we both knew it; we had bad blood dating back to high school.

The hanging bell on The Flower Basket jingled merrily as I entered the perfumed showroom.

"Hello?"

It was eerily quiet—odd. Lori-Sue usually had soothing music playing in the background. It was a small shop, as most stores on Main Street were, converted from former 1800s mansions. The shop felt empty. The bistro chairs scattered around the showroom looked forlorn in their emptiness.

"Lori-Sue?" I spoke quietly this time.

I had to get home. Ellis had a softball game this afternoon. When I missed a game, Ellis wasn't a happy girl.

Still no answer, so I wandered into the back workroom. It was an impressive space with two huge worktables and one large refrigeration unit humming softly. I had been back here plenty of times, going over ideas, brainstorming, negotiating prices. I wasn't ready for what greeted me. No one would be. For there, splayed out on one of the worktables, was Lori-Sue. Her eyes were wide open, but I was fairly confident she was dead. A large amount of blood had pooled on the table from a wound on her chest. I dropped both coffees, the lids of each popping off as they hit the scarred wood of the workroom floor. I should have screamed. I wanted to, but nothing came out. Instead, I stumbled to her and felt for a pulse, then whipped off my go-to-meeting jacket and pressed it to her wound. It didn't seem to be bleeding much. Not the most hopeful sign. I sank to the coffee-covered floor. My hands shook as I struggled to get my cell out of my front pocket. It took me three tries to call 911.

"Nine-one-one. What's your emergency?"

* * *

Later, I still hadn't stopped shaking. A victims' advocate from the town's police force had seated me in a chair in The Flower Basket showroom. She placed a blanket over my shoulders. I kept trying to tell her I wasn't the "victim." Lori-Sue was.

"Now, Ms. Ludlow. Let's go over it again," the stocky female police officer seated next to me said.

I put my head on the table. I was so tired, so tired. We'd been over this three times already. I couldn't tell what I had seen, how I had found Lori-Sue, in any different way. Why did they keep after me?

My legs were trembling. I wasn't sure if it was from nerves or the remaining adrenaline. "Why? Why do I have to repeat myself? I've told you three times already."

The police officer smiled sadly, the dimple on her cheek making a brief appearance. "I know it's hard, Hon, but you *are* covered in the deceased's blood, and you haven't been clear about your relationship with the deceased."

I looked at my hands and blouse. She was right. I was a mess. I had the urge to gag but pushed it down.

I didn't like where this was going. I felt almost like they were accusing me of something. Well, not just any 'something' - *murder*.

I didn't respond right away. "Do I need a lawyer?"

The officer stood. Her buddy-buddy demeanor dissipated. "That's certainly your right, Ms. Ludow. But you have to realize asking for a lawyer will necessitate continuing this at the station tonight, and if you have nothing to hide...."

I'd watched enough *Law & Order* to recognize this ploy, but she did make me feel defensive.

They thought there was something fishy about my story. I could understand, and there *was* that whole thing in high school...

So, I did what any intelligent person would. I exercised my right to counsel. I was loaded into a squad car for the half-mile trek to the police station. My face flamed as several local business owners, and townsfolk took in the scene. I scanned the crowd for Jen, my BFF from high school, but didn't see her.

The station looked like something you'd see on *Gilmore Girls*, all quaint and homey; ivy climbing the brick walls. The front lawn was freshly mown, I could smell the crispness of the lawn clippings. The ride to the station had taken all of a minute and a half.

I was feeling anything but love right about now. My arresting officer, whom I discovered was named Officer Ramirez, didn't want to haul me into the station. She wanted to wrap this up and get home to her kids. Thankfully, she let me keep my phone, and I called the one attorney I knew in town, Charlie Wentworth. Charlie was a high school acquaintance. I'd seen him around some in the year I'd been home. He wasn't a criminal attorney, but he was better than nothing. I deserved a break. When I entered the antiquated station, it was like stepping back in time. I saw one of my clients paying a parking ticket. She seemed horrified her wedding planner was being escorted into the building by a police officer. Please, God, make this go away.

Charlie met me at the station house, bless him.

"Ok, Ms. Ludlow, you can wait here with your attorney." Officer Ramirez indicated a small office and gave Charlie an appreciative glance the way any red-blooded woman would. You wouldn't think I'd notice how well the years had treated him, not after the day I'd had, but I did. He had always been tall, but now Charlie had the physique of a man and a man who knew the inside of a gym. He still had a full head of the most luxurious wavy chestnut hair I'd never had the pleasure of running my fingers through. No man should be so lucky. That hair should be reserved for us women. His eyes matched his hair and were still the warm chocolate I remembered.

"The detective assigned to the case will be here shortly to interview you." Officer Ramirez was curt as she closed the interview room door behind her.

"Don't say anything, Kate." Charlie's brown gaze drilled into mine.

"They can't listen in. This is a privileged conversation!" My gaze wandered around the white, windowless room. The small-town charm was missing here.

The walls were blank, except for the mirror on the opposite wall. We all knew what was behind that, a one-way observation into my interrogation room. At least I wasn't handcuffed to the table. There was a loop for that purpose on the room's generic table.

Charlie quirked a brow. He pulled out a chair for me and wrote on a notepad he had pulled out of his briefcase. "They can't legally listen, but they do. What happened?"

"I walked into the shop, and there she was," I scribbled.

"Ok. That's it?"

"Yep."

"But there was that thing in high school…." Charlie finished.

I frowned at him.

Then the door opened, and *he* walked in the room, Brian McAllister, high school sweetheart, love of my life, and breaker of my heart.

I had done my best this year to avoid him and, not to pat myself on the back, I had done an exceptional job…until now. He was the lead detective on this case. Dang it all.

He smirked when he walked in, shook hands with Charlie, and straddled a chair. So macho. He looked wonderful, better than wonderful. The minimal gray in his sandy hair seemed to highlight it, the blue of his eyes was as striking as ever, and the new lines and crinkles around his eyes promised a story. He was still slim, his long limbs strong but not bulky with muscle. I think I hated him at that moment.

"So, Katie," Brian began, "what happened?" And before I could even answer, he continued, "You know there *was* that thing in high school."

Would everyone just quit with the "high school thing?"

Chapter Four

Even if you choose another dessert than wedding cake, consider a "cutting cake" for you and your groom. It's easy to preserve and freeze. You'll be glad you did on your first anniversary.

"MOM!" My beautiful, leggy, dirt-covered daughter yelled as she stormed into the kitchen. "You *knew* I was pitching today. Did you forget, or were you just too busy?" Ellis stopped dead in her tracks when she saw me huddled over a cup of tea, fresh from a shower. I had thrown away my blood-covered clothes, and was trying to get warm in my favorite bathrobe.

I was seated at the kitchen table, picking absently at its chipped sky-blue paint. I sanded down the kitchen table years ago. I was on a home renovation kick and had chosen the blue enamel from our local hardware store, hoping to brighten up our too-small California kitchen. It worked, and I purchased new 'everyday dishes' to match.

Ellis's blue eyes, not much darker than the farm table, filled with concern. Her brown ponytail, similar to my color, dipped as she tilted her head to me. "Mom? What happened?" She reached down to scratch the head of our mini-dachshund, Chloe, who was seated on my lap, who was breaking the cardinal rule of never being anywhere *near* the table.

Ellis's concerned face, and her sweet everyday act of giving Chloe her love, did me in. I placed Chloe on the kitchen floor. Ellis enveloped me in a loving embrace, and I hugged her back tightly, dirt and all. I finally cried.

"You must have won." I smiled through my tears. I could gauge how hard she played by the filth of her uniform. "Did you win?"

"Mom!" She scolded. "What happened?" Now she was worried.

I told her all about finding Lori-Sue, the police interview, and how my new hero, Charlie, had told Brian, in no uncertain terms, they had nothing on me, and we were leaving.

"It's surreal, Mom. I mean, I didn't know Lori-Sue very well, but to think she's no longer here? I just can't get my head around it."

I felt the same way.

I didn't know how to comfort my daughter. I tried to downplay my interview at the station, but she'd watched her own share of *Law & Order,* and I knew she was worried.

It had been a rough year for Ellis. Grant, my ex, had left us for my former best friend and, uncomfortably…our next-door neighbor.

"I'm so sorry, Mama." Ellis used the name she called me when she was feeling particularly loving or wanted something.

"Thanks, Elle. I love you too." I gave her another hug. I had to get them in when she let me. "Now, tell me about that game. Did you win?"

* * *

Ellis was tucked in for the night, and I could take a breath, no longer having to put on a brave face. My cell phone buzzed. Uh, oh. *Charlie.*

I answered with trepidation. This wasn't good news. "Hi, Charlie."

"Hey, Kate." Silence. This didn't bode well.

"What's up? It's so late."

He sighed. "Ah, Kate, they subpoenaed your cell phone records. A witness heard a particularly nasty argument between you and Lori-Sue the day before she died, and you did find the body…." Eastbury's finest wasted no time canvasing the area, questioning witnesses.

"And that thing in high school," I said for him.

"Yeah, and that." Silence again. "Anything I should know about in your texts or email?"

I thought back. Crap. Those texts between two women who disliked each other but were forced to work together because we lived in such a small town weren't going to help me at all, not at all.

"Well, they won't help."

"That's what I thought. Hang tight. I'll keep you posted."

Oh, God, how was I supposed to sleep tonight? I sat down heavily on the loveseat placed invitingly in front of my cold kitchen fireplace. I wasn't going to sit idly by and be railroaded for a crime I didn't commit. Well, maybe "railroaded" was too harsh. I really didn't look all that innocent.

I decided to take action! I dressed all in black, admittedly my most flattering color, and left a note for Ellis that I had to go out and would be back soon. Yes, my plan was ill-advised...but I couldn't help myself. I had to get another look at the crime scene. This was personal. My freedom was at stake. I no longer had Grant, my ex, to lean on. What would happen to my business, to Ellis, to *me*, if the worst happened and I was arrested? I worried that if additional suspicions came down on me, I'd begin losing clients. That, I couldn't afford.

I shook off the feeling of guilt as I stepped under the crime scene tape at Lori-Sue's shop. Brian would be fit to be tied if he was aware of what I was up to. This was illegal, but I'd no longer pretend I wasn't in trouble, serious trouble, especially with the news my cell phone records were being viewed, probably at this very moment.

I looked both ways as if someone were watching. If someone *were* watching, they'd be all over me, stopping my snooping. It was worse than snooping. I looked under the potted hydrangea bush to the right of the front door, where Lori-Sue kept a key in case of emergencies. Hey, if this wasn't an emergency, I didn't know what was. I prayed the police hadn't set the alarm system; but then, they probably didn't know the code either. The key slipped into the antique lock smoothly, and I turned the handle, sensitive to every creak and squeak. I gently closed the door. I couldn't turn on any lights, and the flashlight on my iPhone was super bright, so I tapped the phone screen to light the home page. I was momentarily defeated. With this weak light, I wouldn't be able to find anything of interest. I'd have to brave it out and use my flashlight. I didn't know what I was looking for and what

I could find that the police might have missed. I started going over every square inch of the showroom with my iPhone flashlight. Nothing seemed out of order except the awful mess the crime scene folks had made. Black powder was everywhere. It wasn't their job to clean, and, sadly, Lori-Sue had minimal family–just Ivy Jackman, my dear, dear friend. H*a-ha*. Two women I really disliked, and they were cousins, go figure. I moved into the workroom. Nothing popped out at me. The flowers in the fridge were doing okay, but several on one of the worktables were dying. It made me sad.

And then I saw it, an opened granola bar, half-eaten and still in its wrapper. Lori-Sue was incredibly allergic to peanuts. I knew this from childhood. I looked closely at the wrapper. I was familiar with this brand and couldn't imagine Lori-Sue would have it in her shop or home. I knew from a friend of Ellis's, who was severely allergic to peanuts, that most people who were so sensitive to the allergen wouldn't even eat products manufactured in a plant that used peanuts in other foods, like this one. The wrapper was something of interest, at least something out of the norm. Most people afflicted with the allergen carried an EpiPen, were careful about eating out, and were diligent about not eating pre-packaged, prepared food or meals. I needed to let the police know about this, but I wasn't sure if it would help me or hurt me. But how was I supposed to go about it? I wasn't supposed to be here. Then I heard it, the squeak of the door and the ever-so-slight creak of the floorboards as the person or persons moved from the showroom to the workroom, where I had hastily hidden underneath the closest worktable. I turned off my flashlight.

The beam of a flashlight shone as he/she searched the room. I was moments away from discovery. I needed to arm myself, but with what? There was a broom next to me, neglected under the worktable. I grabbed it. I didn't know what I'd do with it, but I was ready.

A strong light shown in my face. "I should have known." He kept the light shining in my face, all but blinding me.

I put my hand up to shield my eyes, but it didn't help much. I knew the voice, though. Of course, it'd be him. It was his investigation, after all.

"Get that blasted light out of my eyes!"

"Yes, ma'am. What the heck are you doing in here, Katie? You have to realize this is an open investigation, and you're, at the very least, a person of interest. You also have to know not to cross police tape. Do the words CRIME SCENE, DO NOT CROSS mean nothing to you? Come on," he extended his hand. "Get out from under there."

I didn't take his outstretched hand but extracted myself from underneath the worktable unaided, more awkwardly than I'd like with my bum leg. It was a rather indelicate process. I rose, brushed off God knows what from my black leggings, and glared at him.

"What's with the look? I could run you in for this. You know that, right? And it makes you look even guiltier."

I knew the greatest defense was an offense. But I also knew he wouldn't take me in; Brian still had a soft spot for me. We looked at each other for a moment. And, truth be told, I still had a soft spot for him too. God help me. It was too soon after dear Grant, but it wasn't like Brian was a new being in my life. He'd been in my heart well before my ex-husband had even made an entrance.

"You know this doesn't look good. Is there anything you need to tell me, Katie?"

"No! Gosh no! I'm just trying to save my skin."

He pulled me by the hand back into the showroom. We sat gingerly on the guest chairs. I wondered how much of the fingerprint powder would transfer to my pants. At least they were black. I'd have to remember to take them off as soon as I got home.

"Katie, what were you thinking? What are you looking for? And you have to realize whatever you find here would be useless. The chain of custody of the evidence would be completely destroyed. Any prosecutor worth their salt would get it thrown out." He was angry again.

I looked at my hands. I couldn't see much. The only real light we had was the moonlight streaming in through the windows. I felt stupid. He was right. But then I remembered the granola bar.

I gazed up and met Brian's eyes. "Did you know Lori-Sue was severely allergic to peanuts?"

"No. And this is important because?"

"I found a granola bar on her worktable that Lori-Sue would never allow in her shop. It was half-eaten."

"Did you touch it?" Brian looked at my hands. Then he laughed. My hands were encased in my kitchen gloves.

"I'm not completely stupid." I smiled.

"Does the granola bar have peanuts in it?"

"I don't know, but I'm guessing as she was so allergic, I doubt she'd even allow products that were manufactured in a plant that used peanuts in her house or shop."

"And this one was?"

"Yes!"

"You know she was stabbed, right?" Brian asked with just a hint of a condescending tone.

"Yeah, but..." I must have looked pathetic because he surprised me. "Ok," he stood. "I don't know how this matters. It could have been a client's, but it *is* irregular. Katie, I don't think you're a killer. You have to know that." He looked so earnest, well, as much of him as I could see in the darkness. "Here's what we're going to do. You go on home. I'll lock up. Tomorrow I'll come and 'discover' the granola bar. Who else knew about her allergy?"

"Not everyone, but certainly those who prepared her food, like Jen and close friends."

"Go home and stay there. Don't make trouble for yourself. Did Charlie talk to you?"

"Yes," I whispered.

"So, you know about the texts, and...it doesn't help your case."

I was silent this time. What could I say?

I got up but stumbled on the leg of the guest chair...and right into Brian's arms. He caught me and, for the second, or was it the third time tonight, I was embarrassed. But it felt like home. Brian felt it too. I knew he did. I could tell by the way his arms tightened around me, the way he held me longer than necessary. Did he really feel the pull as I did? I had broken his heart all those years ago...but then he had broken mine.

Chapter Five

Take a photo of how you'd like your guests' tables to be set up. Then your caterer and planner have a reference.

I was in shell shock over my legal situation. But I wasn't under arrest, thank God for small favors, and I still had a business to run; if this whole mess with Lori-Sue didn't crater it.

This afternoon I was "taking tea" at the Simpson home. I was trying to stamp down my panic. I had to find a new florist for Marcy. My brain raced through my short list of preferred florists. I'd have to get a concrete idea of her vision before I recommended someone. That was the brilliance of Lori-Sue. She made the bride's floral vision a reality. She was hard to replace.

The Simpsons' historic Victorian, located on Main Street, was a work of art. It was a cheery yellow with white trim. The porch wrapped around the entire house. I wished we were taking tea there, but it was still too cool. The garden surrounding the house was meticulous. I wondered at the cost of the Simpsons' landscaping bill each month. I smelled fresh and new.

We were seated in the library, with an impressive view of the backyard or "rear garden," as Joyce called it. It wasn't yet in full bloom. Whoever had designed the garden allowed for blooms to be present all through the spring and summer, one group of perennials blooming, and then the next. The tiny, tender leaves on the trees were out, promising plenty of shade in the coming months. I sighed. How I had missed this lushness in Southern California.

I wasn't at all comfortable. I was beginning to wonder if I should have taken on this wedding. My anxiety level was through the roof, and I was a calm, self-assured woman. But then again, I was seated across from Joyce Belmont Simpson, grand dame of The Hartford Chapter of the Daughters of the American Revolution. Marcy looked so much like her mother—both blond, green-eyed, and waifish thin.

The DAR wasn't dying out in the East. It was everything for a respectable pedigree here in New England.

To be a member of the DAR, one must prove one's ancestors either fought in the Revolutionary War or rendered aid to its cause. The documentation process was daunting. The applicant must have all birth, marriage, and death certificates from the Revolutionary War ancestor down to the applicant. These were not always easy to find. The DAR was fairly flexible when applicants couldn't find traditional documentation, however. Family Bible entries were accepted, as well as newspaper birth and death announcements.

Joyce was "pouring out," meaning she was pouring tea into our bone-china teacups. I had read my tattered copy of *Emily Post's Book of Etiquette* the "It Book" for women's etiquette, and learned steeping tea in the teapot was the proper thing to do, versus dropping a teabag in a cup of hot water. In fact, the English called dropping a bag in a mug and pouring hot water over it "workman's tea" or "student tea," meaning one didn't have time to do it properly.

"One lump or two." Joyce even asked me the cliché question. She was intelligence packaged in a no-nonsense ensemble. Today she wore a black cashmere twinset and dun-colored wool slacks. Her shoes were sensible low-heeled pumps, but the leather was so supple and looked so soft, they had to have cost a fortune.

Marcy must get her fashion sense from her mother, as she was dressed very similarly but wore khaki slacks, and her twinset was rose-colored.

"None, please. I take my tea black."

If Joyce was offended by my choice, she didn't appear so. "Marcy, dear, will you please pass our guest a scone and some of the toppings?"

I smiled at Marcy and accepted a scone, still warm, and placed a small amount of strawberry jam on my delicate plate.

Her pouring duties complete, Joyce turned her attention back to me. "We're pleased with how you're handling the wedding details so far, Kate. I trust there won't be any disruptions due to that nasty business of the florist's murder?"

I smiled softly. "Thank you, Joyce, and no, nothing to worry about regarding the murder investigation."

Joyce chose to let it go, although she raised an eyebrow at me as if to say, "Really?"

"Kate, how's it going with locating the ring?" Marcy looked so expectant.

I hated to tell her I hadn't given it much thought.

Joyce frowned at Marcy and placed her saucer and teacup on the coffee table in front of her. "Marcy, I really think you should let this go. It's a fool's errand."

It was obvious Marcy didn't like her mother's displeasure. She looked crestfallen. "Please, Mama. It means so much to me." Marcy twisted her napkin round and round in her lap.

Tears filled her eyes, and I didn't think they were of the crocodile variety.

Joyce looked conflicted. It was obvious she loved her daughter, and they were close. She undoubtedly wanted to please her, so why the hesitation? Joyce didn't seem like a client who worried if she was overstepping.

Joyce acquiesced, "Okay, Marcy, if it means that much to you, move forward. I thought you'd forget about it, as you often do…" This was said gently and with a smile.

Marcy threw decorum to the wind and went to hug her mother. "Thank you, Mama." She smacked her mother soundly on her cheek.

Joyce laughed. It was actually a lovely sound, like a tinkling of crystal. "Marcy, love," Joyce surprised me, speaking with such affection toward her daughter. "if I had any inkling where that darn thing was, I'd be the first to get my hands on it. I dearly wanted to wear it on my wedding day too, but it was nowhere to be found." She placed her hand on Marcy's arm. "I wish you could wear it too, Marcy." Joyce's whole body seemed to relax, and she leaned back heavily.

Awkward! I felt like I was imposing on an intimate family moment. I didn't get the feeling there was a whole lot of warmth in this family, and I was in the midst of it. But why the obsession on Marcy's part for a ring she'd never seen? I imagine her mother's stories of the ring played into the whole cachet of the jewel.

I cleared my throat. "Do you have a photo of the ring? I'd love to see it."

Joyce was silent a moment. "I know my grandmother wore it. I have her wedding photos. Perhaps we can see it if there's a picture of her holding her bouquet in her left hand." She stood and went to the book-lined shelves. She went right to a shelf that appeared to hold several photo albums. Her fingers danced over the album's spines, and she withdrew a faded green one, which had a surprising amount of dust.

"Mom, you mentioned the ring's history to me, and I feel as if I know it, although I've just seen one or two photos. I love the stories you've shared."

Joyce rejoined us and spread the album open to a series of black-and-white photos. The photos appeared to be turn-of-the-century wedding pictures of an exquisite bride. Joyce flipped through heavy pages and came to rest on a photo of a delicate small bouquet. I wasn't a fan of the overlarge bouquets brides were carrying today. I thought it emphasized the flowers and not where it belonged, on the bride. Lucky for us, the hand holding the bouquet in the picture was the bride's left hand and showcased the ring nicely. I could understand why Marcy wanted to wear the ring and claim ownership. It was gorgeous! The main stone appeared to be at least three carats, with much filigree surrounding it. If I were a betting woman, I'd say it was platinum, which was the most popular metal for jewelry back then due to its durability. Today, it was much more expensive than gold, so not as prevalent.

"It's stunning," I gushed. And it was. "Okay, if I take some snaps with my iPhone for reference?"

"Of course," Marcy said enthusiastically.

Joyce didn't seem as gung-ho but didn't resist. I took several photos, hoping this would help in my search because I'd have to begin in earnest.

Joyce said, "The cut was what was called a European Cut, which has fewer facets than a Brilliant Cut. There were two round stones on each side, maybe a quarter of a carat each. There was much filigree, as was the vintage style, and it was all set in platinum."

Ah-ha! I was right about the metal.

While it was gorgeous, something seemed oddly familiar about this ring to me. Where had I seen it before, or one like it? I felt almost certain I had, and maybe recently.

This extra task was becoming complex by the minute. I was curious, though... I had some tiny polite sips of tea and ate the required scone. My waistline was going to pay for this, but I deemed it worth it. The scone was melt-in-your-mouth delicate.

I graciously thanked my hostesses. Marcy got a call as we began the long trek from the library to the front door, where my Suburban was parked in the circular drive, and excused herself. She squealed with delight in the other room. Joyce looked over her shoulder at her giddy daughter.

"Do you mind if I check what's gotten Marcy all in a lather?" She stopped her procession to the front door and smiled naturally, not all that common for Joyce.

"Of course. I can see myself out."

Really, it wasn't hard, but I guess it was. Sallie, Joyce's housekeeper, had recently mopped the foyer floor, as it was still wet, and I slipped like a klutz and fell. The pain in my tailbone was nothing compared to the attack on my dignity, and thanked the saints I didn't seem to have hurt my bum leg. Joyce had rushed off to attend to Marcy and didn't witness my gaffe. I was grateful for small favors. I indulged in a moment of rest and licked my wounds.

"Hello," a man's voice boomed.

I assumed Joyce's husband was calling out to his family. At least he hadn't come in the front and witnessed my fall from grace.

"Darling," Joyce cooed.

Well, this was awkward. I should be gone by now. Instead, here I was, sitting on their foyer floor, rubbing my backside. Crap! It sounded like Mr. Simpson was making his way toward me. Why was he coming this way? Shouldn't he take the back stairs if he wanted to go upstairs?

"Derek, darling, a word before you go up," Joyce spoke in hushed tones.

They seemed to be somewhere close by, but the house was so cavernous I didn't know exactly where they were.

"I want to thank you again for your loving support with that unpleasant business. I would never wish ill on anyone, but with that florist gone, so is our problem."

"Joycie."

Joycie? I never expected that.

"You know I'll do anything for you, and I'm glad you're feeling better about it all, but you know I still think we should have gone to the police. Blackmail is no laughing matter."

Blackmail? This was going to take some mulling over. I couldn't get out of there fast enough. I hoped I moved as stealthily as I imagined. When I made it safely to my Suburban, I remembered again I had forgotten to get the signed copy of the contract.

Chapter Six

Trying to keep your wedding budget in check? Try DIY flowers. Many online companies will send you fresh blooms and instructions on how to create perfect bouquets and arrangements.

The next morning, I decided to head over to Jen's coffee shop for a catch-up. Jen was the best friend a girl could have. We had been besties since we were twelve. She was another huge perk of moving back to Connecticut. I had missed her so. Yes, social media and smartphones made it easier to stay in touch, but there was nothing like a face-to-face.

We were seated at a table as far away from her customers as possible but were still getting quite a bit of attention.

"So, tell me, Katie, all the details about finding the *body*."

I frowned at her. "Jen! It was *Lori-Sue*, not 'the body.' She was your friend too."

Jen looked into her cup. Her face reddened slightly. "Sorry, Katie. I know. It's just so sensational. And I wouldn't go as far as to call her a friend to either of us, to be perfectly honest."

Jen and Lori-Sue's history wasn't a great one either. It wasn't as sensational as mine, though.

It was so long ago, the details were hazy, but not the feelings. I was grateful Jen didn't remind me of my own high-school thing with Lori-Sue. I was getting annoyed with everyone bringing it up.

"There's really not much to report. I went into the shop to place an order, and Lori-Sue didn't answer when I called out to her. I went looking and found her in the back workroom."

"Was it bloody? Had she been shot, stabbed?" Jen was getting too into this.

"Oh, Jen. I hate thinking about it and reliving it. But there's no question she was dead."

"Dead. Was it anaphylactic shock?" Jen smiled. So, Jen *did* know about Lori-Sue's deadly allergy to peanuts. Made sense as Jen handled her food when she frequented her coffee shop. "She didn't like to talk about her peanut allergy, but she felt compelled to tell me 'cause I handled her food," Jen confirmed.

"Ultimately, it didn't matter because she was stabbed," I confided, against my better judgment, but this was Jen. Although, I had to admit she was acting inappropriately.

Jen grinned again.

"Jen…really. You don't have to look so gleeful."

Jen giggled. "Sorry, Katie. I'm being a jerk. No one deserves insensitivity when they're dead."

It sounded ridiculous as she said it, and we looked at each other and broke out into soft giggles. Then I felt guilty, and to be perfectly honest, her glee made me uncomfortable. We knew we'd both wished Lori-Sue dead in the past.

"Jen, what was your complete beef with Lori-Sue? I know it was over, Jack, but you never wanted to talk about it much at the time."

I didn't think she was going to answer me.

She smiled, a faraway look in her eyes. She glanced over my shoulder, looking, I guessed, to see if her daughters working the coffee bar were within earshot. Jen lowered her head and absently ruffled her pixie cut. Everything about Jen was long, her legs, her neck, her arms. But not her hair. If I had been blessed with her luscious thick strawberry-blond hair, I'd wear it long and proudly.

"You know Jack and I were Eastbury High School's second most popular couple, second to you and Brian." She met my gaze and smiled.

My face warmed.

She paused. "I think it all came to a head when we were parked at Cotton

Hollow one night."

That area of Eastbury served many members of the community. For those wishing to get exercise, there were great hiking trails. Picnicking was a popular Cotton Hollow pastime. There was a gorgeous tree, affectionally called simply 'The Tree," that offered shelter and a wonderful place to enjoy a meal. Lovers, old and young, carved their initials in its sturdy trunk. For mothers with young children, a swimming pool was available during the summer months; and for the teen set, it was great parking for make-out sessions. I had been there a couple of times. Cars couldn't be seen from the road, and law enforcement had to drive into the parking lot to evaluate the legitimacy of parked cars. But really? Why would any cars need to be parked there after dark? The chance of getting caught was entirely dependent on what was going on in the sleepy village of Eastbury. If a bored officer wanted something to do, he rousted the parked kids. If he was inclined to park and take a snooze, which was a frequent occurrence among the bored police force, the kids were uninterrupted. If, on the rare occasion, there was something going on requiring real police intervention, the kids were safe again.

"On this particular night," Jen continued, "we had been parked for about fifteen minutes, with no cars driving into the lot. I'd been doing everything in my power to avoid parking with Jack. You know I was mad for him, but we'd been dating so long, he was expecting something more physical from me, more than I was willing to give. It had become quite an issue with him." Jen's face reddened, and she glanced back to the coffee bar again.

"Intellectually, I know Jack hated himself for it, but he still had dropped some not-so-subtle hints that there were plenty of girls who'd give him additional leeway than I would. Chief among them, our friend, Lori-Sue. I knew what I was up against. I knew Jack wasn't bluffing. There were lots of girls who would do anything to be his girlfriend." Jen wasn't exaggerating. He was wildly popular with the opposite sex.

"I had to decide if I was one of those girls. Jack had been patient with me, but I knew we would soon be at a crossroads, and I'd have to make a decision. Prom was coming up. It was understood that, of course, we'd go together. We were a couple, after all." Jen paused here, tearing up at the story after all this time.

"But I also knew what Jack expected at the end of the evening. I was an honest girl, with myself and others. I think you know this, Katie."

I did.

"If I went with Jack, I'd have to live up to his expectations. I wasn't positive I could do that. I had my own expectations of myself. I also knew there were boys out there who were patient with their girlfriends and respected them. Your Brian was one of those boys."

Ah, yes, my Brian. If he weren't so handsome and charming, I'd have never taken a second look. My mother *adored* him enough to turn off any young girl from a potential date. He was the son of one of her best friends. I think they planned for us to be together since we were in diapers. But I couldn't resist him, no matter how much my mom liked him. I wasn't the only one. Everyone loved Brian. He truly was the All-American boy.

Tears ran down Jen's cheeks unchecked, surprising me. "I pushed Jack's hand away again that night. 'I need to get home for curfew,' I told him. As Jack ripped out of the parking lot, I wondered if by next weekend Lori-Sue Johnson would be sitting in Jack's passenger seat... So, yes, Lori-Sue wasn't my favorite person. I don't want to talk about it anymore, Katie. Not today, anyway. Can we finish this later?"

"Yes, I have to get home anyway." I rubbed her shoulder in comfort and headed home.

Chapter Seven

"Social Media"
A ban on your guests' photos at your wedding is a great way to keep those phones silent.

The next morning, after getting Ellis off to school, I scrambled to get myself ready. I pulled out new navy light-weight wool slacks and a cashmere sweater I'd ordered from Talbots' latest sale and got dressed. I had even blown out my hair and added a touch of lipstick and mascara–about all the makeup I ever wore. For today...I had a very important appointment. Until I was notified otherwise, it was business as usual for me. I was headed to the home of Carmella Sepulveda to throw my hat in the ring of planners trying to get her wedding. She was interviewing three other planners, so I really had to bring my "A" game. I reached for my lucky navy pumps. I rarely wore heels these days. They were no friend to my bum leg, but today I felt the extra effort necessary. I went downstairs and into my home office, grabbed my overlarge pocketbook/briefcase, and checked to see if I had enough notepads and pens. I sat down in Ellis's discarded desk chair and picked up my cell. I had to call Joyce before I headed out to Carmella's. I needed to secure that signed contract. I couldn't put it off any longer. I dialed Joyce's number before I could think about it anymore.

"Hello, Kate?" Ah, Joyce had me in her contacts. A positive sign, although she sounded distracted.

"Hey, Joyce, how are you today?" She had finally given me permission to call her by her Christian name.

"Very well, and you?" Distracted or not, Joyce was polite.

"Good, good. Ah, Joyce, is it possible to stop by sometime soon and pick up the planner contract?"

I heard a muffled response, not intended for me. "Go ahead and enjoy a pastry, Ivy. I won't be a moment. Sorry, Kate."

"Ivy!" I said a little too harshly than I would have wished. "Is Ivy there, Joyce?" I tried to keep the panic out of my voice. I did *not* want my rival present.

Joyce actually chuckled. "Not to worry, Kate. I showed Ivy my signed contract with you when she dropped by and wanted to discuss Marcy's wedding again."

"You showed her my contract?" My voice rose. No planner wanted the competition to see their very private contract. The gong of the Simpsons' front doorbell sounded. "Just a moment, Kate. I think that's my bakery delivery. My bridge group is coming in forty-five minutes."

I thought this was said for Ivy's benefit as much as my own.

Joyce's heels clicked on her perfect floors. "Hello, Jennifer. You can put the tray in the kitchen. Thank you so much for the delivery."

"Thanks," Jen said.

I wasn't surprised Jen would make a delivery to Joyce's. It wasn't something Jen liked to do, but Joyce was always hosting a DAR event or a personal party. She'd be a fool not to bend over backward to sell her baked goods. I was getting impatient. I was ready to hang up when Joyce came back on.

"Come by anytime, Kate. I'll put the signed contract in an envelope on my desk, and if I'm not home, Sallie can find it for you."

"Thanks, Joyce. I'll be by soon." And I would. I didn't like the fact Ivy was lurking around. Oh, how I disliked her. That task accomplished, I grabbed my bag and headed out to Carmella's.

* * *

I had admired Carmella's historic mansion even as a child. Of course, she didn't own it then. Her home was seven doors down from my mine, although my house was no mansion. Carmella's home was made entirely of brick that had been painted white. Four columns supported the substantial porch, which was decorated with four wicker cushioned chairs, a love seat, and a glider swing. The front door, painted in glossy black enamel, looked to have been recently painted. From my own experience, it had to be done about twice a year. I bet Carmella's was painted double that.

Carmella answered the door herself, even though I knew a home of her size had to have staff. She was dressed in slim black yoga pants and an oversized coral T-shirt. I felt overdressed in my slacks and heels.

"Kate! Thank you for coming. Please come in." She opened her shiny door wide.

I walked into dark coolness. The house was historic but well-maintained. Although I was aware the kitchen was new, and the plumbing and electric wiring up to code, it still had an antiquated feel. The furnishings were luxurious. There must be potpourri close by; I smelled roses and another floral scent. She ushered me into her personal sitting room. A fire cracked cheerfully, taking any possible chill from the room. The sitting room was done up in all shades of yellow, from deep butter to the palest shade of wheat on the window drapery.

"I have a tea tray coming. I hope you brought your appetite. I do love a tea party. Meeting with you planners has given me a great excuse to put on the dog."

I was so curious who my competition was, but it wouldn't do to outright ask. I was going to have to wheedle it out of her somehow.

The luscious, raven-haired Carmella was engaged to her future third husband. Mr. Sepulveda had been husband number two. He passed away a year ago. Husband number one hadn't lasted much longer. She divorced him after 18 months. I didn't know why and certainly wasn't going to ask, but I *was* curious. I estimated Carmella was about 27 or 28. She'd done well for herself financially via her marriages. I didn't know much about her life before, but there were rumors, and while I wasn't a big gossip, I was going to listen closely.

A tiny maid brought in the tea tray and, running around her feet, surprisingly not tripping her up, was the cutest Pomeranian. Cute, that was if you could stand its incessant yapping. His barking was sharp and put my teeth on edge. I stood to help the maid with the tray as I was afraid she was going to stumble over the yapper and drop it on the antique rug.

"Oh, thank you, miss." She seemed grateful.

"Really, Lola," Carmella scolded. "You've got to be more careful."

I set the tray on the coffee table with deliberate care, glad I did so quickly, as a searing pain radiated in the back of my heel. The tiny dog had just bitten me. I was proud I didn't scream, not so much from the pain but from the shock.

"Ouch." I had to say *something.* The dog had just *bitten* me.

Carmella giggled. "He's a minx, isn't he, Lola? He bites her all the time too. You'll get used to it."

No, I didn't think I would. But I decided to let it go. This was a great opportunity, and I wanted this job…a lot. And then…the teeny "minx" bit me again. This time I did squeal.

"Dang!" I almost yelled. "That hurt." I snuck a look at my ankle, and yes, he'd drawn blood.

Carmella smirked and then ruffled the dog's luxurious fur. "Rocky, you stop that, precious, or Mama is going to have to put you in your room for a time-out." Carmella picked Rocky up and held him on her lap.

I caught Lola's glance, and she rolled her eyes at me.

"Kate, would you be a doll and pick up the notepad and pen on the desk in the corner?" Carmella indicated a lovely Chippendale piece.

"You bet."

"I heard you're doing the Simpson girl's wedding," Carmella said it as if she were a matron discussing one of her friend's daughters. In fact, I bet she was younger than Marcy.

"Yes." I smiled. I hoped she had heard positive things.

"And Addalee Baker's?" She gave an odd expression, somewhere between glee and anger.

Whoa, was something up there?

"Um-hum." I grabbed the mentioned notepad. I was determined to be noncommittal. There was information she wanted, and even if I knew what it was, I wouldn't share. Addalee was one of my brides, a relationship I held sacred, but she was also a friend from high school. She had a tough time growing up. Her dad was a drunk, her mother less than reputable. She had never had two nickels to rub together, but what she did have was a sweet spirit and unearthly beauty. It was as if she'd won the beauty lottery. Did this make her life easier? On the contrary, Addalee didn't realize how stunning she was with her almost white-blond hair and aqua-blue eyes. Her figure was like an old-fashioned Barbie doll.

Not the Barbie doll of today, where the Mattel Toy Company was pressured to make the dolls realistic, but like the olden-time dolls. Those with the teeny tiny waists and the generous bosoms. One boy refused to be put off by Addalee's shy rejection, like she rejected all the other boys. He was Cory Bloomfield, the town's golden boy. It didn't hurt that his family was the wealthiest in the county, either. His attention made Addalee the envy of every girl, and she was hated. After a rocky road, Cory and Addalee were finally getting married.

Carmella was watching me closely as my mind flashed back over Cory and Addalee's story. She rested her chin on her closed fist, her elbow on the sleek arm of her chair. "A birdy told me there may be trouble in paradise, something out of Addalee's past. I heard she is accompanying her future mother-in-law to Joyce Simpson's bridge party today. I can't tell you how long I've been trying to get an invitation to that gathering."

Hum... Was it sour grapes at not being invited to bridge or was there really an issue with Addalee's relationship with Cory?

"I wouldn't know anything about that." I cut her at the knees. Was this a test? Did she want to see how I responded to people fishing about my clients' personal lives?

And just as suddenly as she began her query, she moved on, well, with a little help from Rocky. He chose that moment to leap off his mistress' lap and bite me yet *again* in the back of the other ankle. This hurt more aggressively than the first bite, and I howled. This was over the top, and I couldn't put up with it.

Carmella felt she must offer some sort of disapproval. "Rocky, that's just enough. You apologize to Kate right now."

Apologize? What? The only apology I received from Rocky was to watch him do his business in the middle of the expensive carpet.

"Rock-ky." Carmella's voice was slightly louder, displaying mild amusement rather than actual anger. "That is *so* an outside thing. Lola, please give him three minutes of time out."

I had had enough. Yes, I wanted this job, but if Carmella was this ridiculous with her dog, I had a terrible feeling she'd be a bridezilla to work with. Time to take my leave.

"Carmella, thank you for the tea and treats, but I don't think this is the most ideal time for Rocky. Perhaps when he's feeling up to it." Like never. I rose.

"Kate, aren't you such a doll. I so appreciate how sensitive you are to Rocky's moods. I wish both of my former husbands had been so kind."

Ah, ha.

"Yes, let's do reschedule. Perhaps in your office next time? And I'm sorry about the tea. You didn't touch it, nor the pastries. Ivy and Esther didn't stay long either. You girls are so busy!"

I knew Esther Carmichael. She was a doll, but Ivy! I hated to hear her name again. She was becoming quite the thorn.

Sadly, I hadn't touched the treat tray. The pastries looked so delicious too… But maybe if Carmella would compromise and meet me at my office, there was hope.

"I'll email you my calendar link, and you can get back to me with what day and time works for you." I made my hasty escape.

Lola walked me to the door. "Goodbye, miss, and good for you. Wish I could get away that easily. I'm starting to get scars on my ankles."

I knew she wasn't kidding.

"Oh, and just so you know, she'll be bringing that little mongrel to the meeting at your office. She doesn't go anywhere without him."

Well, that made up my mind about Carmella's business. I all but ran to my car.

Chapter Eight

Consider a long weekend honeymoon right after the wedding and then a longer vacation six to twelve months after your wedding. You may enjoy it more this way.

The next morning, Ellis had just caught the school bus, and I was looking forward to another cup of coffee in front of the kitchen fire when there was an impolite knock at my front door–not the mudroom door, where everyone generally knocked, but the front door. I don't know why I hesitated, but I did. I had a bad feeling. No friend would be knocking on that door, especially at this hour. Before I could even get to it, the knocking escalated to pounding, with a male voice shouting my first and last name and "Eastbury Police."

I opened the door, and Brian was there with some legal-looking documents. He had the grace to look down. He seemed to be having a hard time meeting my gaze.

"Brian?" The name came out more harshly than I intended, but I was confident of what he held.

"I'm sorry, Katie. You know I would have given you a heads-up if I could have. I hate being in this position." This was said softly; there were officers behind him. "Not my call for the search," he said softly as the men entered.

"This position?" I wanted to scream, but didn't. He was the one running the investigation on Lori-Sue's murder. But I guessed the warrant had been issued by someone above him.

I held out my hand for the papers. "I'll call Charlie to look this over, but you might as well come in and get started. I'm sure everything's in order, and the sooner you get started, the sooner you'll be done. I want you gone before Ellis gets home." Then it occurred to me. "Thank you for waiting until she left for school."

Brian and his team entered my home, my sanctuary. I remembered all the times he visited me at my parents' house in high school. This time, however, felt wrong.

"Least I could do," he answered over his shoulder.

Charlie arrived in ten minutes and suggested we sit together in the family/great room. I'd seen the police dramas where homes were trashed during a search warrant. Thankfully, Eastbury was small-town enough that our finest respected their own. My personal items were handled with care. The warrant said they were "looking for anything that could link me to Lori-Sue Johnson's murder." Brian took a moment and spoke to Charlie quietly. Brian then returned abruptly to continue supervising the invasion of my home. Three other officers were conducting the search, none of whom I knew.

"What did he say?" I asked Charlie as soon as he returned to my side.

He hesitated.

"Spit it out," I said more sternly than he deserved.

Charlie was being a true friend. He didn't have to sit here with me, and no mention of payment had been made, although I'd have to broach the subject soon. I just couldn't today, and besides, where would the money come from? I was stretched to the max with the launch of my new business here in New England.

"You have always been a person of interest, but this search was authorized and executed based on an anonymous tip called in yesterday, well, and the angry text messages you exchanged with Lori-Sue." Charlie looked anxious.

I stood from my living room sofa, my cozy sofa I sometimes napped on during a rainy afternoon. I didn't think I'd feel relaxed enough to do that again anytime soon.

"An anonymous tip?" A frown was forming on my brow. "What did this person say?"

"I don't know much. Brian really shouldn't have even mentioned it to me, but it's *you,* Katie. He's willing to bend the rules for *you*. So, don't be greedy." He smiled a half smile.

"He had to have said something additional."

Charlie sighed and patted the seat next to him on the sofa. I sat.

"He said someone called the station, asked for him, and told him you had the murder weapon somewhere in your home."

"That could be anyone! What gave weight to this anonymous caller?"

Charlie looked solemn. "One of your contracts, with what is believed to be Lori-Sue's blood type on it. The caller said it could be found under her desk in her floral shop, and it was."

"Let me guess. It was Marcy Simpson's contract, right? Come on, Charlie. You know that contract had to be planted. The police would have found it during the initial search."

"How'd you know it was Marcy's contract?"

I put my face in my hands. Please, please don't let me cry here, not in front of Charlie or the police officers, and especially not in front of Brian. "It's the one contract I have loose. On top of that, I can assure you, there are so many people that could have grabbed it from the Simpson home, including the people attending the bridge party Joyce Simpson had at her house yesterday," I said between my fingers covering my face. Why oh, why, didn't I go to the Simpsons' and pick up that contract after Carmella's meeting? Cause I had to dress my wounds from that mongrel's bite, I thought.

"I'm being framed." I bravely looked at Charlie, hoping to see some belief there.

What I saw was a stricken friend. "I think you need a criminal attorney, Katie." Charlie's warm brown eyes looked deeply into mine. He really was a prince of a guy.

I knew he always liked me in high school. I was crushing on him my junior year too, but then Brian happened. Even as a teen, I was aware Charlie's infatuation with me didn't dissipate. I thought back guiltily how I innocently used that to my advantage—help with my science project and last-minute homework copying. Was I doing the same thing now? Was I innocently using Charlie until I figured out what to do with my legal situation? I hoped not but wasn't so confident. I knew he was still attracted to me. And, heaven help me, I was still attracted to him too.

* * *

Brian and his crew left, carrying very little in the way of evidence. It hurt my heart, not to mention my business, to see my computer carried out the door. Luckily, I had everything backed up, and Ellis would have to get used to sharing her laptop with me in the short term. I was innocent, but that didn't seem to count for much. What I couldn't understand was why I wasn't being arrested right now. Finding the bloody contract seemed a shoo-in for a room at the county jail. Charlie said it was too circumstantial. He thought Eastbury Police "liked" me for the murder, but, so far, they didn't have enough for a conviction.

When Charlie again suggested I find a criminal attorney, I shut him down. Maybe it was my way of denying I was in real trouble, but, also, I didn't know how I'd pay for it. My parents would do what they could to help, but what adult child wanted to ask their parents for money to pay for a criminal attorney?

Charlie left about noon, and I collapsed on the kitchen loveseat in front of my cold fireplace. Chloe tried her hardest to comfort me, cuddling into the bend of my knees. I cried at the invasion, the disruption of my life, and the feeling of total lack of control. After a couple of minutes of boohooing, I went to the powder room, washed my face, and blew my nose. Makeup right now was a waste. I finger-combed my hair and went out the mudroom doorway. It was time for a serious walk, some distraction, and a cup of coffee. Only one place to go, Jen's.

My cell rang as I was walking out. Oh, terrific. I looked at the screen. I needed a happy talk. I just loved Bethy Rogers. She was a dream to work with.

"Hey, Bethy!" I was trying to sound upbeat.

"Kate."

"How are you?"

"Not well, not well at all," my sweet bride answered.

I had chills. This call did *not* bode well for me.

"I'm afraid we'll be going in another direction with our planner, Kate."

Crap. I was silent for a moment. The professional Kate kicked in. "May I ask why?"

"Oh, Kate, I don't want to," there were tears in her voice. "But with all the trouble, what if you're in jail during my wedding?"

There it was. "I can assure you that won't happen." Could I, though? In all honesty, I couldn't. "But I understand," and I did. "I wish you great happiness," and I disconnected.

Chapter Nine

Signature Cocktail? It can be a brilliant solution to shortening those nasty lines at the bar. Have several of your signature cocktails premade. You can also save money by offering just beer, wine, and your signature cocktail.

Jen took one look at my face and hustled over. "What in God's name happened?" She reached for my hands and held them in her warm ones.

"Do I look that bad?" I would have thought the cool April air would have helped my tear-splotched face return to normal.

"Katie...I know you. What happened?" Jen guided me to a table in the corner, adjacent to the built-in shelves which held all the gourmet treats Jen made a fortune selling to Eastbury's well-heeled clientele.

I was never bored if I had to wait for Jen to finish up a task at her shop. All I had to do was gaze with lust at the delicacies she stocked on her shelves. They were crammed full of packages of dark chocolate-covered biscotti, chocolate-covered espresso beans, and chocolate-covered graham crackers. Oh, she had other items, too, generously blue-cheese-stuffed olives, rich buttery crackers, and sea-salted nuts. Today I had no interest.

Only the other patrons in the coffee shop prevented me from breaking down right then and there. I wasn't ready to tell Jen about the search, the blood-covered contract, my sense of invasion, my fears. What would happen to Ellis if I were arrested? I knew Jen would be willing to take her. Grant would put up a fight, but she'd be more comfortable with Jen and her girls than Grant and the evil Heather. And she wouldn't be uprooted yet again. Ellis was happy here. At least, I thought she was. I hoped she was. That conversation with Jen wasn't something I wanted to have in a busy coffee shop, however.

Just a twitch of Jen's head in her daughter Sylvie's direction brought immediate attention in the form of two coffees and a plate of biscotti; then, she was gone.

"This will make you feel better," Jen soothed.

And it did. We were quiet for a moment. I would ask her to continue the second half of her high school heartbreak with Jack, knowing this would distract me for a bit.

I looked at Jen. She had shadows under her eyes, something I hadn't noticed in all the years I'd known her. A sleepless night?

"How is *your* day, Jen?" I asked kindly, not just as a segue into her story.

She just shrugged. "Ok." But she sighed and took a deep breath.

"I know you want to hear the rest of my story; misery likes company." She smiled., then jumped in. "I should have made Jack break up with me, but I had my pride. If I was going to lose the second most popular boy in school," she smirked, "I was going to be the one doing the breaking up. I asked him to go for a drive. There was nothing Jack liked better than to take his vintage sixty-five Mustang out for a spin. His engine roared, and I ran out to meet him. I wanted to get this over with and didn't want any prolonged visit with my family. My younger brother, Ethan, worshiped Jack, and I wasn't up to listening to his adoring chatter. Jack was getting ready to come to the door to get me as I tapped on the passenger window. My mom had insisted he come to the door when we first started dating. Jack was nothing if not a gentleman...in that regard, at least. Jack grinned when he saw me and leaned over to pull the handle on the passenger door to let me in. I knew what he was thinking. Maybe I was getting it. Maybe I realized we needed to come to some sort of agreement on our physical relationship. There were plenty of girls who would do almost anything to be with Jack, the town's great baseball star.

He truly seemed enamored. He really did love me; I think, well, as much as any seventeen-year-old boy could love a girl. I got in the car and pulled the stiff door shut; it creaked with age. Jack leaned over and kissed me, trying to be gentle, but his sense of urgency radiated to me. He squealed off. I hoped my mother didn't notice but knew she would. He asked where I wanted to go, but I could just laugh. I suggested the high school parking lot. He frowned.

As dense as he could be at times, he was starting to get a bad vibe. Parking in the school parking lot wasn't his idea of a good time. He said he had a better idea and placed his hand on my leg and softly squeezed. I then moved his hand and said I wanted to talk.

Jack sighed and pulled into the high school lot. He parked, turned the engine off, and turned to me. 'What?' he asked."

I was transfixed. I couldn't believe she had never shared this with me.

Jen continued, "I said, 'I know things aren't going like you want, Jack.' And he agreed, but he leaned over and attempted to kiss me. I shook him off and said, 'Jack, it's over. I can't give you what you want and know some other girl will. So, I give you your freedom. Can you take me home now?'

Jack leaned back. He was stunned. 'What the heck, Jennifer? What the heck?' he said and started the Mustang and ripped out of the parking lot. It was one thing to pressure me to expand the physical side of our relationship and threaten me with other girls. Quite another to have me break up with *him*. What would his friends say? What would the school say? Now he was mad, very, very mad. We got back to my house in record time. Jack came to a rapid stop and told me to get out.

I wasn't at all positive if I had done the right thing or how it would affect my life."

I covered Jen's hand. "I'm so sorry I wasn't there for you. I knew you broke up, but not why. I asked, but you never wanted to talk about it. I thought I was respecting you, but instead, I wasn't being a best friend. I'm so sorry. I should have...done more, probed more." I left the questions of why silent.

Jen looked over my shoulder. "I think I was ashamed. Ashamed Jack didn't love me the way Brian loved you. That I wasn't good enough."

"Oh, Jen." I didn't know what to say.

At that moment, Ivy walked in, or should I say 'strutted,' and we were both distracted. Ivy didn't look like a nice person. She had all the outward appearances of physical beauty. She was blond, smartly dressed–this morning in a pair of skin-tight jeans and a cheetah print sweater. Kind of youthful, but it worked on her. Ivy seemed to have a perpetual snarl. In all honesty, I couldn't quite put my finger on it, but that was my impression. Her gaze met mine, and she tried to smile, at least, I *thought* she did. It was no secret she was a big Botox follower. Her *smile* had no warmth. I thought she'd come over and rub my current legal situation in my face, but she didn't. Lori-Sue was her cousin, after all.

Ivy had never been a nice girl, and she wasn't a nice woman. Some people didn't have the 'nice' gene. Even though she hadn't gone to Eastbury High, but instead had a Catholic School education at South Catholic, I saw her often enough, palling around with Lori-Sue. She was always snarky. I had lost track of her after I moved to Orange County, CA, but boy, did I feel her wedding presence once I returned home and started my business. Until my return, she really was the go-to wedding gal. I still had a long way to grow, but I was cutting into her space.

Jen ignored her and changed the subject. "I've been fixated on myself long enough. What happened this morning? You look like death."

"Gee, thanks." I didn't smile. "The police just left. They searched my house."

Jen's eyebrows flew into her hairline, her mouth dropping open.

"A bloody contract was found at the scene–one of *my* contracts. And they found the nasty texts Lori-Sue and I were exchanging the day before her murder. Not looking good for Kate. Oh, oh!" I pounded the small barista table with the flat of my hand. "And…an anonymous caller phoned in and said they'd find the murder weapon at my house."

At this, Jen frowned. "Please…" Her voice dripped with sarcasm. She paused. "What does Charlie say?"

"That I need a criminal attorney."

"You do, Katie." Jen covered my hand.

"Jen," I had to ask her this now…but it was hard, so very hard. Hard to imagine, hard to face, "if," I choked up.

She squeezed my hand.

"If I have to, if I…"

"I'll take her, Katie," Jen said kindly.

She knew, without my even asking. I wanted her to be the one to comfort Ellis, to house her, to love her if I was arrested or, God forbid, convicted of Lori-Sue's murder. At least I could put that worry to rest.

My dark mood was distracted by Addalee Baker, another high school pal, walking into Jen's shop. She was the bride Carmella Sulpelveda had referred to as having "trouble in paradise." Addalee's usual "glow" was absent. It was as if the aura that usually surrounded her had been distinguished. Even her luminous hair looked limp. She saw me and smiled briefly, then made her way over to my table. Jen smiled at her, then got up to go back to work. Addalee sat down. One thing I had always admired about Addalee was her calmness. She was unflappable, but not today. She was, for lack of a better word, twitchy.

Addalee was concerning me. She was such a sweet girl.

Jen sent one of her baristas over to Addalee with her favorite latte, I guess she had pre-ordered. She took a sip, closing her aqua-blue eyes briefly. Addalee had learned how to apply makeup to make those eyes her strongest feature. Then her eyes went from breathtaking to other-worldly. A natural blond in high school, her hair remained shockingly light. It always looked strong and healthy, but not today. She wore it in gentle waves above her shoulders. I had asked her once if she curled her hair every morning. "It's natural," she replied. I was jealous, still was. My own hair was pin-straight.

"How are you, Addalee?" I hoped my concern for her wasn't obvious in my expression.

Addalee met my gaze. "I'm fine." She brightened considerably. "I'm so excited about my wedding dress and the wedding. It's been a long time coming." She giggled.

And then some.

She still looked young and beautiful. I hoped she and Cory had time to have kids. Addalee had always wanted them, at least she had when I knew her long ago. I was worried about her, about how she looked and what Carmella had hinted at. Was there any substance behind her words? What past was

Carmella referring to?

"How's it going with the vendors? Did you and Cory decide on a DJ? And wasn't Lori-Sue going to do your flowers?"

This was awkward. As a photographer, Addalee was picky about her wedding details.

"Lori-Sue wasn't all that. Even though she thought she was." Addalee's face seemed colder than I would have expected.

A slight chill covered me. Apparently…I wasn't the only one who wasn't a fan of Lori-Sue.

"I know the The Rose Petal can do a better job."

"Joe is very talented. I know you two are friends. Frankly, Addalee, I'm surprised you didn't ask him to begin with."

She just shrugged. Weird.

"How are *you* doing, Kate?" Concern showed in those show-stopper eyes, and she covered my hand. "I heard what happened with the police. You know I'll always have your back. No one's a bigger fan than I."

I squeezed her hand back. "Your support means the world to me, Adda. I'm working through it."

She let it go. I was grateful. I didn't know if I could talk about it yet.

"Well, there *was* that whole thing in high school. That can't be helping."

This brought a smile to my face.

"Hey!" Addalee bent down and rooted around in her oversized pocketbook. She pulled out her iPhone. Her fingers flew across the screen. She smiled and turned her phone to me. On the screen, obviously, a photo of an old photo was an ancient picture from high school. There was my younger self next to Brian, his arm around me. I looked like such a baby. On my other side was the breathtaking Addalee, with Cory next to her.

I smiled. "Where was this taken, Addalee?"

Addalee turned it back to herself and looked longingly at the photo. "It was Cory's family lake house. Remember when we went out there that fall Saturday, our senior year? It was such a beautiful day."

I did remember. But I also remembered Cory and Addalee had had one heck of a fight that day. Now, this was before cell phones, but there was something about a message on the lake house answering machine...Why not ask Addalee? It had to be water under the bridge by now.

"As I remember," I paused here. I could stop right now and not bring it up, but I was curious. "You and Cory had a doozy of a fight that afternoon."

Addalee looked away. She didn't say anything for a bit. "Yeah." I didn't think she was going to say anymore, but then she did. "It was that hateful Lori-Sue. She had to know we were going to the lake for the day and called and left a message on the machine. I really don't remember exactly what she said." Addalee looked off to the right and didn't meet my gaze. "She never liked me and left a hateful message on the machine, knowing Cory would get it. We had the worst fight. I thought we'd break up. At least we got this picture," she tapped her phone, "before the fireworks started and Lori-Sue worked her magic and stole a beautiful day. That was her goal all along. I don't know if she was jealous or just hated me."

"What happened, Addalee? What did she say, and why would you ask her to do your wedding flowers?" I asked softly.

Addalee didn't answer me. "Love you, Kate, but I've got to go." She still didn't look directly at me.

We both took a last gulp of our coffees. I gave Jen an abbreviated wave. I wanted to tell her about the latest development with Addalee, but I also knew she'd tell me to keep my nose out of it. But I had a vested interest. I was Addalee's wedding planner. Did I imagine it, or was Addalee hypersensitive to all things Lori-Sue? I got that chill again.

Chapter Ten

Brides, remember to have a table at the reception for your vendors to rest and enjoy a meal. You will be greatly appreciated.

I slept in the next day. I almost always got up with Ellis, barring an outbreak of the flu, made her breakfast and lunch, and talked about her upcoming day. She had slid a warm "Moon Rock" muffin and a piece of melon onto my nightstand and deposited a cup of honey-laced tea next to it.

She whispered in my ear as she smoothed my sleep-tangled hair from my face. "Sleep in, Mom. I love you."

Who could argue with that? I never thought I'd sleep, but I nibbled on the muffin, took a couple sips of the sweet tea, and was out. Little Chloe snuggled next to me in bed–another no-no. I awoke again at 10, grabbed a shower, stepped into some khakis and a button-down shirt, and went into my home office. I didn't really like working from home. I was the kind of person who needed to distance home life from the job. But I didn't have the energy to make the trek to my downtown office, located above Jen's coffee shop. She was, in fact, my landlord, cutting me an incredible deal on the rent–almost nothing for my first year. Jen's Coffee shop was on Main Street, of course, located in a converted old mansion. She had knocked down walls on the main floor and created a wonderful open space filled with cozy groupings of tables and eclectic chairs. Nothing matched at Jen's, and it all worked. I was on the second floor, as well as a few other small businesses. We were able to access our offices either by an outside staircase, or the internal stairs via the coffee shop. My suite of rooms was barely that. I had a tiny waiting area for clients, a closed-door main office along with a tiny powder room and a kitchen nook—comprised of a mini-fridge, a hot pot, a microwave, a small counter space, and don't tell Jen...an espresso machine. But at least for the next several days, my office was too close to Lori-Sue's shop. She had been a tenant of Jen's as well.

I was lucky to have enough space in our home for an office, and I had decked it out with a used desk, several bookcases, and a ladder-backed chair that had originally been part of Ellis's juvenile bedroom set from Ethan Allen. Lots and lots of her school years' art framed the walls. I had added a comfy armchair and ottoman in the corner, and the space looked like me. In fact, it was more "me" than my fancy office downtown. I returned some emails, Chloe content in her extra dog bed at my feet, but worried about the murder and the police's perception of my role. Just being associated with this whole mess could prove ruin for my fledgling business. I decided to grab some lunch, and before I knew it, it was time to head to the high school for Ellis's softball game. But first, I needed coffee. Ellis's tea hadn't done the trick. She was pitching again, and if I knew what was best for me, I wouldn't miss another game. Jen would have a cup of my favorite brew waiting for me this time of day. Was I that predictable?

I walked into The Coffee Roasters and was greeted by an unusually long line. 'The Roasters,' as the locals called it, was everyone's go-to coffee shop. I loved the eclectic style Jen had used to decorate her shop. Local artists' art hung from the coffee shop walls, the lights were low to give off a "chill vibe," and cool Jazz played over the sound system at all times. The long line was a plus for Jen's business but bad for my time schedule.

I got a melancholy feeling as I thought of Lori-Sue. She wasn't my friend, but I was sad at her passing and horrified at the way she had died. I was worried about my legal situation. Was that what bothered me more than her passing? Could I be that self-absorbed? I put those thoughts on the back burner as Jen caught my gaze and indicated with her head to move over to the pickup bar. She handed me my dark roast with room for cream. I had never paid for a cup of coffee at Jen's shop, but compensated by heavily tipping her daughters whenever they were working.

"I was hoping you'd come in today." Jen's short, straight hair was swinging around her face.

I smiled my thanks for the extra-large coffee.

Almost everyone in the line was looking our way, and it wasn't because I had jumped the queue. New Englanders were too well-bred to come over and bombard me with questions. Thank goodness because I was not ready to discuss my situation. I was already late for Ellis's game.

* * *

Ellis and her team lost the game. As well as being bone tired, I had to deal with an already surly teen in a terrible mood. I got home before Ellis, as she had to have a team debriefing.

I greeted her warmly when she entered our mudroom, bringing in the smell of the softball field with her.

"I have a pork roast and new potatoes in the slow cooker and Cream Cheese Brownies for dessert. Let me add the green beans, and dinner will be ready in about twenty." I was hoping for a civil response as she entered the warm kitchen.

Dream on.

"Not hungry." Ellis then proceeded to stomp up to her room, spreading a cloud of fine red silt with every step.

If it made her feel better to ignore our rule of removing those filthy softball clothes in the downstairs laundry room before traipsing through the house, I could deal with it.

What I couldn't deal with was the phone call that came next. My cell buzzed and my delightful ex appeared on the screen. To answer or not to answer...

"Hi, Grant."

"How's my little murder suspect? Ellis let me know." He sounded smug.

I rolled my eyes. See what living with a teenager would do to you? "Thanks for the sensitivity, Grant. This whole thing is no laughing matter."

He cleared his throat. "Sorry, Kate. Didn't mean to come across as such an insensitive jerk." Uh, oh. He wanted something. Grant never apologized.

I pulled out a kitchen chair and sat down. Might as well get comfortable. "What do you want, Grant?"

"Wow, Kate."

"How long were we married? You think I don't know you? What's up?"

Silence. He was plotting how to formulate his request. You'd think he'd have it all mapped out, but not Grant. He liked to gauge his audience and then decide how to play it. He had my tough self today. I was in no mood. I actually thought he might call back tomorrow, hoping for a happier Kate. I was so irritated, I put him on speakerphone and began scrolling through work emails. But what he said next brought me sitting up straight. He had my full attention.

"Well...Heather and I decided last minute to kick back and throw caution to the wind. We're going to Hawaii for a week...." Caution to the wind? That was the story of Grant's life.

I met Heather when Ellis, Grant, and I moved into our new "McMansion" in Huntington Beach, California. She and her husband lived next door. We had so much in common, we talked about everything, and I really thought I had found my female soul mate. She consoled me when Grant and I had a fight, took Ellis when I had the flu, and was the shoulder I cried on when I had a miscarriage. We even vacationed together. I now hated her, and it was maddening that I had to share my daughter with the woman who broke up my marriage.

I was still silent after Grant's statement.

"We want Ellis to come with us."

Seriously? "And when would this be, Grant?"

"Next week."

I laughed, actually laughed. When he first mentioned Hawaii, I thought I'd be in for a battle royal with him, with Ellis. But next week began the state tournament for the softball team. Ellis would rather sever a limb than miss it.

"You find this amusing, Kathryn?" Oooooh. Grant was throwing down the big guns, calling me by my formal name. What was he, my dad?

I went back to scrolling through my emails. It was do that or scream at him.

"What I find amusing, Grant," I wished he had a formal name I could throw down, "is that you know neither your daughter nor me well. I'd never agree to a week off school, and your daughter would never miss the state tourney. I'd think you'd at least know that. You were her coach for a long time, remember? You know how much softball means to her. But then you didn't even know when it was, did you? Excellent job of staying up to date with her life." And then I was mad, not just at him. I was mad I had stumbled across a body and seemed to be in hot water over it, mad my daughter was being such a snot tonight, and mad I didn't have the confidence to wear dresses anymore because of the scar on my leg from my bike accident. I wished I had the option to slam the receiver down. Maybe some brilliant engineer would develop that feature on the next new-and-improved iPhone. So, instead, I ended the call.

Chapter Eleven

Make sure your planner has extra copies of EVERYTHING, from your vows to seating assignments.

After much pleading, Ellis agreed to help me at a wedding. I was excited and grateful. What a wonderful way to spend a Saturday. I had to start going through those resumes in my inbox for an assistant. It would be a tough job to fill. My assistant would be part-time. It would be a great second job for someone, but I knew it would be asking a lot for a part-time worker to reserve time to work a wedding as much as a year in advance. But that was the nature of event planning.

"Mom!" Ellis came hopping over to me in the barn where the reception was being held.

Yes, it was another barn wedding. Here in New England, barn weddings hadn't gone out of vogue. This venue was right off a two-lane road, but once we entered the property, it was as if we were in another world. The fields were being prepped for the new spring plantings, the barn had a fresh coat of red paint, and I had heard a rooster crow, for goodness sake. I hoped the farm family didn't rely on him as an alarm clock. His timing was way off.

"The cake's here." Ellis loved all the bells and whistles of a wedding: the dress, the cake, the favors.

"Wonderful." I had begun to worry.

The cake was an hour late. And to add insult to injury, the bride, against my advice, was using a baker I'd had nothing but trouble with. The last time I used this baker, the cake fell apart after the bride and groom cut it. Did the guests witness this catastrophe? No. I took care of the disaster. The baker had pushed the bride and groom into using buttercream frosting, a bad choice in warm weather. They didn't know this, but the baker did. It was much cheaper to use buttercream than a sustainable substance like fondant.

It was the baker's responsibility to advise and direct. A couple should feel confident and comfortable with their baker, knowing he or she wasn't trying to drive the price up but had their best interest at heart. To be perfectly honest, it was my job too, to advise and direct the bridal couple I was working with. If I saw a garish error, I was duty-bound to point it out and point it out I had.

"But, Kate," my former bride whined, "I love buttercream, and Tina promises my cake can be refrigerated until it's time to display it for the reception."

"How can Tina promise that? She's not in charge of the kitchen. Your caterer is. She can make no legitimate promises as to the storage of your cake. What if your caterer needs the space in the fridge?" But there was no reasoning with Louise.

So...I was less than pleased when tonight's bride and groom hired Tina, the queen of the cake disaster. I was relieved when Tina and one of her staff members finally sauntered in, carrying their heavy burden, grunting, and sweating. No apology was made for their tardiness.

"Where do you want it?" Tina wheezed, a drop of sweat dripping down the side of her face.

"On the table with the two vases of lavender roses, in the empty space. You're an hour late."

"I just finished it," Tina snarled.

And hello to you too! I thought but didn't say.

"Yeah. Tina's an artist. You can't rush art," the short redheaded fireplug carrying the other side of the cake chimed in; she wasn't smiling.

"Kate, can I borrow you for a minute?" Kim, today's caterer, rushed in.

I hated to walk away from the cake set-up, but Kim looked stressed.

After I helped Kim locate the missing prosecco, I headed back to the cake. The two women were gone, but the cake sat in the middle of the table I had indicated. A troubled Ellis stood in front of the cake table; her head cocked first from the left and then to the right.

"I think the cake is leaning," she deadpanned.

Oh, my word. That was the understatement of the day. "Ah, yeah. Run and get those two buffoons before they finish packing up and drive off."

"Oh, they're gone, Mom." Ellis's gaze still didn't leave the cake.

I understood her fascination. It really looked as if it might fall right over. And this cake wasn't cheap, either. It was a beautiful, save for the leaning bit, concoction of buttercream lavender icing with darker spun sugar lavender flowers. I had to admit, the spun sugar flowers were so expertly done one might mistake them for natural. A true work of art. It cost upward of $1,500. Today's bride had been almost secretive with her bakery invoice after I had encouraged her to go with someone instead of Tina. She shared the other vendor invoices with me, but nothing to do with the cake.

Dang. There wasn't time to call them back because dollars to donuts, if I called the bakery, they wouldn't return my call. I'd have to fix it myself.

"Game to help me fix the cake, Ellis?"

Ellis, with difficulty, tore her "deer in the headlight" gaze from the cake and stared at me with open-mouthed horror. "Whaa??"

I almost giggled. But I refused to be cocky till this ridiculous cake was set to rights. Ellis knew me as the mom who was a proficient cook, but not much of a baker; add to that, I didn't much like it.

"I can do it, Elle. But I'll need a second pair of hands. You in?"

A small glimmer of admiration lit in my daughter's eyes. Fixing the cake for her approval now meant as much to me as the repair itself.

"Grab my bride bag in the office, please, Ellis."

My bride bag was a source of pride. I had everything in there to fix any kind of problem. Needed a cake repaired. I had a spreader; I needed to sew the bride's bustle, no problem! Your time of the month, I had that covered too.

She scampered off. I walked around the cake. It really wouldn't be that hard of a fix.

Ellis came back in with my bag, and I sent her into the kitchen for a glass of warm water.

She returned in thirty seconds flat and placed the full glass on the cake table. I rooted around in my bag and came up with some white cocktail napkins, kept tidy in a plastic bag, and a spreading knife–the kind with a wide flat blade you used to frost a cake.

"So, Ellis, when you look at this cake, what do you immediately think?"

"It's leaning, like the Leaning Tower of Pisa."

"Okay, so what we're going to do is lift the offending layer; the whole cake isn't leaning, just the middle layer, put some cocktail napkins under it, and repair the frosting we disturbed." Luckily, Tina had yet again used buttercream. It was easier for me to smooth buttercream than it was fondant. And we did just that. I didn't have piping tools, so there was an obvious area where it had been messed with, but we had done it at the back of the cake and then moved the cake table against the wall so people couldn't admire the cake from all angles. I had taken a "before" and "after" picture. I was shocked Tina had delivered it that way and shocked she'd set it up flawed.

"Now we have to tell our friend Kim, the caterer, about the napkins so it's not a surprise when they cut the cake to serve, and the bride as well. A wad of paper wouldn't go over well if she's not expecting it." It would serve her right, though, for not listening to me. After the wedding, I'd email the photos to Tina but felt certain I'd get no response. I didn't expect one, but I'd keep the photos in my files in case another bride wanted to use her bakery.

Things flowed smoothly for the wedding after the cake fiasco. Ellis and I enjoyed a lovely dinner courtesy of the bride. She had also thoughtfully provided a dining table for the vendors. Not all brides had the luxury of extra floor space, but it was so nice when they did. Sometimes we vendors were on our feet as much as twelve to fourteen hours on a wedding day. A comfortable, out-of-the-way place to call our own during the day was a godsend. And, with my leg aching tonight, it was a double blessing. Ellis and I were lucky enough to have the table to ourselves for the moment.

Dinner was delicious. I had chosen the salmon, Ellis, the chicken. The creamy new potatoes were my favorite side, or was it the buttery asparagus?

"Mom?" Ellis asked.

I finished chewing a bite of the luscious salad. "Yeah, hon?"

"I'm having a bit of trouble at school."

Knock me over with a feather. I had no idea. Was Ellis that slick at hiding her feelings, or had I been that inattentive with the Lori-Sue fiasco?

"Oh, God! Are the kids giving you grief about the murder investigation? I'm so sorry if this has affected...."

Ellis put her hand over mine. "Mom." She squeezed my hand into silence. "Don't stress. I *have* been talking about it; everyone has. I thought it wouldn't hurt to ask around, see what everyone's thinking, if anyone knew anything...."

"Ellis!" I was appalled. My poor kid. What was I doing to her with all this mess? "I'm so sorry, hon. It's going to be okay."

"Oh, I know it is, Mom." She took a bite of her chicken.

I had to stop myself from telling her not to talk with her mouth full. Now wasn't the time.

"It's just that when I started asking questions, I started getting weird, kinda threatening texts from an unknown number."

Crap! I became lightheaded.

Ellis laughed. "Mom, chill." It was her turn to try to comfort me. "It really is going to be okay."

I wasn't going to let her get me off track. "What did those texts say." My mama-bear ultra-ego was kicking in. I could do some damage if anyone hurt my baby.

Ellis smiled. She knew my look. "Whoa, Mama-Bear. Not much to report. Just along the lines of 'Quit asking questions about Lori-Sue. It's none of your damn business...or else.' That was it, well, I got some more, but the message was the same. A few of them had some wicked good swearing in them." Ellis snorted.

"Let me see them, right now! Do you have any idea who's behind the texts?" I held out my hand for her phone.

"Uh, phone's at home, per your mandate." She smirked. "But I have this weird feeling it might be Lori-Sue's cousin's kid.

"Whaaa? You mean Ivy's kid?" As I had lost track of Ivy, I didn't know anything about her family situation. "Okay, as soon as we get home, I want to see that phone."

Ellis saluted, "Yes, ma'am. And thanks, Mom." She was still my baby.

Chapter Twelve

Printing your invitations on your home computer can save quite a bit of money in your wedding budget.

Ellis showed me the hateful texts as soon as we got home. I didn't like the anonymity of them, nor the nasty, threatening tone, but it seemed to be kid-stuff. Not to be ignored, of course, but not an emergency, either. I'd investigate, but sadly, it would have to be on Monday. I had another party tomorrow night.

I wasn't in the mood for an event, not after the wedding last night. Oh, my aching leg *and* my aching feet, but we had to eat. I tried to book just one party a weekend, but a Sunday evening at the engaged couple's favorite venue, the Eastbury Country Club, was the only night available for months.

Eastbury Country Club was very understated, not at all like the gaudy clubs of the south. The course was breathtaking, especially in the fall when the trees were all kinds of orange, red, and yellow. The clubhouse itself was a Cape-Cod-style structure, complete with shake siding. The interior had undergone a major remodel and was tastefully updated with refurbished hardwood floors, luxurious draperies, cozy wing-backed chairs and love seats. The bar area was the perfect place to unwind after a round of golf or to close a business deal. The main dining room had an overlarge dance floor and a view of the course that was to die for.

Tonight's engagement party was an over-the-top affair. The event had all the components of a wedding, except for the ceremony. The mini-wedding had a cocktail hour, sit-down dinner, and full band. I had made it through the dinner and just had the cake-cutting left. They actually planned to cut a cake, just like at a wedding. Really? What was the deal? They would be doing all this, almost exactly the same way, in twelve months' time; perhaps it was for the gifts? Now I was being crass. But I knew, for a fact, that with a crowd of 300, (about 150 couples), the engaged couple could rake in approximately $75,000 tonight. A nice nest egg to get the couple started, and they could expect to double that for the wedding.

Tonight's couple was Barbie Mission and Steve Chrisly. Barbie was a bit of a diva and instructions had been sent to all engagement party guests to wear black and only black. Barbie wore red; it was quite stunning. We hadn't gone over all the wedding details, but I had a feeling she'd do the same for the main event; but, of course, she'd wear white. Barbie even boasted a tiara tonight; the diamonds were real. Was it a bit gouache that she wore it, as tiaras were usually reserved for titled, married ladies? Perhaps, but what the heck? It was her night.

The cake was commonly known as a "Groom's Cake." It was a novelty cake in the shape of the groom's favorite car, (and he had plenty), a 911 Porsche twin-turbo. When it came to debating who was more gouache, the bride or the groom, I'd had to pick the groom. The cake was silly. It looked like something Buddy, from the reality show *Cake Boss,* would make. Cute, appropriate for a child's birthday party, yes. For a party that was trying to be elegant, no. But no one listened to me. I was beginning to regret my decision to take on their wedding. The last thing I needed was to be associated with tackiness. No one really watched the "cake cutting," even though I did my best to round up the guests. People were too interested in the cigar bar, tequila tasting station, candy bar, and Ben and Jerry's cones. A true example of too much was too much.

Barbie was headed to the bridal suite to change into her second dress for the evening. She had chosen a short red frock for dancing. Barbie had hinted to me she had a third dress for the after-party, but I would be long gone by that time. My contract said my services ended after the cutting of the cake. At least I had been wise enough to depart early. Really, with such a formal event and so many servers waiting on the couple, there was not much for me to do after the cake was cut/dessert served.

I was ready to make my getaway when I felt eyes at the back of my head. I turned slowly around and met the eyes of…Sarah Deloro, my high school nemesis. She was dressed in a drop-dead gorgeous black sheath dress. If possible, she looked better than she had in high school. It appeared she had had breast augmentation. I didn't remember her being that big, but boy, was her surgeon skilled. 'They' looked so real. I thought of my own natural breasts, not so perky after breastfeeding. Sarah was slim, and her dress looked to have cost a fortune. It clung in all the right places. I hated her as much as in the past, if possible. Sparks flew from her eyes. She still hated me too, it appeared.

The reason for our mutual dislike? Well, Brian McAllister, of course; for Brian was Sarah's boyfriend before he was mine. Did I steal him? Well…not exactly, but the case could be made I didn't help their relationship. Brian and I were in the same Home EC class. It wasn't so much a thing anymore, many high schools having done away with the cooking/sewing classes, just not enough funds. But back in my day, almost everyone took it. If you could read and follow directions, you got an A. My cooking partner, Tiffany, was absent one day, and Brian became my chocolate chip cookie partner. I was a nice-looking girl, but not a knock-out like my Ellis, but it was as if he saw me for the first time and liked what he saw. At the end of class, he asked me out.

* * *

All that seemed to flit across Sarah's face. "Well, Katie, how nice to see you." There was no smile. "Oh, my, I'm oh so thirsty. Can you get me a glass of water? You are the hired help, right?" This was said with a snarl.

I initially said nothing but stared at her toes and made my scathing appraisal up to the top of her head. I had my own lip curl going. "I'm so sorry you're parched, Sarah. There are a couple of half-empty glasses on the table over there." I carelessly waved my hand over in the direction of the guest tables.

Sarah opened her mouth, but nothing came out. She never was very quick, and really, what I had said wasn't very clever. She could have come up with *something!* How about a jab at my legal woes? Instead, she stomped off. Huh. I knew she was now a big-shot Realtor. One couldn't go anywhere without seeing her photo on a "For Sale" sign, or billboard, much to my annoyance. It *really* was time to go especially as I didn't want any run-ins with Sarah.

I was heading to the cloakroom to fetch my pocketbook and coat but heard female whispers coming from the direction of the ladies' guest restroom. I'd admit it. I was nosey, so I stopped and consulted my Apple watch for my "cover" and listened.

"Sarah Deloro is here! John says it was absolutely going to the Board of Realtors, but then Lori-Sue was murdered!" The first voice hissed.

"And without her statement, the complaint was dead in the water," the other said with a giggle.

"Great choice of words, Liz."

"Nobody liked Lori-Sue, anyway," the other replied. "And once again, Sarah

Deloro skates free. When is she going to get her comeuppance?"

"I was playing bridge with Violet and her group last Tuesday in the ladies' card room, and she said she'd do anything to get a look in Sarah's club locker. She heard a rumor she keeps all her nasty secrets there instead of somewhere secure like a bank safety deposit box," the other woman replied.

"Now that's weird," commented Liz.

I'd have to agree, and wow, Wow, WOW! But my eavesdropping cost me. I didn't quite make my getaway before the bride-to-be returned in her dancing dress. Dang it!

"Oh, Kate! Thank God you're still here! I need you to run out to my car and get my box of tampons." Barbie said all this in a hushed voice, handing me her car keys.

Okay. There were three things I don't do for a bride or any client at an event. I didn't stand on ladders, I didn't carry anything over ten pounds, and I didn't do *anything* related to food, i.e., refill platters, serve drinks, or clean up refuse. I now realized I needed to add fetch tampons out of the bride-to-be's car to that list. I really didn't mind helping out wherever I was needed. But I did take offense at being someone's errand girl, especially after the lady in question knew I was done for the night. But then...perhaps I was a mite cranky. I made short work of retrieving the tampons and returning the bride-to-be's car keys. This short errand hadn't lessened my desire to investigate, though.

I had to see in Sarah Deloro's club locker if it was the last thing I did. I decided on a bold move.

I knew where the club's business offices were located. I looked left, I looked right. No one was around. I approached the door. I bet it was locked. My hand hovered over the office doorknob. I was crossing another line, and this time, I was infringing on a client. This could really come back to bite me in the behind. I almost hoped the door *would* be locked. It wasn't, though. I prayed there wasn't an automatic light that would shine on as soon as I entered. The room remained dark, thank God for small favors. I silently closed the door behind me. The soft moonlight streaming in from the one office window helped me see the general layout of the room, but it didn't prevent me from banging my shin into a desk leg. Dang! I muffled my rarely used swear words and rubbed my shin aggressively. Yikes, that hurt. I risked it and turned on my cell phone flashlight. I quickly looked at the family photos on each of the three desks. I recognized one family and thought I'd have a better chance of guessing her computer password than the other two. Because we all knew, secrets were kept on computers, be they cell phones or desktops. It would be a long shot that I could guess anyone's password, but hey, it was worth a try. I sat down at Teresa's desk and thought. I knew her in high school, she was a sweet girl and LOVED cats. Ok, I rolled the office chair closer to the desk and moved the mouse to wake up the computer. Boom! The screen saver was a photo of a darling kitty. We didn't change, did we? What was the name of her darn cat she was so crazy about? I had limited time and attempts. Patches! I remembered looking at the photo of a kitten on the screen saver. "Patches 1 2 3," I typed in. The password box jumped at me, indicating my incorrect attempt. What was Teresa's birthday? How in the world would I know that? I flipped through her calendar blotter on her desk until I came to November. *Anniversary!* was written on November 8. Okay. We were in business. "Patches 11 8," I tried. The password box jumped again. This wasn't going to work. Would she, would she be so careless? I typed "Teresa 11 8." Boom…I was in. Someone had better have a talk with Teresa about her internet security.

I went to the folder on the desktop that said "Member Locker Numbers." I scrolled down to Deloro, Sarah. Number 304, combination: 13-23-43. This was too easy, but who was I to complain? I carefully closed Teresa's 'Member Locker Numbers' file and put the computer back into sleep mode. I put her office chair back exactly as I found it and then quietly exited the office, mindful of any stray party guests in the hallway. I needn't have worried. I could hear the dull noise of the party but saw not a soul. Which way to the women's locker room?

I headed straight down the corridor and turned right. "Women's Locker Room" a sign boasted. Well, ok! What would my story be if discovered inside? Hmmm… I'd just say I was retrieving a personal item for the bride. Kinda true! Barbie *did* ask me to fetch her some tampons. But once again, I encountered no one. I went right to locker number 304 and tried the combination. I had to do it three times, my hands were shaking so. It reminded me of finding Lori-Sue and having to call 911. The locker door groaned open with a creak. The interior smelled like all lockers, musty and yucky. I rooted around inside, feeling dirty doing so, but my life was at stake here. I found nothing of interest, some toiletries, a smelly T-shirt, and a pair of questionable socks. But at the bottom was a photo of a house. Not a surprising find considering Sarah was a realtor. But the house looked familiar. I heard the locker room door open and quickly threw the photo back in the locker and closed it with a soft click. I went in the opposite direction from the intruders and slipped out of the locker room and into the dark parking lot to make my escape.

Chapter Thirteen

It is imperative you have a rain plan for your Wedding Ceremony and Reception.

It was Monday morning. I wasn't going to let the whole anonymous bullying of Ellis thing go. I wouldn't ignore it under normal circumstances, but given that someone had been *murdered,* not to mention I was a person of interest, it was a no-brainer. But how did I infiltrate the high school, find the culprit, and make sure my girl was safe, all the while not arousing her suspicions or anyone else's? Because Ellis would most certainly not want me butting in. Suspicious behavior was reported by teens at lightning speed with the advent of smartphones. I longed for the days when kids could have phones but never ever use them at school, at least not out in the open. Now the schools *gave* them devices and insisted they use them for academics. It really was a mixed bag. I hadn't decided how I really felt about it. I knew they were a great teaching/learning aid...but...

So, this morning, as tired as I was after *two* events this weekend, I decided the safest thing to do was to find out who was sending those texts. You'd think I'd know about Ivy's kid from living in Eastbury, because, in a small town, most people knew, or knew of, everyone's extended family. But I had been gone a long time.

I drove to the high school. Eastbury High was a red brick building that fit in ascetically with the New England architecture of the town: historic and staid. But on the inside, the school was state-of-the-art, especially the science wing. It was on par with most college labs. These days, everyone had to check in at the security desk and declare where they were headed. I put the library. If anyone asked why I didn't know what I'd say. Maybe my cover would be I wanted to look at the yearbooks to research for a party.

The librarian gave me a dirty look as I walked in the door. Ha, I guessed they hadn't changed much since I was a student here. The librarians were the crankiest of all the high school staff then and, so it seemed, now. She didn't question my intentions, however. But I could tell she was keeping her eye on me. The librarian noted I was wearing my Visitor sticker.

If I remembered correctly, the yearbooks, one for each year since the school had been in existence, were housed against the back wall by the magazine shelf. I headed over that way, and, yep, there they were.

Once I grabbed a couple of yearbooks, I questioned my strategy. Ellis didn't mention if Ivy's kid was male or female, what year they were, or their name. What was wrong with me? Did the teen have the same last name as Ivy? I should have quizzed Ellis, but I was afraid she'd be on to me and ask her own questions. *Why did I want to know? I wasn't going to do anything, was I? I wasn't going to the high school, was I?* I was weighing my options when someone whispered my name.

When I didn't answer, they said it louder, "Katie!"

I looked up. And there, working the library desk, she must have been in the back when I walked in as I hadn't seen her, was my high school friend/acquaintance Rainey Shaker. Rainey and I were in the same graduating year and had several classes together. We were both on the cheerleading squad and friendly, but never close friends. She was a nice girl, and I had always liked her.

I walked over to the library desk and awkwardly hugged Rainey over the counter. She grinned widely. I remembered *why* I had always liked her. She was warm and genuine. Her figure had become generous over the years, just like mine, but I'd know her anywhere. Her soft blond hair tickled my nose.

"Katie Manet. I heard you were back. It's been about a year now, hasn't it? I meant to call, but life, you know...." She grinned again.

"No worries, Rainey. I could have, and should have, called myself. How *are* you?"

She grinned again and smiled. "Married Glen Westfield and have three boys. And look at us, back at high school!" She motioned me around the desk.

I was lightheaded. Who would ever think I'd be *behind* the librarian's desk? We went into the glassed fronted office, giving us some privacy, but we could still see out into the library.

"It's quiet out there. Let's have a cup of coffee and a chat. I won't beat around the bush," she popped a coffee pod into the machine and placed a paper cup underneath the spout. "I'm dying to hear all about Lori-Sue's murder. She was never a favorite of mine, but I'd never wish *that* on her. Are they really looking at you as a suspect?" Rainey wasn't shy. She shook her head as she reached into the mini fridge and grabbed a carton of Half and Half. Rainey put a generous dollop into her cup and mine. She didn't ask, just created her concoction as she talked. Rainey didn't offer sugar, and I didn't want it. We each had our cups at rapid speed, and she guided me to two industrial chairs. I wouldn't be surprised if those same chairs were here when we were.

"I heard you have a daughter at the high school, but I would have known even if no one had told me. She's the spittin' image of you as a girl."

I smiled a proud smile. Nothing pleased me more than to hear that. "Love that, Rainey. Thank you."

"Now, about that murder!" Rainey wasn't letting me off the hook.

"Rainey, the police won't let me discuss it. I'm a person of interest. But you can help me with something."

While she looked slightly shamefaced, Rainey recovered quickly. She always did have a sunny disposition. "Hogwash. You couldn't hurt a fly, Katie. What do you need?"

"I'm trying to help Ellis, my daughter, with something," I smiled. "Do you know if Lori-Sue's cousin, Ivy, has a child who goes to school here?"

"Well, you've come to the right girl." Rainey crossed her legs and settled in. Was she on break? She looked as if she hadn't a care in the world and ignored the nasty frown the librarian up front shot through the office window as she checked out students' books. "No one knows all the dirt in town like the high school librarians." She snorted as she laughed.

"And yes, Ivy does have a kid who attends here, and, between you, me, and the fencepost, not a nice kid, either. I can say that cause I'm not a teacher, just a library aide. If I were a teacher, they'd have my head for spouting off about a student."

Helpful to know.

"Anyway, Kelly Jackman isn't someone you'd want your kid hanging with. Ivy married up. Her ex-husband owns a Chevy dealership in Hartford. That girl has too much money and not enough supervision. Runs with a fast crowd."

"I've been gone so long. Were Ivy and Lori-Sue still close? I remember they fought like cats and dogs when they were kids."

Ivy and Lori-Sue's moms were sisters, and they really wanted their girls to be close. Supposedly, they planned to get pregnant together, and it worked. The one thing they didn't plan for was their offspring's intense bickering.

"Tell me about Ivy's daughter, Kelly." Hey, if Rainey wasn't going to become unnerved about the increasingly nasty looks she was getting from her coworker, then neither was I.

"I rarely see her in here, but when she does come in, it's to cause trouble. She seems to get a kick out of picking on others and causing a stir. There are some people who are mean, and I'm afraid she's one of them."

"How old are your boys?" Quick change of subject, but I should be polite. Besides, I was interested.

A look of pure mama love came over Rainey's face. "Sophomore, junior, and senior. They're great boys, straight 'A' students, athletes, and nice people."

I knew Ellis could do worse than one of the Westfield boys. I'd have to coyly ask if she knew one or all. Dollars to donuts, she did.

I gave Rainey a warm hug, thanked her for the coffee, and started to head out of the library. I looked over my shoulder to give Rainey one last wave (but she was busy back at work checking out students' books). Then I noticed Ellis and her group of friends in the very back of the library. Huh. How did I miss them before? I imagine they came in while I was in the back chatting with Rainey. This was a golden opportunity. What could a little eavesdropping hurt?

I had no excuse for contemplating eavesdropping on my very trustworthy daughter. Who was I? I hid behind a shelf, trying to appear like I was looking for a book in case I was caught. Guilt stabbed me. I had been a less-than-attentive mother to Ellis as my marriage was breaking up; the fact I was clueless to the destruction of my union was no excuse.

Ellis had left a boy behind in Orange County, California, when we moved east. It was a new romance, and even I wasn't aware it had become more than a friendship. His name was River, a quiet boy, tall with soulful brown eyes. He was a gifted musician and played the viola like nothing I had ever heard. I could have listened to him play for hours. They had been friends since middle school, an easy relationship. With River, Ellis could be completely herself. She said he laughed at her jokes, was a shoulder to cry on when her girlfriends were typical mean girls, and never judged her. I knew she missed him, missed his music.

Ellis confided in me that her changed feelings caught her completely by surprise. They were on the bus riding home, neither had their driver's licenses yet. I wouldn't let Ellis ride with her older friends who had cars, which she sometimes did if she thought she wouldn't get caught.

She said their gazes met as they laughed over something silly, not someone. Neither would do that, just a shared joke. And Ellis said she got a weird feeling in her stomach like she did when she rode a roller coaster; the feeling like you'd stayed in one spot, but your stomach dropped out.

River met her gaze head-on and didn't blink. He leaned in and gave her a chaste kiss on the lips. It was just a moment, but it changed Ellis's world. She said she opened her eyes, looked into River's, and said, 'Wow.'

"He grinned, Mom," she'd shared. "I've been wanting to do that for a year," he said.

"Why now, then?" Ellis told me she'd said.

"I saw in your eyes you finally felt the same way." River had shyly placed his hand over Ellis's.

I got goosebumps when she told me about it.

Ellis said she wrapped her hand around River's, interlocked their fingers, and hung on.

Nothing else was spoken, and, by mutual agreement, they both got off at Ellis's stop and walked to our house, where they were warmly greeted by me with homemade hummus and wheat-free crackers. I was quite the California mother at that time–nutritious food and all that.

I didn't know about their romantic tale when I asked, "How was school, kids? Do you have a class project to work on or something?"

Ellis hadn't given me a head's-up River was coming over, so I thought it must be school-related.

"No." Ellis hadn't quite met my gaze.

Weird, I thought at the time.

I was preoccupied those days and didn't notice the new dynamic between Ellis and one of her friends for a while. River was a fixture in our home, had been since seventh grade. I was an attentive mother, but something wasn't right with Grant, and it was occupying my thoughts. He was coming home late, was on his phone *all the time,* and seemed to be miles away, not from just me, but from Ellis too. I had hoped there was nothing wrong at work. Was I blind or what? He usually shared his business concerns, liked to bounce ideas off me, valued my opinion. A terrible thought crossed my mind at the time. What if he had been offered a promotion that required a move? I had made it very clear to Grant I wouldn't uproot Ellis while she was in high school. I had had the luxury of attending the same school district for my entire education and wanted the same for my daughter. That was it, I decided at the time. Grant was just too scared to tell me about the possible move. Well, we'd deal with it as a family. Maybe I'd stay behind with Ellis and allow her to finish high school here. We could visit Grant on random weekends and holidays, and he could do the same. *Just please, please don't let it be overseas,* I thought. I could deal with a domestic long-distance family thing, but not if he wasn't in the same country. But, in all honesty, I still had a nagging fear. What if it was something else? I had a bad feeling. If I had only known…

When it was time to move, Ellis was cranky and out of sorts; I wasn't surprised. Her parents were splitting up, she was moving across the country, and she was starting a new school. At the time, I hadn't dug any deeper than that. I couldn't face that I was the cause of Ellis's first romantic relationship breaking up. I had enough guilt over my failed marriage, I couldn't add additional guilt. Was it partly my fault? Was I not attentive enough, attractive enough? But I knew, intellectually, this train of thought was toxic and moved away from it. My herculean effort didn't help Ellis, though, as she struggled with the loss of her first love. Oh, yes, River and Ellis planned to keep in touch, and social media made it easier than days past. But both were mature enough, and realistic enough, to know it wouldn't last.

So, was it important to me that Ellis had loyal friends here and that I be emotionally present in her life? Yes, yes, it was.

* * *

"So, Elle," Candy, official best friend and star girls' lacrosse player, said as I listened to them from my spot behind the library stack. "What's with all the cloak and dagger stuff? I have practice."

"Yeah," chimed in Whitney, second best friend and the good sport in their group of four.

The girls gave Whitney a hard time for being head cheerleader on the varsity squad. Cheerleading wasn't the big deal here in New England that it was out west or down south. It was tolerated, barely. Whitney had to continually remind her friends it was a *sport*. The girls were merciless when it came to teasing her about it. They secretly acknowledged it really was an athletic endeavor.

"I've got cheer practice. Stop… don't start," she warned the group, holding her hand up.

"And I've got an ortho appointment in," Peter, the only male at the table, said, "twenty minutes." Peter was the girls' token male friend.

I think he was in love with all three, but they treated him like an annoying but reliable younger brother.

"Ok, thank you all for taking time out of your oh-so-busy lives to help a friend," Ellis said with a smile. "I have softball practice. Don't forget. States and all." States were all Ellis had talked about lately. "You know my mom found Lori-Sue Johnson's body, and the police are giving her a hard time. They even trashed our house looking for evidence." This last was said and received by her friends with a seriousness that belied their years. "There's something going on weird with Kelly Jackman. Did you know her mom was related to Lori-Sue? I'm wondering if her weirdness and Lori-Sue's murder are related."

Whitney said, "You think she had something to do with the murder?"

"Maybe, Whitney," Ellis started to say.

"I heard her talking about the murder in Trig. Everyone was hanging on her every word. She was trying to cry but couldn't quite get it right. I hate her," Candy said unapologetically and with very little emotion.

"You hate everyone, Candy," Peter said what Ellis was probably thinking.

"She didn't mention your mom, so what does skanky Kelly Jackman have to do with this meeting?" Candy was obviously trying to speed things along. Candy wasn't as skilled at lacrosse as she was at soccer, which she played in the fall, but she was more than adequate. Her powerful young body was sturdy and strong.

I really liked her mom, and Candy looked just like her.

"I just have this weird feeling about Kelly. I was asking people some questions about the whole murder and her family connection, and I started getting these super nasty texts from an unknown number. My mom found them," Ellis said.

"Crap," Whitney said indelicately.

All of Ellis's friends knew how involved I was in Ellis's life. Ellis pretended to be bothered by it, but I think it helped to have one parent who really cared. And honestly, Grant didn't seem to.

"So..." Ellis said, "I need someone to hack into Kelly's social media."

Peter said, "No way. You know I love you, Elle, but no way."

The girls murmured nos.

"Come on, Petey," Ellis wheedled.

Peter acquiesced surprisingly easily. I was betting he was thinking of that ortho appointment he had and that he might as well give in; he eventually would anyway.

He sighed heavily. "What do you want me to do?"

"Yessss!!" Ellis screeched quietly.

The ever-present librarians were circling.

"Oh, knock it off, Elle," Peter said. "You knew you'd get me to do it. I have that ortho appointment in…fifteen minutes now."

"Thank you, Petey. Now I need you to hack into all Kelly's social media—Snapchat, Instagram, Facebook, Twitter."

"Yes, Elle, I know what social media is," Peter sounded like his former happy mood had evaporated. "I'll text you when it's done."

"Hey," Candy said. "I want in on this! I want all the deets! Let's meet at Elle's after everybody's practices or *ortho* appointments."

"Wait!" Ellis said to her retreating friends. "I can't be found hacking into Kelly's stuff. My mom will freak!"

"Too bad. It's your idea. We're just along for the ride and to help," Candy added. "See everybody at seven at Ellis's." And Candy was gone.

Whitney hustled off too.

"Seriously, thank you, Peter," Ellis said. "I owe you."

"Yeah, you do," Peter grumbled. But he'd do it. He'd do anything for Ellis.

I waited a beat and then slunk off like the coward, eavesdropper, sneak that I was.

* * *

Later that afternoon, I decided to pay a visit to Ivy. Would it be uncomfortable? Yes. Would Ellis have my hide? Yes, again, but I decided to pose it as a condolence call. Lori-Sue was, after all, a coworker in the wedding industry, and Ivy was her sole relative, to my knowledge. In *actuality*, I should be doing this. I pulled a pound cake out of the freezer. I always kept one or two in the freezer in case Ellis needed to take something to a team event or potluck. *Please thaw quickly*. The fact that I was a person of interest in Ivy's cousin's murder and was trying to get information and rat out her brat of a daughter was beside the point. It was a slippery slope as I really had no proof

Kelly was sending threatening texts to my daughter, except her instinct and my own common sense.

Ivy lived in a lovely home in South Eastbury. It was a Cape Cod. The wooden shingles had aged just enough without looking shabby. Would she be home at this time of day? Like me, she could make her own hours. She was stiff competition.

I rang the bell, and it gonged softly from within. In no time, Ivy answered the door. Had she been watching me?

"Katie," Ivy said with mild surprise. "Come in." It seemed she was going to play nice today. She opened her substantial front door and welcomed me in.

Ivy was dressed all in Lululemon exercise lounging wear for women who didn't mind dropping $100 to $125 on yoga pants. I minded. I just couldn't see the value.

"I just put a fresh pot of coffee on. Will you join me?" Why was she being so cordial? This wasn't the leopard-clad woman in Jen's shop.

"I'd love some coffee. Here," I pressed my foil-wrapped, still cold, cake into her hands. "I make a mean pound cake if I do say so myself." I paused. "I'm so sorry for your loss, Ivy. Lori-Sue had become a supportive business associate since I've been home. I should have formally reached out sooner."

If Ivy was surprised at my unexpected condolence, she didn't seem it. She accepted the cake graciously. "Thanks, Kate. It's nice to be recognized as family."

Ivy led me into her spacious kitchen, facing the front circular drive. It had everything I loved, Viking stovetop, Subzero fridge, and white-washed cabinets. The granite and marble were a soft green that made the whole room warm. She finished it off with a deep farm sink and buttery-yellow walls. Ivy guided me into her kitchen's seating area, decked out with unpainted wicker furniture grouped around the room's used-brick fireplace. And yes, that fireplace even had a fire roaring. The yellow-flowered cushions on the wicker were surprisingly soft. I was mentally uncomfortable, though, and wondered if it showed.

"I thought you and Brian McAllister would be one of those high-school couples that got married and lived happily ever after. What happened?"

I was surprised at the personal question. "It was a long time ago."

Ivy changed gears quickly, stating the obvious. "So, you're back and a wedding planner, significantly cutting into my business, may I add. You have a daughter, AND you're a person of interest in my cousin's murder." She placed a cup of coffee, cream, sugar, and dessert plates with a generous slice of my almost-defrosted cake on them. If she noticed my cake's cold state, she didn't comment on *that.*

Nothing got past Ivy. I decided to ignore the person of interest dig. "You have a daughter too, Kelly?"

Ivy beamed. "Yes. The light of my life. Worth putting up with her idiot father for." She sounded bitter, and her face twisted as if she'd taken a bite of lemon.

How to respond to that? *What is my mission here today?* I took a bite of my delicious cake, the grass-fed butter I had used seeming to add a creamy texture, as I contemplated my next move. *Remember, ugly as it is; I'm here to offer my condolences.* I was also there to find out information about Kelly and why she was bullying my daughter, not to mention do some digging into Ivy and what was going on with her. But one couldn't just say, "Hey, I have no proof, but I think your daughter is cyber-bullying my daughter. Will you please tell her to knock it off? And, by the way, what's up with you? Your behavior is slightly suspicious."

"I think the girls know each other," I ventured, a slight edge to my tone.

Ivy looked up sharply. She must have heard the tone.

In the corner of my eye, I saw the ever-present Amazon van pull into the circular drive (well, ever-present at *my* home), but instead of a drop-off, the doorbell rang. Ivy frowned at the sound of the doorbell.

I could tell she didn't want to be interrupted, but she said, "Sorry, it's a delivery that requires a signature." She hustled off to the front door.

Huh. In my experience, the Amazon drivers dumped and dashed; I wondered what her delivery was.

Ivy had been fiddling with her phone as we talked, thus, it was open, and she had, carelessly, I may add, left it on the wicker end table. Dare I? Would I be so bold? Was I that rude? Yep, yep, I was. I grabbed the phone, put it in my lap, and went immediately to her texts. Thank God it was an iPhone, or I'd have been hopeless at navigating through it. There were texts to her ex, her daughter, someone called Becca, Joyce (yikes!), and then...my daughter's number. I read through quickly. Idiot! Why didn't she erase her texts? Well, I couldn't talk. I didn't, either. The nastiness appalled me. I looked over my shoulder and, while I couldn't see Ivy at the door, I heard her arguing with the deliveryman. Excellent! So...the texts hadn't come from Kelly, but her mother. I slowly replaced the phone after returning the screen to the home page where it had been and took a deep breath. How was I going to *not* rip Ivy's face off when she came back to the table? I took three deep yoga breaths. Ok, I hadn't done yoga in two years, but I promised myself to get back into it right then. This was for Ellis, I kept reminding myself as Ivy's voice rose along with the deep grumble of the deliveryman. The door slammed, and Ivy stomped back into the kitchen empty-handed.

She looked at me. "Damn Amazon. Are you okay? Your face is all red." She sat back down.

"Yep, fine." I managed to get out. "So, the girls..." I still had that edge to my tone.

"Yes," she cocked up one brow—impressive!—and gave me an icy stare. She said nothing further.

So, another Mom had perfected the "keep quiet and wait out the other person you're talking to" thing. "It will break them," said the experts. But I was better. I wasn't better at much, but I was better than Ivy at the waiting game.

Yep, she blinked. "How do they know each other?" she finally asked.

"Well, maybe I was overstating it when I said they know each other. I think there's some communication going on. Texting and all." And I was silent again.

Ivy squirmed and pulled at her skin-tight yoga pants. She wasn't very good at this. "Oh?" was all she got out.

Still, I waited.

"Is there some sort of problem?" She looked concerned but irritated at the same time. She stood and began clearing the dishes away, rattling them in her haste.

I guessed I had worn out my welcome. But I didn't budge. I hadn't yet said what I'd come here to say.

"I think there is. There are unwanted texts, Ivy. As one mother to another, I'd appreciate it if you'd make them stop. I'd like to keep this between us because kids are kids and they don't always realize the ramifications of their actions. It's always better to try to nip these things before they escalate and the school becomes involved." Blaming her daughter for texts I now knew Ivy had written just might make them stop. I didn't think she was such a terrible mother she'd let her daughter take the fall for her misdeeds.

"I don't know what you're talking about," she said but looked worried.

"I'd advise you to find out and make it stop. I don't want to have to go to the school or even the police, but I will. And, oh…by the way, our conversation had better not come back to me or to Ellis; because, if it does, our deal is off. And I'll take this as far as I need to. I'm not above payback." I stood.

If she was going to throw her daughter under the bus by way of not owning up to her actions, let her. The texting better stop. Yep. I had made a friend.

"I'll walk you to the door." Ivy slid past me and headed for the foyer. She showed amazing restraint. She had more class than I would have thought.

"I truly am sorry about Lori-Sue," I said, and meant it.

The door slammed in my face. Too soon?

I thought Ivy got the message, but would my daughter kill me if she found out what I had been up to? I knew Ellis wanted to take care of this situation herself, but I had to do something. It was a situation that begged to have parent involvement. I didn't think Ivy would rat me out. The cost would be too great, especially as I now knew it was Ivy sending the texts. I didn't think she'd call my bluff about notifying the school administration, or the police, if she didn't stop the threatening texts. And, oh, I wasn't bluffing.

Chapter Fourteen

Will you have children as guests at your wedding? If not, make sure everyone knows in advance so there are no misunderstandings.

Ellis seemed too relieved when I told her I was so very sorry, but I had to go out to a local business owners' networking event that night. I asked would she and her friends be okay without my hostess duties? Ha-ha.

"Don't worry about it, Mom. We'll be fine. No worries." Thank GOD! I could hear her thinking. Boy, was she going to be disappointed when I informed her my meeting had been canceled.

I didn't think under normal circumstances, Ellis minded me being around when her friends were over. I tried hard to make them feel welcome. I offered something to eat or drink, but I admit I had a hard time leaving them alone. Teens were an interesting group of people, and I loved talking to them. I think Ellis suspected I was a bit lonely. I was.

Whitney was the first to arrive that evening. She shrugged out of her cheer warm-up jacket as Ellis opened the door to her. "You're not going to believe what Tiffany Ashford did!" She was all in a huff.

Ellis looked over her shoulder at me. She was wishing me gone. Poor kid.

"Hi, Whitney!" I said warmly, greeting the lovely girl. "Here, I'll take your jacket."

She sweetly handed it to me.

"Can I get you one of my Cream Cheese Brownies?" I knew these were a particular favorite of Whitney's.

"No, thank you, Mrs. L. I just had a huge dinner."

I bet you did. Whitney's mom was known for being a fabulous cook, unlike yours truly. But Whitney looked remorseful. I think, as full as she was, she wanted one of my brownies.

Ellis didn't care but knew she had to ask. "What did Tiffany do, Whit?"

"Gained about ten pounds over spring break. Her family went to Fort Lauderdale."

Tiffany Ashford was the top of the pyramid for the Varsity Cheer squad. This *could* be a problem... There was no time to contemplate this new crisis. Candy was right behind Whitney, sporting a shiner.

"What happened to you?" Both Ellis and Whitney asked at the same time.

"Stick to the face," Candy replied nonchalantly. "Have any frozen peas, Mrs. L.?" Candy asked. "Have to ice it every hour the trainer said."

Ellis ran off to the kitchen to look in the freezer. She knew I kept peas for her own injuries. I smiled as she wrapped the bag in a tea towel and hurried to join the girls. They all went into the 'parlor' we used as a 'family room.' They would ice Candy's injury and await Peter.

Peter arrived about five minutes later, looking smug.

It had taken him no time at all to hack into Kelly's socials. Peter was a total tech nerd. Heck, he could probably get into the Eastbury Public School System's account and change all his grades to "A's" if he wanted to, but then he had all "A's" anyway. Even I knew the secret to *that* system, not that I could hack it. The school allowed all access to part of their system via their student/parent portal, where both could check grades and teachers' websites. But restricted "all-access" to the rest of the website–too easy to get in the private side with that setup, or so I heard.

The girls greeted Peter with more exuberance than he was used to, and he lapped it up.

"Petey!" Ellis embraced his lanky frame.

"Let's get you out of this jacket," Candy pulled off his Northface sweater jacket.

"Are you thirsty, Pete? Bet Ellis has soda." Whitney didn't want to be outdone by her friends.

I had to smile. Ellis glanced over my way. She seemed anxious for me to head to my meeting.

Peter grinned and allowed himself to be pulled into the east parlor, which we used as the family/great room. Our house was a historic property from an era where, upon entering the house, you stood in the entry hall. The house boasted twin parlors on each side of the hall. I used the west parlor as a home office, and we used the east as a family or great room.

"Okay, Peter, what did you find?" Ellis couldn't keep up the nice-guy act any longer. She liked Peter, a lot, but she had to find out what he knew.

Ellis glanced into the kitchen, where she knew I was still "cleaning up." I could tell she had hushed her friends because the volume had gotten lower. I could see her, but she couldn't see me. Problem was, they were speaking so softly now, I could barely hear.

"I hacked into Kelly's Snapchat. There was something weird going on with Mr. Williams. But there were a couple odd photos of them together—in his office mainly." Peter said it flatly, but the timber of his words wouldn't matter.

All the girls would hear would be his explosive words.

Mr. Williams was a guidance counselor at Eastbury High. The implications of this relationship washed over the group. I was aghast. What should I do about this? I was an adult, after all.

"What kind of pictures were they?" Candy asked again, maybe hoping for Peter to say they were more titillating than they were.

"Nothing risqué. Kelly was kind of hanging on him and mugging for the camera." Peter said, "But they were intimate enough to know there was something weird about the teacher/student relationship. Cozy-type shots, though not technically inappropriate."

"Wait," Ellis stopped Peter. "I thought Snapchat pics are supposed to disappear after mere seconds."

"Images are *supposed* to be erased in seconds, but there's always a way. Remember, *chicas; I* keep trying to tell you, nothing truly goes away on the internet. I'm just a high school kid, and *I* found it." All four of the friends knew that wasn't entirely true. Peter wasn't just a high school kid. He was very smart and very talented.

"Why was she mugging with Mr. Williams?" There was skepticism in Candy's voice. You could tell she didn't quite buy it. "Kelly Jackman adores Zack Ramano. She wouldn't do anything to jeopardize her relationship with him. Would she?"

"Bizarro," Whitney said.

Silence. There was just silence.

"Well, why would she *post* a photo of the forbidden when someone could so easily see it?" Whitney asked.

Peter gave her a look that said, "Excuse me? Nothing about hacking into Kelly's Snapchat account was easy." It was for Peter, but he wouldn't want the girls to think that.

The four friends were more confused than they were when they hatched the plan for Peter to hack into Kelly's social media that afternoon. Ellis didn't even seem to care that I never went to my meeting.

Chapter Fifteen

Consider a formal portrait taken of you in your gown a month before the wedding and display it at your reception.

My heart was heavy the next morning. I was worried about so many things. Some self-care was needed, so after I got Ellis off to school, I made myself a cup of tea. I really wanted a fire but was just too tired to build one. I promised myself I'd set one tonight so it would be ready to go tomorrow morning if I felt the same. It was the small things in life. I curled up on the love seat in front of my cold kitchen fireplace, pulled a ratty afghan my grandmother had crocheted over me, and sipped the tea. I put my worries in order; first of all, the murder. I *had* to do something to get the police off my back, but what? Then there were the nervous clients. I had another call last night after Ellis's friends left. This one was from the mother of a bride. I tried to reassure her all would be well, but she had hinted she was looking for a replacement. It could be like the 1920's run on the banks. If a client or two started jumping ship, I might lose all my clients. My business would be sunk before it even took off. Then what would Ellis and I do?

I was also worried about the situation with Kelly and the guidance counselor, Mr. Williams. I wasn't supposed to know about the weird photos on her Snapchat, but I did. Did I have any responsibility to report them? My guess was no. According to the kids, nothing unseemly was captured. But it was still troublesome.

Then...Marcy's grandmother's ring. With my business on the line, I needed to do anything and everything to make any remaining clients super happy. I was going to have to find that ring. I decided then, and there that I was going to *find the ring*. Ok…but where was I supposed to start? Well…assuming someone had the ring, and it wasn't lost, it would have to be a family member or someone who had happened upon it. I gulped my now lukewarm tea in one long swallow, anxious to take action. I'd visit the local jewelry stores. There were a couple reliable ones in town, and I knew both owners. Call it a bonus or hazard of my business; everyone needed a wedding ring.

I flew upstairs and got dressed in my uniform of khakis and a button-down shirt, today pink. I was moving with such purpose I didn't even notice my bum leg. My sweet dog, Chloe, looked at me with pleading eyes. She really needed some exercise. "When I get back, I promise we'll go for a walk, girl." I meant it.

I arrived at Eastbury Jewelers and lucked out with a parking spot right in front. A soft chime announced my arrival, and Russ Parker, owner and a gem of a gentleman, greeted me, no pun intended.

"Well, Katie Manet. To what do I owe the pleasure?"

No matter how many times I tried, Mr. Parker never remembered my married name. I had given up reminding him. I guessed it was fair. He had asked me repeatedly to call him "Russ," but I just couldn't. He would always be Mr. Parker to me.

"Hey, Mr. Parker. How are you today?"

"Not too busy. April is slow, but we'll gear up for Mother's Day. What can I do for you?"

I pulled out the photo I had taken of the Simpson ring. "Have you ever seen a ring like this?" The photo wasn't very detailed, and it was small.

"I do believe I have, Katie. One came in here not too long ago for a cleaning and some maintenance. Jewelry of this era was usually made of platinum and held up well, but the filigree that comes with this style is delicate."

Whoa! "Who brought it in?" I hoped my eagerness didn't show too much. I tried to contain my hope by bouncing from foot to foot.

Mr. Parker smiled. "Ah, Katie, you know I can't tell you that. It's privileged."

Privileged? What was he, a priest? So, I said with what I hoped was a smile in my voice, "What are you, a priest, Mr. Parker?" And I gave him my Katie smile.

And Mr. Parker smiled back. "No, Mrs. Ludlow," and here he was serious, and ths time he remembered my married name. "I'm not a priest, but my customers trust me with their financial matters and their treasured jewels. I never speak of those things to anyone."

He shamed me...a little. "I'm sorry, Mr. Parker." I looked at my feet, properly chastened. I paused. "Can you give my ring a steam?" I had a jewelry swirling machine at home, but it just didn't do the trick, and ok, I'd admit it...I still wore my gorgeous two-carat pear-shaped engagement ring from Grant...on my *right* hand. I handed it over to Mr. Parker.

"This is a beaut, Katie. Colorless and almost flawless." He bounced the ring in his hand, then disappeared into the back.

I confirmed he was concentrating on the steamer. He had a big picture window in his workroom where he could see out into the showroom, but one couldn't look away from that scary steamer. You'd be scalded if you were careless. I indelicately slid over the glass-topped display case, not caring about the pain from my bum leg, feeling foolish when I spied the wooden swing gate a couple of feet away and grabbed Mr. Parker's old-fashioned claim-slip book he kept for repairs. I madly went back a couple of weeks, stealing glances at Mr. Parker. He was polishing my ring with a microfiber cloth now, and I suddenly found what I was looking for. "Antique platinum ring, three-carat diamond: check, repair, and clean." I ran my finger down the page, stopping at the owner's name and contact info.

I nearly dropped the book when I heard the sharp, "Katie!" Instead, I placed the book back in its spot with care, gave it a pat, and turned to face the music.

But instead of the tongue-lashing I expected, Mr. Parker smiled and handed me my ring. "You always were a minx, Katie," and he winked.

I gave him a quick peck on the cheek, whispered a rushed thank you for the cleaning and for not scolding me, then exited–via the gate this time.

Chapter Sixteen

If you plan a formal procession into your wedding ceremony, the mother of the bride enters AFTER the mother of the groom due to her more important status.

Well, this was going to be awkward. The owner of the ring was... well, the ring Mr. Parker had repaired; I'd have to investigate to determine if it was the Simpson ring.

The owner was Tina from Tina's Bakery, the more-than-rude baker with the leaning cake. I was now sitting in front of her bakery, gearing up to pay her a visit and get a look at her ring.

I sighed audibly and hung my head over my Suburban's steering wheel. I really did not want to do this. I slowly opened my car door and slammed it shut, and walked resolutely to the bakery entrance. "This will please the Simpsons; this will please the Simpsons," I kept saying to myself. I needed to do anything and everything to keep my remaining clients happy.

No merry bells jingled on Tina's door. The bakery was quite cool to keep the baked goods chilled? Tina's bakery showroom was impressive I'd give her that. The cakes she had displayed were true works of art, one ivory-colored wedding cake with spun sugar roses in particular.

A harried employee came scurrying out from the back room. "May I help you?"

Tina must have the help working at double speed. I smiled. My beef wasn't with her.

"Hi. I'm Kate, a wedding planner, and I'm looking for Tina." I smiled again.

The girl's eyes darted to the workroom door. "Um…"

"Laura!" Tina bellowed. "I need you!" The baker came out red-faced and sweating. She abruptly stopped her hurried stride into the showroom when she saw me, then frowned. "Kate."

"Tina." I needed to make nice. So, I smiled. It wasn't easy. I didn't think it seemed genuine because she didn't smile back.

"Are you here to give me more grief about that cake?" Drats! I shouldn't have written that email about the cake in such a nasty tone.

I smiled again, better this time, I thought. "Aw, no worries, Tina."

She cocked an eyebrow at me. Tina was no fool, she looked me with suspicion. She wiped her hands on her frosting-crusted apron. "Coffee?"

Huh? Tina had a gracious side. "Sure. That would be great."

"Laura, two coffees with the fixin's and two crullers." She gestured to a table with two chairs in the corner by the picture window. Several tulips were making their appearance in the window box outside the window. They gave a cheery feel to the bakery.

I sat. So did she.

"Okay, Kate. Why are you here?" Right to the point.

I weighed my words here. She might respond better if I was upfront. Laura put two cups of steaming coffee, along with cream and sugar, on the table and two of the most luscious-looking donuts. Tina pushed some stray strands of hair behind her ear.

"Do you have an antique diamond ring?" Could I have been more direct?

Tina leaned back and crossed her arms over her ample chest. There was that smirk again. "And what business is it of yours if I do?"

It was my turn to smirk. I didn't know why. "I'm looking for one. It's a mystery, and the family desperately wants it back."

You could see the wheels working in her pea brain. "Let's say I do have an antique ring. What's in it for me?"

I guessed we were mincing no words. "I'm confident the family would pay you full market value if it's their family ring." My curiosity got the better of me. "May I see a picture of your ring, if you have one?"

Tina looked at her hands and twisted a plain silver band around. There it was, in all its glory, the most beautiful antique ring and what I believed to be the missing Simpson ring.

"I know it's silly to wear it when I'm baking. I get all kinds of gunk in it, but I just love it." And just like that, Tina's face softened. Maybe she wasn't so bad. Then the old Tina was back. "Again, Kate, what's in it for me? I'm quite attached to this ring." She placed her hand protectively in her lap as if I'd rip it from her finger.

I pulled up my picture of the Simpson ring on my phone.

Tina leaned in. "Looks to be a dead ringer to me."

I fired off a text to Joyce. **Any engraving or defining marks on the antique ring?**

I waited a moment and saw the Apple bubbles working on the phone, indicating either reading or typing.

Engraving inside "Always, my love." Why? Do you have a lead????

I ignored Joyce and said to Tina, "Look inside. It has an engraving."

Tina attempted to remove the ring, made all kinds of faces, turning red in the process. Whether it was effort or embarrassment, I couldn't determine.

"I'll get some butter." Tina returned in short order. Wiping her ring and fingers on her even-more-soiled apron, that poor apron. "Always," and here she moved closer to the window for the light, "my love."

Whoo-hoo!!! The calm tone of my voice surprised me. "I think it's a match, Tina." I stood.

Tina looked up from the ring with a cunning look. "Who's the family, Kate?"

"The Simpsons." I sat back down at the table. This was going to take a while.

Joyce chose that moment to send another text. **Kate??? Anything???**

Still, I ignored her. I had to be certain of this situation.

Tina grinned. "Oooo, la la. Grand Dame Simpson. I have something Joyce Simpson wants."

Chapter Seventeen

Consider getting your engagement ring steam cleaned at your local jeweler right before your wedding. Undoubtedly, your photographer will want some close-ups.

I had texted Joyce that I thought I had a lead on the ring. Tina had smugly informed me she wasn't sure she wanted to part with her precious ring. I thought she wanted to work out a deal with the Simpsons herself. I didn't care as long as I got the credit for finding it. I wondered about her story of how she came about acquiring the ring. According to her, she had found it at a tag sale here in town.

I wanted to have something to offer Joyce about the trail of the ring and how it was found. I was putting off thinking of scary, pressing issues. Like...being the number one suspect in a murder investigation. When did I become such a procrastinator?

The most logical place to glean information would be the farm where Tina claimed to have purchased the ring at a tag sale. I knew the farm. It was a historic property that had been in the same family since, I thought, the Revolutionary War. It was located in South Eastbury. South Eastbury had its own zip code, but everyone in Eastbury/South Eastbury went to the same schools. Some said it was a mistake to build a new middle school five years ago, that the funds for it should have gone to build a second high school, but I disagreed. One high school united the town. Two would have divided it.

I pulled into the dirt road leading to Sunset Ridge. I hadn't been out here in a long time. The one and only time I had been was for a high school party. One of the sons of the house had had a rager. I thought half the school population had attended. The beauty of a party out here was the cops didn't bother patrolling it because it was private property, and it was all outside. No one's house was destroyed.

I parked next to the farm trucks and walked up the wrap-around porch steps. The farmhouse was a white clapboard structure and well-maintained. The front door sported a beautiful stained-glass window depicting a colorful garden.

I got a wave of apprehension. I really better come up with the name of my high school chum, or this could be embarrassing! Joe, yeah, that was it…or was it Jack?

I didn't even get a chance to knock when the door opened.

An attractive strawberry blond was standing before me, younger than I, with a toddler on her hip. "May I help you?"

It seemed like an odd thing to say. This wasn't exactly a neighborhood setting. I doubted she got many surprise visitors way out here.

I smiled. That always went a long way. "Hi." I extended my hand. "I'm Kate Ludlow. I'm a wedding planner in the area, and I have sort of an odd set of questions to ask you."

She tipped her head to the left and looked me up and down as if to assess whether I was to be trusted or not. "Better come in then. I'm Peggy."

This was easier than I thought it would be. I walked into a time capsule. Everything was pristine and renovated, but the furnishings and appliances were true to an earlier era–which, I'd have to ask.

"This, this is *awesome*!" I got a genuine smile from the stoic Peggy.

"Yeah. We're gearing up for a historic tour of the farm. I think we can earn some extra income with a homemade ice cream shop, corn maze tours, house tour, farm stand, and pumpkin patch. It's not easy to make a living farming these days." She looked melancholy.

"I think you're on to something. I wish you the best." I meant it, and she smiled.

"A wedding planner, huh? You want to do weddings out here?"

Wow…it was a fair question, and one I'd revisit after this. I'd think about it.

I'd be the exclusive planner. I'd bring all my brides looking for a venue out here first, and if a bride came to the farm before she had a planner, they'd direct her to me. I liked it! I hoped there would be weddings in my future. Right now, I had bigger problems, and I was there for another purpose.

"Maybe, but that's not why I'm here." I felt awkward. There was no easy segue. "I understand you had a tag sale recently."

"You want a cup of coffee?" Peggy rose. "Forgive my manners for not offering you a cup earlier."

"I'd love a cup. Cream, please." I knew she'd have fresh cream, maybe even from her own cow.

Peggy efficiently grabbed a cup from a hook under the cabinet, shifted the toddler to her other hip, and filled the cup from a percolator on the stovetop, my kind of girl. She splashed a generous dollop of cream from a small cream pitcher on the counter. I had a feeling that cream never got warm. She didn't offer sugar. I bet Peggy and her husband were drinking coffee all day long. After my first sip, I knew I would have been too.

"You were saying," Peggy sat back down, smoothing hair out of her miniature guy's eyes and settling him on her lap. "This is Joe Jr., by the way."

Ah-ha! I was right. My acquaintance's name was Joe. I couldn't help myself. I took another sip of the nectar of the gods. I thought I'd swoon when she placed a plate of warm chocolate chip cookies in front of me.

The baby reached for one, but she gently, but firmly, moved his hand away.

"So, the tag sale?" I prompted.

"Yes," she grabbed a cookie and bit into it lustily, sharing a tiny bite with Joe Jr. "It was more of an estate sale, really. My grandmother-in-law was moving to assisted living. She knew she was mentally slipping and gathered everything that wasn't of sentimental value, but she thought it was worth something and made me promise I'd have a tag sale. I thought it was ghoulish, but she made me promise. She asked that I put all the proceeds into a college fund for her great-grandkids. So, I did."

I held up my hands. "Hey, I was just askin'...."

"I'm sorry," Peggy flushed. Ah, the curse of the fair-skinned. "I'm sensitive about it. My sister-in-law, Vanessa, Joe's sister, was very critical of the sale."

"Your grandmother-in-law sounds like a practical lady." I had to turn this conversation around. It was getting away from me. "Why I'm asking is that one of my friends purchased a ring at your tag sale, and it turns out it was a long-lost heirloom from the family of one of the brides I'm working with."

Peggy's mouth formed a perfect O. "I bet I know the ring you're talking about. I told Vanessa that ring was worth something. It just had that look, ya know, but she said, 'How valuable can it be? It was loose in a shoebox!' I think the lady who bought it paid about twenty bucks."

So, Peggy remembered it. "Do you know anything about the history of the ring?"

"Sorry, no. I'd never seen it before, and neither had Vanessa. But you could talk to Joe's Gran. She has good days and bad. You might find her on a lucid day, and she may remember something."

"Awesome!" I'd take anything I could get at this point. "Where does she live now?"

"She lives in an assisted living community out on Lebonon Road in town. Poor thing. They haven't put a name to her kind of memory loss, but does it really matter?"

No, it didn't, I agreed. "What's her last name? Do you think she'd mind if I dropped in on her?" I was hopeful.

"Rizzo, and I don't see why not. She loves visitors. I can call the facility ahead of your visit and let them know you're coming."

"That would be great, Peggy. I don't think I can get there today, but..."

"I'll call today, anyway, let them know you'll be coming." Boy, I'd likc to work with her. She was personable *and* organized. "And think about our place as a wedding venue. You can save me some time. I was going to reach out to some local event planners—"

"I'm in." I picked up my coffee cup and napkin as I stood.

Chapter Eighteen

Wristlets are a much better option than pin-on corsages.

I was headed over to Comfort Living the next morning. It was a state-of-the-art assisted living compound. Word was it had its own movie theater, beauty salon, and mini-mart. When the residents wanted to get out and run errands, there was a shuttle that provided transportation. The meals were first-rate and nutritious. Sounded pretty wonderful to me.

I should have enough time in between appointments. Joyce Simpson was after me nonstop to tie up loose ends and return the ring to its rightful home. What a turn-around from disinterest to her present demands. I'd asked myself before, was it really my duty? Of course not. But it was keeping my mind off the murder investigation, and, honestly, I enjoyed it.

I went right to the reception desk, where a girl of about eighteen smiled brightly at me. "May I help you?"

"Yes," I smiled back. "I'm here to see Mrs. Rizzo. Her granddaughter called ahead and said I'd be stopping by?" I didn't know why I phrased it as a question, but I guessed it was. I *hoped* Peggy *had* called ahead.

The young lady, her name tag read Robin, consulted some sort of log on her desk. She ran her finger down the page…and stopped. "Oh, yes. Mrs. Peggy Rizzo did phone and give her the okay for you to go up and see Mrs. Marion Rizzo. She's on the second floor, room 207. Elevators are on your left," she gestured as if she were the hostess on *The Price is Right.*

"Thank you, Robin." I smiled brightly as I turned to make my way to the elevators. I hoped I had retirement funds available when it was my time for such digs. This place was swanky.

The elevator ride took moments. I stepped off, took a left, and was in front of room 207. I raised my hand to knock but hesitated. Why was I nervous? Because I was going to quiz an elderly lady about her past when it really wasn't any of my business. But I knocked and, much to my surprise, got an immediate response, in quite a hearty voice, no less.

"Come in," she boomed.

I entered, still feeling uneasy. I was in a sitting room that was prettily furnished with a loveseat and armchair that didn't overwhelm the small room. I could see there was a bedroom through the half-open door to my left.

"Mrs. Rizzo?" I queried.

"Yes, and you are?" Mrs. Marion Rizzo asked.

I fidgeted. "Kate Ludlow, a wedding planner."

Marion laughed, a hearty laugh. "I don't think I'll be needing one of those anytime soon, but I'm bored, so have a seat." She indicated the soft loveseat in the corner of her suite.

I sat down gingerly, crossing my legs primly. There was something about this lady that put me on my best behavior.

Mrs. Rizzo looked me up and down. "Well, say your peace."

Yikes. Could you say awkward? I repeated my story of the lost ring, yada yada, and it sparked no interest. Maybe the memory loss? But then I showed Marion the picture of the ring. She knew it, that much was for certain. Her hands shook slightly. The paper I had printed from my cell phone photo fluttered in her hands.

She raised her gaze to mine. "Where did you get this?" Her face had lost color.

"So, you know it, the ring?"

Marion lowered the paper to her lap and let it rest there. "You need to leave now. RIGHT NOW!" She screamed. "IRENE!" she bellowed.

I was frightened now. I didn't want to upset this poor old lady. I also didn't want her to have a stroke.

Two lavender-clad women came bounding in, their faces awash with worry.

"Miz Rizzo, whatever is the matter?" The shorter of the two asked.

I assumed this was Irene. The taller, stouter lady efficiently smoothed back Mrs. Rizzo's thin gray hair that had come loose from her severe bun in her frenzy.

"Shush, Miz Rizzo, it's going to be okay," she cooed.

"Get her OUT OF HERE," she screamed, pointing a crooked, shaking finger at me. Her face had turned an ungodly shade of purple. Mrs. Rizzo grabbed onto Irene's scrub top, her gnarled fist white from the effort. "And promise me, Irene, PROMISE ME, you won't let her read the journal. PROMISE ME!!"

"No, Miz Rizzo," Irene said in a calm, soothing voice. "I promise. No journal for this lady." She turned to look at me, but I was already on my way.

I grabbed my pocketbook and was making my way to the nearest exit.

"And don't come back!" Mrs. Rizzo yelled the steam beginning to fade from her rant.

I didn't wait for the elevator but took the emergency stairs two at a time. I felt horrible. What had I done? One thing I knew, however. This memory hadn't faded from her fragile mind...and somehow, I was going to get my hands on that journal.

Chapter Nineteen

Have extra material from your wedding dress left over? Ask your seamstress to save some when she hems/alters your gown. Consider making handkerchiefs for your nearest and dearest to carry on your wedding day. The handkerchiefs are especially appreciated by the men in your life. They look so smart peeping out of their jacket pockets.

I was in my downtown office early the next morning. I was moody. The events yesterday at Comfort Living had unnerved me. Well, it was nothing a cup of tea couldn't solve. I flipped the switch to my hotpot and watched it go to a rolling boil in seconds. I poured the hot water into my favorite mug, "Don't Stress. Hire a Wedding Planner." I popped one of my prized 'Prince of Wales' teabags into the steaming water, then sat in my desk chair and put my head down, letting the tea steep. I just didn't know what to do; I didn't know how to help myself. My attempt at undercover work had produced little. I had no idea who killed Lori-Sue. I just knew I hadn't done it. I took a gulp of my tea and burnt my tongue. Darn it! I sat up straight in my chair. *Okay*. I grabbed one of my notepads and a favorite pen. I started making lists and charts. I thought better when I wrote, I always had. What did I know? Not much. So, I put Lori-Sue's name at the top of the paper and started a list. I wrote: "Suspects" and then at the top of the list: Sara Deloro, of course. The simple act of putting my arch-enemy's name on my list of suspects felt delightful. Besides, there was something weird with the Board of Realtors and Sarah, and what about that picture of a house in her club locker? Why would one lone picture be stored in what was purported to be her secret hidey-hole? And why did that house look so familiar? And what about Joyce Simpson? What had her husband been referring to when I overheard him mention blackmail? I added Addalee. Carmella Sepulveda wasn't subtle when she dropped Addalee's name at our consultation, and I hated to admit it, but Addalee's behavior was off. I knew Addalee didn't like Lori-Sue, especially when she reminded me of the ill-fated lake house day in high school. Then why did she ask Lori-Sue to do her wedding flowers? I would have thought Lori-Sue would be Addalee's last choice. And what *had* Carmella been referring to when she referenced Addalee's past?

Ivy was a suspicious character. What grown woman sent a teen threatening texts unless they were up to something hateful?

There was an additional name I had to add to the list. This one I really didn't want to put down. How could I? What kind of a friend was I if I even suspected her? How long had I known her? Since middle school. She was my rock, my friend through thick and thin. She was more of my happily ever after than Grant had ever been. But still...I couldn't ignore what I knew to be true. She was oddly guilty looking. And she had hated Lori-Sue since high school and didn't even seem sad she was dead. My inner voice wouldn't be quiet. Jen *was* at the Simpson house when my contract was there, the contract that had mysteriously shown up in Lori-Sue's shop with her blood on it, framing me. She could have easily taken it and planted it in the flower shop. How could I even think this? But I knew I couldn't keep her off my list of suspects because she was my greatest friend in the world.

I added Jen's name to the list.

All the names seemed to be weak suspects, but someone killed Lori-Sue... all I knew was it wasn't me.

* * *

The day passed with only a quick trip downstairs to Jen's for coffee. The fact I had put her name on a list of murder suspects wasn't lost on me. I continued to feel awful.

At least I made use of the remainder of the day and got caught up on paperwork. There is a lot of paperwork that goes into planning a wedding. The all-important timeline must be written, along with the bridal procession, recession, and introduction of the bridal party into the reception. That was just scratching the surface. This was my least favorite part of event planning, and I tended to put it off. I had to get home to Ellis soon.

The sun had gone down, but it wasn't completely dark. I loved this time of night when the evening hadn't decided if it was day or night, when the light was soft and blurred the edges, when the heat of the day had dissipated, provided the finicky New England weather had had any heat that day.

I had just turned on a small desk light, and the golden glow was soothing. I was shocked at the timid knock on my outer door, which I had locked when I entered, not my common practice. I walked with trepidation to answer it. I had never been anxious about opening my business door, but a lot was going on these days… I need not have worried. Standing at my door was a small woman with elfish features anxiously wringing her hands.

"Kate? Kate Ludlow?"

"Yes," I answered. "and you are…?"

"May I come in?"

I was embarrassed. Where were my manners? "Yes, please, come in," I opened the door wider and ushered her into my reception area. When she was seated, sitting on the edge of her seat, back ramrod straight, I offered her some tea or coffee.

"No, thank you. I won't be long. I understand you visited my grandmother." She jumped right in.

"I'm sorry, I didn't catch your name."

It was her turn to look embarrassed. "I'm sorry. I'm Vanessa Fleming, Marion Rizzo's granddaughter. The reception desk alerted me you were a visitor. May I ask why?"

This must be the Vanessa my new friend, Peggy, from the farm had mentioned, Joe's sister. Her being here was odd. Why would the front desk tattle on me, and why would Vanessa feel the need to find me to ask why I was visiting her grandmother?

"I'm sorry," I wasn't, "is there a reason you need to screen your grandmother's guests?"

Vanessa's eyes darted around, stopping at a photo of Ellis in her Eastbury High softball uniform, then at the framed photos of some of my brides on the wall behind me; she looked out my office window at the almost-dark sky. Finally, she met my gaze.

"She's very dear to me. I really don't know anything about this ring you're asking about. But I do know your questions upset her very much." Her voice had become sterner, her expression stormy.

What was I doing? Who was I to upset a senior? This was just a lark for a rich woman, Joyce Simpson. I'd stop right away. I opened my mouth to say so, but Vanessa beat me to it.

"I'm warning you, Ms. Ludlow. Stop asking your nosey questions, or else." Vanessa stood, grabbed her pocketbook, which she had not so thoughtfully placed on my desk, and charged out of my suite.

I sat there, my mouth agape. Huh. *Methinks her reaction is over the top.* And I knew what that meant. She and her grandmother had something to hide. And a big something, from the venom of her threat. I wished I could say I was going to stop now, but Vanessa had just ensured I would keep digging. I had to. Tina wasn't giving up the ring easily, and Joyce was very curious, and now, so was I.

Chapter Twenty

Perhaps you won't wish to dance the entire song for your first dance with your new spouse...a full song is longer than you think...

I was meeting one of my fall brides today, April Summers. I was trying to get my head back into wedding mode after my call from Charlie this morning. He had called with a referral for a criminal attorney. He flat-out said I'd need one sooner rather than later. But he also assured me he'd be available for me until I hired the criminal attorney. I had to stop burying my head in the sand.

My bride, April, lived in London, so I had been tasked with planning and executing her entire wedding. All was approved by April, and her fiancé and I had run into no dissatisfaction. I had met April just once when she signed her contract at my office in Eastbury. Her fiancé was a New England boy, and it was his wish to be married here. I was looking forward to seeing April again. She wanted to meet at a restaurant instead of my office, so I chose my favorite, Harry's Fish in Somerset Square.

I walked into Harry's, the coziness of the restaurant surrounding me like a warm embrace, and was greeted by the owner himself, a short Italian man.

"Kate!" Joe said with great enthusiasm and a kiss on both my cheeks. He reached out and grabbed my hands, speaking to me as he wrapped my hands in his larger ones. "It has been too long!"

It had been only days.

"Are you cheating on me, Bellisima? Are you eating your fish somewhere else?" He grinned.

I gave his hands a final squeeze. "Never. I'm meeting a client here, April Summers. Is she here yet?" I looked around the tables, not spotting her.

"*Si*, she is," he gestured with his chin to the corner table.

I followed his indication, but she wasn't there.

"I don't see her. She's blond, has brown eyes, is about five-six, average build." I continued to look around the restaurant, my eyes stopping briefly at a full basket of Joe's famous bread. Yes, I was going to splurge today and have one of the whole-wheat rolls and one crostini.

"Yes, yes, Kate." Joe ushered me over to the original table he had indicated.

And then I saw her, the very slight similarity. April *was* the woman seated at the table Joe had shown me. But she had gained about forty pounds. Oh, no. This was a disaster.

I smiled as I walked over to greet April.

"April," I all but squealed. Ok, a little over the top, but I didn't know how to react. Had she been sick? Was she emotionally troubled? I knew how hard it was to maintain one's weight. I had faced my own battle after my bike accident...wait...was she pregnant?

April struggled to her feet. "Kate," she grinned, opening her arms to me.

I walked into them to be enveloped in a warm embrace.

"So lovely to see you. It's been far too long!"

She motioned for me to take the chair at her half-booth, half-chair table.

"Yes, it has, April."

April ordered a nice chardonnay, so I felt certain she wasn't pregnant. We engaged in minor small talk. Then April was the first to address the wedding.

"Kate, I've been so pleased with all you've done for us. In fact, George and I couldn't be happier, except," she paused and looked at her plate heaping with pasta alfredo, the rich cream sauce puddling between the noodles.

"Yes?" I prompted.

"Except," April stalled again. "Except for my dress."

"What's the problem, April?" I think I knew.

"Why, it doesn't fit, Kate. You've been so spot-on with all your vendor recommendations, but I have to say, I'm very disappointed with your alterations woman. My dress does *not* fit. In fact, I don't know what to do, and, frankly, neither does she."

I was speechless. Was I surprised? No. But I also didn't know how to answer her. Something had to be done. She needed a dress, and preferably, the one she purchased. I needed to have a sit-down with Barbara, my most professional and favorite independent wedding seamstress. Normally, the salon in New York, where April had purchased her gown, would do the alterations, but with April's bi-country status, and the wedding being held in New England, we decided on a seamstress here.

I had to be diplomatic, but I was worried, extremely worried. It was no big deal to make a big dress smaller, but it was almost impossible to make a small dress larger.

"Let's enjoy lunch today, April, and I'll set up an appointment with Barbara for tomorrow. We'll get to the bottom of this issue. I give you my word we'll fix it to your satisfaction." Oh, boy. Did I really just say that? But what choice did I have?

I called Barbara after lunch when I returned to my office.

"Hey, Barbara, it's Kate Ludlow."

Silence.

"Barbara?" Okay, I was really borderline panicked.

"I'm guessing you've spoken to April Summers?" No mirth was in Barbara's voice.

"What are we going to do, Barbara?"

She sighed heavily. "We have to basically make an entirely new dress. Oh, I can use the basic pattern, but the alterations will be extensive. I'll have to make sure I have additional material, but you know me. I have about everything you can imagine, and what I don't have, I have friends who do. But you have to get her here tomorrow. We'll be cutting it close." And then she laughed dryly. "No pun intended."

* * *

April and I answered Barbara's summons the next day. It was tense and embarrassing. She wasn't pregnant. I had hinted around as to when they might want to start a family, and she assured me that was a way off.

We began with April trying on her gown and standing on Barbara's pedestal. The dress had a back zipper and it gapped about six inches from the widest point across her shoulders. Barbara at first said nothing, just put her hands on her ample hips and walked a full circle around her. April took the aggressive approach and got mad.

"I have to tell you, Barbara. I won't be recommending you to any of my friends. Your alteration work is atrocious. It's not just a tiny bit off, it's nothing short of ridiculous!" April's face was scarlet by this time.

Barbara met April's angry gaze in the mirror. "April, you must have gained thirty-five to forty pounds. You know it, I know it, and Kate knows it. Now quit insulting our intelligence and let's figure out what to do."

And then April burst into tears. I handed her a hanky; yes, I still carried old-fashioned cloth handkerchiefs, call it a hazard of the business.

"Now go step out of your dress," Barbara said kindly, "and we'll fix this."

April hurried off, and I looked at Barbara. I had no words; yes, I did...

"Barbara! Can you really fix it?" I highly doubted it.

She smiled bemusedly. "Just you watch me. But it comes with a price."

"There will be no problem on that score. April has never said a word about any of the wedding bills." Heck, I'd pay Barbara's sure-to-be-exorbitant alteration bill if I had to. Just the thought of it made me feel weak in the knees, and I sat on the folding chair Barbara provided for her clients.

Barbara grinned almost wickedly at me. "I'm not worried about the monetary payment. I know April pays her bills. A bride with no dress will do anything to get her dress fixed. The payment will be coming from you, Kate." And she sat in the second folding chair next to me.

Whaaa?

Here was that evil smile again. "I hear you're doing up the Simpson girl's wedding," Barbara said in the quaint New England way of someone planning a wedding.

"Yesss..." I drew out the word. Something about this was making me uncomfortable.

"I remember the grandmother's wedding." Barbara lowered her voice.

How old was she? "How old are you, Barbara?" Oops!

Barbara gave me a look and frowned. "Kate."

"Sorry."

"Anyway…I remember the grandmother's wedding and the scandal. You're working so closely with the family now, have they made any reference to it or the ring?"

Suddenly I was no longer annoyed but interested. "Ring, what do you know about a ring?"

Barbara stooped to pick up some pins that had fallen on the thread carpet. "Not much. That's why I'm asking *you*. I remember a big 'ole hoopla about a rushed marriage between Eveline Crawford and Johnny Bellmont. And too soon, along came baby Joyce. The wedding was tiny, not at all in keeping with the grand Crawford style, and she didn't wear the famous ring. Everyone had a different idea about where the ring went from, 'her mother didn't give it to her because she was angry the wedding had to be rushed,' to 'she lost it on her wedding day.' Or 'she threw it at a former beau out at Cotton Hollow by the tree.'"

Barbara didn't have to remind me about the 'tree.' It was a cherished town landmark at Cotton Hollow. Lovers carved their initials in it, families picnicked under it, and its branches sheltered those caught out in a rainstorm.

"I was about twelve at the time," she continued, "but I sure was curious. And I swore to myself that if I ever got the chance to ask someone who may know, I would, so I am."

I was absolutely convinced that was the most I had *ever* heard Barbara say. "Wow, Barbara, I do believe that's the most I've ever heard you say." I smiled as I said it. I didn't want my favorite seamstress mad at me. "I wish I could tell you more, but I don't have your answers. If I do find out a tidbit or two, I'll share." Normally, I wasn't a gossip, but Barbara had always come through for me, and I was certain she would again with April. Information was a form of currency. And I'd pay if I could.

"Umph. See that you do." She seemed satisfied.

April handed her gown, through her sobs, over the dressing room door, and Barbara received it. She immediately turned it inside out, slid her reading glasses off her gray head onto her nose, grabbed her seam ripper from the multi-pocketed apron she always wore, and began ripping.

Had Barbara gone mad? April heard the sound of ripping fabric and came running out of her dressing room, barely holding her changing robe together.

This time her face was white as a sheet. She tried to speak, but nothing came out as she witnessed the horror of her dress being destroyed.

Barbara smiled at her, a wee bit maliciously. "It's going to be okay, April. Trust me."

April sat down right there on the floor with a thud. I felt like doing the same. I liked Barbara, had always trusted her with my best clients–well, all my clients were my best; perhaps I should say my most discerning clients. But this time...oh my gosh.

Chapter Twenty-One

Limit your "Cocktail Hour" to one hour. Any longer is too long and your guests will either: drink too much, eat too much, or get bored.

I was still sweating after the emotional charge of the dress disaster with Barbara and April as I headed to my next appointment. What did I see on the shoulder of the road? A giant billboard with the face of my least favorite person, Sarah Deloro. It put my teeth on edge to see what a wildly successful Realtor she was. She had a big slice of the Greater Hartford area and had cornered the market in Eastbury. My curiosity was tickled regarding the conversation I overheard, ok eavesdropped on–I was getting proficient at that, at Barbie Mission's engagement party and the single photo of the nondescript house she kept in her club locker. Could she lose her license over possible infractions? I didn't know enough about the Realtors' Board of Ethics. So far, she had avoided sanction, but it could be catastrophic to her reputation and livelihood if those rumors were true. The more I thought about her, the more I thought she was my number one suspect for Lori-Sue's murder.

One reason Sarah was so financially successful was she sold houses as fast as she could with no regard for neighborhood prices. Many a neighbor had suffered seeing the value of their own home plummet when Sarah sold her listings for rock-bottom prices. A deeply discounted house closed quickly, and from what I had heard, Sarah wanted to: 1) collect her commission fast and 2) get the numbers needed to be ranked a quick closer. The fact she cost entire neighborhoods to have their home values plummet wasn't on her personal radar. I had done my homework. Why homeowners continued to use her, I wasn't sure.

She had never married. Her heart had been set on Brian McAllister, in fact, if Jen was to be believed, it still was. They had dated briefly in high school both before me and after Brian and I broke up, but it didn't last. Our last fight had been about her and a situation she had manufactured. Brian had gone off to college. Jen confided that Sarah had flitted around and finally settled on her current career. She dated frequently, but it was mostly to make business connections. Of course, she had heard that I was back in town. In the year I'd been back, we had avoided one another like the plague. We still hated each other. Did that mean I hadn't seen her? No. I had, but we hadn't had a confrontation until the engagement party.

* * *

This afternoon I had an appointment with a client to plan her goddaughter's engagement party. I pulled into the Rosenbush residence and saw a for sale sign in the yard. And whose face was beaming out at me? Sarah's, that's who.

I pulled my Suburban right behind the Porsche Cayenne in the drive. I glanced at the woman standing on the front porch, waiting admittance. Dang, dang. Sarah Flippin' Deloro. We had done a decent job of avoiding each other for the year I had been home. But obviously, our luck had run out. Twice in one week? What were the odds?

Sarah narrowed her eyes at me. Yep, still hated her.

We'd have to be civil. I got out of my Suburban and walked to the door of the mock Tudor residence. This town, and especially this setting, with one of my clients, demanded it. Hopefully, we'd be somewhere in the near future where we could let our real feelings fly.

"Well, well, Katie Manet," Sarah struck first. "I don't see you in the whole year since you've been back, and now twice in one week. Sorry about your divorce; shame for your kid. Hope she'll be okay if you go to jail." Her smirk was hateful; I bet she'd been planning this.

I smirked back. "No worries, Sarah. You'd just love my Ellis. Smart, beautiful, kind. In fact, if you thought *I* was pretty back in the day, you should see Ellis!"

Sarah turned away and focused on the closed door, muttering a disgruntled, "Humph." She rang the bell…with her left hand. I always wanted to be left-handed. My dad was, and he was artistic. A person seemed able to use more of their brain if they were a leftie. Was that science-based? Probably not. But just another reason to hate on Sarah.

I smiled but was glad when the door was opened by the harried stay-at-home father of two, Chad. Chad had a smear of what looked like baby squash on his cheek, at least, I hoped it was baby squash. He had a baby on his hip, a golden lab barking at his heels, and a four- or five-year-old tugging at his shirt. I almost laughed. He looked like I felt when Ellis was a baby. Sarah, I noted, looked at him longingly. Something was up there.

Chad invited us in, then bellowed for his wife. "Helen! Down here, please, people to see you!"

Sarah quickly corrected him. "Chad, you don't have to bother Helen. I'm sure Kate has some things to discuss some trivial function or other with Helen. You and I can take care of the real estate issues." She smiled her brightest smile.

A harried Chad thrust a smelly, food-covered baby at Sarah. She had no choice but to accept the baby. She tried to hide her displeasure, but I knew the old Sarah. Well enough to know she was less than pleased. To her credit, she hid it pretty well.

"Oh, okay," Sarah held the child at arm's length, and I could see she was trying hard not to wrinkle her nose in distaste and keep her black suit pristine. "I think this one needs a change."

I had to grin. I was most certain this wasn't the morning she had planned. "You're right, Sarah. Helen and I have 'some trivial event' things to discuss. Have fun, you two, ah…discussing your real estate issues." And I breezed into the large eat-in kitchen, where Helen had set up some lovely pastries and a pot of tea. *Round One, Kate.* I smiled. Now, if I could just ferret out what was up with Sarah, the Board of Realtors, and Lori-Sue…

"What do you think of a themed party, Kate?" Helen asked.

I was trying to formulate my response. I was not a fan of the theme party. A blood-curdling scream erupted from the next room. I didn't know which child it was, but it sounded serious.

"Helen!"

I got chills when Chad bellowed.

"Sorry, Kate, back in a flash. I swear, what does he do when I'm not home?" She didn't seem worried.

I would have been, hearing that death scream. But moments later, I heard her laughing. Thank God!

I sat on one of the island barstools. I had a feeling this was going to take a while. I looked at Helen's impressive cookbook collection. Huh, most people got their recipes online these days. Then my eyes wandered over to her teapot collection arranged artfully on top of her cabinets. I *loved* teapots! Growing bored, my eyes lit on Helen's kitchen computer screen, which hadn't gone into screensaver mode. She had Facebook open. And there, for all the world to see, was a photo of our Helen playing bridge with Joyce Simpson. Huh. Helen was a little young for bridge, wasn't she? It seemed like an older lady's activity to me. I looked closely and saw two tables of four women each. The ladies looked like they were having fun. I looked more closely still. In addition to Helen, I saw Addalee and her future mother-in-law and, oh my word, Sarah! *I bet she plays bridge to get chummy with potential clients.* The gang's all here. It appeared Joyce was the photographer, taking a selfie. She seemed very pleased with herself and her party. Something was nagging at me. I took a step closer to the computer, first looking toward the family room, where the kid disaster had occurred, to see if there was any sign of a returning Helen. Nope, not yet. What was it about this photo? I knew! I had thought Joyce was a leftie, but 'she was holding her cards in her right hand in this photo. I was convinced she had signed the deposit check to the Wadsworth with her left hand, but I guessed not.

"Kate, I'm so sorry!" Helen laughed as she walked back into the kitchen. "Emory smeared lipstick all over herself, and Chad is just beside himself."

I quickly jumped back from the computer. "What a minx. I remember when Ellis did something like that! What a mess. Although, I think she used my favorite lipstick all over her cloth doll, and we had to lose her." I grinned, trying to hide the guilt I felt being such a snoop.

Helen smiled. "Let's enjoy these wicked good scones before diving into my goddaughter's engagement party." And we did. It was worth putting off my resolve to eat better for one more day.

Chapter Twenty-Two

Would you consider having your pet in your bridal procession? Many brides are doing that these days...

I was headed home from the Rosenbushes' when I got a call from my mother. I loved my parents, and the wonderful thing about being back in New England was that I was physically close to them again. Neither was getting any younger... but sometimes they called when it was inconvenient, like...right now.

I saw Mom's number on the display of my cell and, shame on me, considered not answering it. *I really should answer.* They just had my sister and me. Vivian lived in San Francisco, so wasn't as available as I was.

Okay...I had a brother too. But he had decided to be a free spirit and travel the country with his band. He had had moderate success, if you defined success as earning just enough from one-night gigs to pay for food, hotels, and gas to get from town to town. He was happy, so I guessed I shouldn't begrudge him his lifestyle, but...I did. My parents worried about him and his restlessness. He was thirty-four now and hadn't a thing to show for his years on this earth except for his truck and guitar. Was part of my reaction jealousy? Maybe it was. Perhaps I envied him his carefree existence. He was responsible for no one and answerable to no one. But what about when our parents got older? Would he be there for Vivian and me? I know Mom and Dad missed him. Jeb made it home about once a year, not nearly often enough in my book. He had recently started dating someone...did you call it dating when you were in your mid-thirties? Sharon wanted to settle down, maybe even start a family. I had great hopes Jeb would come home and do just that; I worried about him. Would he ever lose his wanderlust? Time would tell. I knew he seemed to be more serious about Sharon than he ever had anyone else. We had met her at Christmas, and they were still together. One could hope...

I decided I better answer my phone and immediately wished I hadn't.

"Kate!" Mom screeched into the phone.

I tried and tried to tell her she didn't have to yell into a cell phone, but she didn't get it.

"Hi, Mom," I replied softly, hoping she'd get the hint. I glanced over my shoulder and changed lanes. How did I ever talk on the phone and drive safely before the hands-free option?

"Well, he's done it again." My mother declared with a hint of exasperated satisfaction.

I knew what my dad had done, but I had to ask just to make Mom happy. "Done what, Mom?"

"Took the car. You know he has no feeling in his right foot."

Yes, yes, I did know that. And it put the fear of God into me every time he drove the car. We were doing all we could to persuade him to voluntarily surrender his driver's license. So far, we had been unsuccessful. He insisted he knew what he was doing or that he had been driving for so long, he could easily compensate for the minor inconvenience of his non-feeling foot. My mother drove the two of them 99% of the time, but sometimes he got away from her. He wasn't diminished mentally in any other way except that he thought he could safely drive a car.

I sighed heavily, the casualness of my tone belying the terror in my heart. "Where's he going, Mom?"

"Town Hardware. I said I'd take him, but I wanted to finish the final prep for dinner first. He didn't want to wait."

I wasn't too far away. "I'll get him, Mom. But you and I will have to go get the car later, perhaps even tomorrow. Or you could Uber over to get it."

"What?"

I kept forgetting Mom and Dad didn't keep up with the times. They did have a computer, but it was twelve years if it was a day, and all Mom used it for was email; Dad didn't use it at all. "Nothing, Mom. We'll get the car no later than tomorrow. See you soon. Love you."

I made a slight change to my route and swung into the hardware parking lot. I spotted my stout Dad walking out of the store, carrying two gallons of paint. Oh, boy. No wonder he didn't want Mom to drive him. Dad wanted to paint a room in the house every week. Mom was tired of the smell and the mess. Their house had been updated in every possible way. There was nothing else to do but paint rooms over and over. Dad seriously needed a hobby. I wish he'd use what I knew to be his considerable artistic talent instead of repeating the painting task over and over. He should put his left-handed talent into something productive.

I pulled up alongside my dad. "Hiya, Dad. Need a ride?"

Dad had the grace to look shamefaced. He knew he shouldn't be driving. It must be truly awful to be perfectly fit, mentally and physically–except for one thing. And a foot that one couldn't feel really could put a crimp in your driving style…

"Dang it, Katie. Your mom ratted me out, didn't she?" He walked over to an empty parking place, and I parked in the one next to it.

"Yep, Dad, she did. She just cares about you." *And all those innocent people out on the road.*

"I know, Katie. It's hard, ya know, after being independent all these years and then having to ask your wife for a ride." He looked so sad, my heart broke for him.

"Hey, Dad, you should enjoy it. Mom and I owe you after being our chauffeur all these years."

He grinned. What else could he do? He picked up the paint cans, popped them in the back of my Suburban, and hopped in the passenger seat. We were off.

"I saw Jen inside," he shared.

"Oh, yeah?" I wasn't surprised. Her husband was a dentist and, while a hard worker in the office, not so much at home. I never was sure if he was inept or just didn't like a "honey-do" list.

"She didn't look like herself, barely said hello. Made me remember that time in your girls' senior year."

"What time, Dad?" I glanced over at him.

"Oh, you know, that time she came to the house all worked up, tears running down her face, said she really had to talk to you, but you weren't home. I think it was spring, cause it was fairly late. We were waiting for dinner on you, but it was still light out." He chuckled. "Jeb was all put out. You know how hungry teenage boys get."

"I don't remember that, Dad. Did she say what it was about?" I was shocked. All these years, and I had no idea what he was talking about. Maybe it was about Jack. But something told me it was something else. "Why didn't you tell me?"

"Heck, I thought you girls worked it out. You always did. And she said she'd find you. She didn't?"

I thought I'd remember if Jen came to me in a hysterical state. "No, Dad, can't say that she did." Made me wonder, though.

My thoughts drifted from Jen to my parents. Inconvenient or not, it was wonderful to be here. Who else would be picking up Dad if not for me? And it was good for Ellis to know her grandparents. There was something special about what the younger generation could learn from the older. Why did it seem my mother and I could offer Ellis the same advice, but when Mom said it, it was wisdom. If I repeated the same sage advice, it was annoying. Was I ever the pain to my mother that Ellis was often to me? Probably.

Chapter Twenty-Three

If you wish to display family photos at your wedding, make sure you make copies and use those. Keep your originals at home.

My calendar said this morning would be slow, so I decided to snoop around Comfort Living. I'd be making no points with Vanessa after her very direct instructions to stay clear of her grandmother, but I thought it was my greatest chance of getting information.

I was making my way into the luxury building when a florist van pulled up. *Humph*, it was a shop from Manchester. It always riled me when people didn't use our town shops. Then an idea struck. I was thankful, too, because up until this moment, I had no idea how I was going to get into the care facility. I felt confident Vanessa had my name removed from the approved visitor list.

I blocked the florist van's progress into its desired parking space. "Excuse me," I held up my hands.

The driver rolled down her window. "Yes?" She smiled.

"Are you going into Comfort Living?" Duh. I felt stupid asking. Of course, she was. I could tell by the look on her face she thought it was a stupid question too. But she was too polite to say anything.

"I am."

"I'm running in too. Can I take your delivery? I used to work for a delivery service too, and I know how overbooked you can get. They just don't get it at the shop, how long it all takes."

This time her smile was genuine. "Oh my gosh. That would be so great!

I'm super behind, and I would love to have lunch today." Her face twisted into a sour expression.

Oh boy. I thought lunch, or lack thereof, was a sore spot with her.

"No prob," I said as she pulled over, jumped out, and threw the side door of the van open. She rooted around and then came up with a huge bouquet.

"Thanks so much. I'm Deb, by the way. You can just leave this at the front desk, and Robin will see it's delivered." Deb slammed the van door shut, jumped back in her driver's seat, and was off. I must be a terribly suspicious person. No way would I trust me. And I would be right too. I did have a less-than-altruistic motive for offering to deliver the flowers. I was going to use this mammoth mass of blooms to gain entrance to Comfort Living.

I was thankful for the automatic doors that opened when I approached the entrance. I didn't think I could have opened a door with this giant bouquet in my hands. The better to hide behind.

"Hey, Deb," Robin called out to me. "Saw your van. I guess you're behind there." She giggled.

At least, I *thought* it was Robin. I could see nothing.

"You can leave that on the front desk, and I'll have it delivered."

"That's okay." I tried to cough as I spoke so as to muffle my voice. "Think the family wanted me to take it right up."

"Okay," Robin answered the phone in her next breath.

Wow, easy-peasy. I made my way to the elevator and entered. No way was I climbing the stairs with this burden. I held it away from me. It really wasn't all that attractive, too many carnations and mostly white. The elevator doors dinged back open on the second floor, and I stepped out of the elevator and placed the arrangement on a side table. I'd better read the card and see who it was addressed to. "Jonah Robbins, Suite 224," the card read. Lucky. This meant I had to walk past Marion's room to make the delivery. I made my way hesitantly down the hall. Everyone was hustling back and forth down the passageway. It was a sunny place. It warmed my heart to know such places existed for the elderly. Oh my gosh! Was that Vanessa in Marion's doorway? I couldn't see well around my giant shield, but I think it was. Coincidence that she was here the morning after reading me the riot act at my office? I thought not. I slowed my pace.

"I know, Gram. I know. It's going to be ok." It appeared Vanessa was trying to make her escape, but Marion was making it hard for her. "Have to go, Gram, but I'll take care of it. I promise."

Marion mumbled something I couldn't hear. Then she said loud and clear. "Promise me, Vanessa, promise. You will go there and make sure it's safe."

I slowed even more. This information was gold.

"I still think you should leave well enough alone, but if I do go check on it, I think I should destroy it unless you want it?"

"For God's sake, no." Now Marion sounded exasperated and a little irritated.

The voices were getting fainter as I slowly made my way down the hall away from them. Drats!

"See if it's still there, and if it is, put it back. And don't read it!"

The journal Marion had referenced before? What else could it be? But where was it? By this time, I had arrived at Mr. Robbins's door. His suite was open. I stuck my head in, but no, Mr. Robbins, probably for the best. I placed his arrangement with care on the coffee table and made my escape.

Chapter Twenty-Four

Some brides ask their grandmothers to be...flower girls! What do you think?

This afternoon, Charlie called to nag me about the criminal attorney *again*. He said Brian had done him a solid and informed him that, while they found nothing in my home to implicate me, the blood on Marcy's contract was indeed Lori-Sue's type. This didn't help my case.

"Better to be ahead of the situation than behind it, Kate," Charlie had warned me.

Had I called the attorney yet? That would be a big fat no. I felt pulled in so many directions, from trying to take care of Ellis, to keeping my business afloat, to keeping my behind out of jail.

And tonight, I was in a compromised position. I really shouldn't be here. Intellectually, I knew this. I wasn't a stupid person. But I just couldn't help it. Yes, I was outside Ivy and Kelly Jackman's house, the home of the ruffian who Ellis *thought* was bullying her...and I was peeking in the windows. As I figured out Ivy was the mystery texter, I had to see what her agenda was. Yes, I was looking in her windows like a regular "Peeping Tom." Ok, my nose wasn't pressed against the window, but it was invasive. I was behind a beautiful mature oak tree, dressed in my signature sleuthing black attire, looking in the open windows of Ivy's house. What was I looking for? I didn't know. I just knew those two were hiding something. Kelly was into something odd with her school guidance counselor, and Ivy was anonymously texting nastiness to my daughter. Did it have something to do with Lori-Sue's murder? At this point, everyone looked suspicious to me, even dear Jen. Ivy had a large property, and her blinds/curtains weren't closed. Good for me, bad for Ivy when she had someone like me lurking around. My risk of getting caught was slim. There weren't motion detectors, dogs, or a security patrol. And I prayed no camera doorbell system. With that in mind, I wasn't going to get too close. There was no way either Ivy or Kelly could see me. Yes, the fact I was here was, in essence, an act of desperation. I didn't know what else to do. I didn't know how to help Ellis or myself, and the walls were closing in.

Could I get closer? I was fearless. Yes, yes, I could. I crept closer. I really didn't need to move with such stealth; I didn't think they couldn't hear me. I was now behind a paper aspen, peering around it, hoping to see something besides Ivy doing dishes–nice that her kitchen faced the front of the house. Her home was a generous one. I liked the Cape Cod look. I could easily see this home at the shore, but it fit here too. My gaze flitted to the Jackman's enormous front door. No movement.

I was startled out of my musings as the hair on the back of my neck went up, like a dog's. I heard nothing, but I knew, just knew someone was behind me. A hand went over my mouth, and I was pulled against a hard body; I was in trouble. I was somewhere I shouldn't be and couldn't call for help. Oh, my God! I decided not to struggle until we stopped moving and I could evaluate how to escape, what weapon I might be able to grab. It was true. Deadweight was heavier than a body struggling, at least, that was how it seemed. My captor was having one heck of a time dragging me.

We got behind a hedge, and they turned me around, their hand still clamped firmly over my mouth. When I saw who it was, I tried to bite him. Brian! What the heck?

"If I take my hand away, will you be silent?"

My eyes shot daggers into his, but I nodded.

"What the heck, Bri?" I hissed.

He looked at me like I'd lost my marbles…and maybe I had. *"What the heck, Bri?"* He mimicked, incredulous. "What the *heck* are *you* doing here, Kathryn?"

Kathryn, really?

I said nothing. It was obvious what I was doing here. The one question was how much trouble I was in because we both knew in this situation we weren't equals. He was the law, and I wasn't. I had been warned, and I blatantly went against his orders.

"God, Katie. This can't go on. You know what I told you before. I'd have to run you in if I caught you trespassing again."

But I knew he wouldn't.

Brian hung his head. "Katie..."

"I'm sorry, Brian, I am. It's not just about me now. Kelly, Ivy's daughter, is up to some weird stuff. Ivy has been...."

A door from the residence opened and closed.

"Shhhhhh," he warned. "We have to get out of here and now."

We ran. His car was parked right outside the entrance wall to the property. Thank God Ivy hadn't invested in gates.

"Where's your car," Brian asked.

"I didn't bring one."

"Get in the car." He shoved me in, and not too gently, either.

We roared away, but not fast enough to arouse suspicion.

"Kate, how did you get here?" He turned to look at me.

"Drive," I scolded.

And he drove directly to Cotton Hollow, our old parking spot. Did I remark on his choice? No, it was too awkward.

He put his car in park and turned the engine off. "How the heck did you get there then? Too far to walk...Oh, God, please don't tell me you had Ellis drop you off." Brian turned and looked at me.

I was glad it was dark. My face was hot. "Uber," I whispered.

"What?" he leaned toward me. It seemed he didn't hear.

Crap. I had to say it again. "Uber."

And he laughed, thank God. He laughed. "Katie, you Ubered here?" He had a tough time getting it out, he was laughing so hard.

"Well, I couldn't leave my car there and didn't want Ellis to drop me off, as you seem to agree would not have been a good idea."

"Actually," he turned serious, "Ubering wasn't a great idea. If you were ever apprehended, there would be concrete proof of your whereabouts. You would be, no, let me rephrase, you *are* your own worst enemy."

He was right. But luckily, he was the one who found me. My gaze drifted to our surroundings. The high school lovers' lane. I didn't want to remember, but I did.

He did too, because the next thing I knew, he was leaning into me.

But at that moment, my cell buzzed. Ellis.

Mom, Emergency! Come home now! Not the danger - Dad kind.

Yikes...Dad kind. Did she mean Grant? She couldn't mean Grant. He was on his way to Hawaii with the *lovely* Heather by now, wasn't he?

My thumbs threw across the screen. I felt Brian's eyes on my phone. He wasn't shy about trying to read my texts.

I turned to him. "Excuse me!" I shifted my body away from his as much as I could.

"Hey," he responded. "Must be quite interesting to shift your attention from me." He grinned, his face an eerie blue from the dashboard light.

What's going on Elle? I typed.

Dads HERE!!!!! Help!

"Oh, my dear Lord," I muttered.

Brian looked genuinely concerned. "What's wrong, Katie?"

I couldn't get it out right away. "My ex. He's at the house."

It was his turn to be momentarily silent. "I thought he lived in California."

"He does. Take me home now, please. This had disaster written all over it."

Maybe it was because he was a cop. Maybe it was because I knew he still had feelings for me. But whatever the reason, I didn't argue when Brian said he'd come into the house with me. This whole scenario was bizarre, and I was glad for the backup. Did Brian fear a domestic dispute? Maybe. I knew I was on edge.

Grant had been an uninterested father since the divorce. He had eyes only for his new love, my former best friend. Yes, it stung, but it crushed Ellis. She practiced an air of indifference, but I knew how it made her feel, discarded, unloved. Maybe I had been wrong in declining Grant's invitation to Hawaii without asking Ellis her thoughts. Although, I would never have okayed a week off of school for a frivolous trip to Hawaii, of all places. What was Grant thinking? Was he trying to buy her love? Did he want to try to lure Ellis away from me, back to California–the land of warm weather, school dance teams, and year-round softball? I started hyperventilating at the thought. I couldn't lose her too. And yes, all these thoughts went through my mind at lightning speed as we entered the house.

Chapter Twenty-Five

Remember, it's your day. Don't let anyone from the caterer to the wedding planner hijack your day!

"Grant." I walked into my home feeling like a visitor.

Grant had a way of making you feel as if he owned the place.

He had been traveling, but Grant looked as fresh as if he had just stepped out of the shower. Had he already been to his hotel and freshened up? He was wearing a sunny yellow Vineyard Vines shirt and jeans I swore had a crease. He smiled that smile...that smarmy smile. What had I ever seen in him? Yes, he was handsome in a slick kind of way, and he *did* have dreamy green eyes and that dimple on his left cheek...but still...

He stood from his relaxed position on the family room sofa; his gaze immediately shot to Brian. A flicker of recognition passed through him. He had seen my high school yearbooks. Did he recognize Brian? Did he know Brian meant something to me? Grant would use it against me somehow if he did. He was just that kind of guy.

Grant stuck out his hand to Brian. "Grant Ludlow, Kate's husband."

Brian was slow to extend his own hand, but he eventually did. They held onto each other's hands a mite too long.

"*Ex*-husband. Grant, really!" I glanced at the hand-wringing Ellis, looking like a deer caught in the headlights.

She darted her gaze left, and then I heard it, running water. NO! He did NOT bring her here. He did NOT bring HER into my home. My home, that I purchased with my own money, where my child lived, my sanctuary.

Grant caught my eyes. I shot daggers at his. I tilted my head as I glared at him, as if to say, did you actually drop into my home across the country with your girlfriend?

Brian, for all his detective skills, seemed clueless at this point. He stood next to me awkwardly. No way was I going to be the gracious hostess, but I wanted Brian and Ellis out of the room so I could have a chat with Grant. "Ellis, can you and Detective McAllister please get our guest and the rest of us some water?"

The two went into the kitchen, Brian throwing me a questioning look as Grant gave me a crooked smile, a signature move of his that he thought was more attractive than it was, or maybe I was just immune to him. I didn't invite him to sit back down, something I knew he noticed. My mother raised me that a guest in your home was treated like visiting royalty. Grant had lived with me long enough to recognize the slight.

"What are you doing here, Grant, unannounced and especially with HER? You are barely, and I mean barely, welcome here. She is not. I don't want a scene. The last thing I want to do is prove myself un-lady-like in front of two people I care about, and I don't mean you and Heather. Please leave." I walked toward the door.

Grant sat on my new sofa, soft with buttery leather. Typical Grant. He did what he wanted when he wanted. Why did I never see that when we were married? Had he changed that much, or had I?

"Lovely home, Kate. And who's the guy?" He jerked his head toward the kitchen, where Brian and Ellis were preparing our refreshments. Knowing them, they were being more hospitable than my stingy offer of water–and tap water if I were serving it.

"You don't mess around." His eyes narrowed. "Hey, is he the high school heartthrob?" Jealous, really? But he was. Didn't want me, but didn't want anyone else to have me, either.

What *was* Heather doing in the bathroom so long? The water had long ago turned off. Maybe she heard my voice and was scared to come out. She should be.

I refused to sit. "Again, Grant, what are you doing here? I'm guessing this isn't the way to Hawaii." I was all about the sarcasm now.

"No, Hawaii's on hold. We'll wait until Elle can go with us. And you're right. States is a big deal. Ellis would want her dad there to cheer her on. Heck, I was her coach all those years before high school. I miss seeing her play." That was the first genuine words that had come out of his mouth since I got home. Grant always did love the beautiful combination of Ellis and softball.

"And besides, the company may transfer me to Hartford. Now wouldn't that be something?"

I thought I'd faint, and, at that moment, Heather chose to exit the bathroom. Was it wishful thinking, or did her skin look aged? She was a runner, and I always thought women who ran in excess looked a little haggard. Did her hair lackluster? I had always been jealous of her thick, wavy blond hair. Our gazes locked. How had this incredibly awkward, maddening moment happened?

"You can't be here." My calm voice shocked me, but this was my home, my safe place, and she just couldn't be here.

Heather turned on Grant, anger in her voice and on her face. "I knew she'd freak out. I'm out of here." She grabbed her Louis Vuitton on my sofa table - why had I not noticed that when I walked into the room? - and stomped to the front door. Had she put on some weight? I certainly hope so. Surprisingly, Grant let her go. How she was making her escape, I didn't know, as I saw one car in the drive when we pulled up. Would she take the rental or perhaps Uber? My family and I were keeping them busy tonight.

"Not running after her, Grant?" I said with a wee bit of snark.

He sighed heavily and scooched down lower into my sofa with a comfort level I wasn't happy with. Yes, we had been married sixteen years.

Brian chose that moment to come back with Ellis, carrying a tray of my Waterford iced tea glasses filled with...iced tea. The fact that the crystal was a wedding gift wasn't lost on either Grant or me. He met my gaze and gave me a small smile, and I had to give one back.

I went to help Brian with the tray. "Where did you find the iced tea?" I whispered. It wasn't something I usually had in the fridge.

"Ellis found some cold brew tea bags in the pantry," he whispered back.

"It's time I head out," Brian said to the group in general. He stuck out his hand to the now-standing Grant. "Nice to meet you."

Grant grunted something, which wasn't like him. He was usually Mr. Personality, and this time it was he who grudgingly gave his hand.

I showed Brian to the door and would have walked him to his car. I felt we were leaving this whole evening unfinished.

But he held his hand up to me when I started to walk out. "No. We'll talk later." His look promised that, and it wasn't entirely friendly.

I closed the door and locked it. It seemed Ellis had made her escape upstairs because there was no sign of her.

"What the hell, Grant?"

"Now, Kate," Grant made himself comfortable on my sofa again.

"Don't get too cozy. It's time for you to go." But I had to know. "Why are you here? This is beyond weird, and I really don't appreciate the drop-in. You know you can see Ellis anytime, but I need notice." I never thought I'd need to say this. A trip across the country wasn't a spur-of-the-moment thing. "What's really going on?"

Grant sighed deeply. "Nothing but inconsideration, I guess. I really do have an interview for a promotion here in Hartford, so Heather and I flew out, and I thought we'd surprise Ellis." He actually seemed embarrassed.

I sat next to him. "Grant, you have to realize it wasn't a brilliant idea to bring Heather here." I had to laugh. It was so ridiculous.

Grant smiled weakly. "I thought maybe we could see Ellis play some games. What you said about me, not even knowing she was in states, got to me. I was an awful husband, but I never saw myself as a bad dad."

What a jerk. "Leaving your wife and child for your next-door neighbor makes you a bad dad, Grant. How you go forward from there is up to you. But you can't just pop in with your girlfriend and expect me to be ok with it. She is never welcome here, nor is she welcome at Ellis's games or events. Now if you're still together when Ellis graduates from college or gets married, I'll be civil, but beyond that, keep her away. I don't want Ellis to feel uncomfortable, but if she comes into my world, or Ellis's, I'll make a scene. And I don't think either of us wants that." I stood. "Are we on the same page, Grant?"

Grant stood too and frankly surprised me with his next words. "I'm concerned about this murder investigation and your involvement. I want you to know you have my support and Ellis as well. How worried should we be?"

His concern touched me. You couldn't be married for over a decade and not have *some* sort of feelings for your former partner.

I put my hand on his forearm. "Thanks, Grant. So Heather isn't in a good mood?" I tried to lighten the mood.

"Well, things aren't great with Heather. It's not what I thought it was going to be."

"Really? I could have told you that."

"I imagine she's on her way back to Huntington Beach right now."

"I'm sorry."

He cocked his head at me. "Really?" He seemed shocked. "I kind of thought you might be happy."

I walked toward the door, hoping he'd take the hint. "Really, I don't care. I want Ellis to be happy. If your parting ways with Heather makes her happier, then wonderful. If she doesn't care, neither do I."

I'd hurt him. But really? He left in his sporty rental car. He always was flashy, so Heather hadn't taken the car. He'd be back. My life was going to become more complicated.

Chapter Twenty-Six

If you're getting married in the summer, it's best to choose fondant for your cake topping. Buttercream or a whipped cream base may melt in the summer heat. And fondant doesn't have to be refrigerated.

The next day was a Saturday. In a rare occurrence, I didn't have a wedding today. Ellis had softball practice this morning, but we had a little time to spend together. We needed coffee, the *really* good stuff, and nurturing. So, this morning it was Jen's shop. I needed my friend more than I needed a substantial breakfast at our local breakfast spot.

I grabbed a table, and Ellis went up to get our coffees. She was ordering Jen's famous scones, and I insisted she *had* to pay. Free coffee for me from my best friend was one thing; coffee and breakfast for my daughter and me was another. Luckily, Jen's assistant was working the register and didn't bicker with Ellis over payment. I was so tired, physically and emotionally, I didn't even rise to help Ellis with her load. She placed the coffees on the table first and then the pastries. Today's scones were blueberry; you had to love New England.

"I haven't put cream in them yet." She set down the two coffees. She was tired too and apparently hoping I'd do it.

"No worries, kid. I'll get it." I rose and headed over to the condiment bar.

Jen came out of the kitchen at the same time. She stopped mid-stride. "You look like death."

You could always count on your best friend to tell you like it was. I hadn't asked her opinion, however. It didn't help my mood that every hair on her head was in place and while I knew she was working, her apron was pristine.

"Gee, thanks." I gave her a lopsided grin.

She was right, and I knew it. The positive and the negative about having a lifelong friend–they spoke the truth…but did they?

Jen noticed the frown. "What's going on, Katie?" Her concern was genuine.

"Grant," I decided to go with that.

"Grant? Is he still pressuring you to let him take Ellis to Hawaii?" Her expression was somewhere between worried and angry. Jen had never liked Grant. I guess she was a better judge of character than I was.

I glanced over my shoulder. Ellis looked impatient. She wanted her coffee. "Hang on." I splashed some cream in each coffee cup and ran the cups back to our table. "Be back in a flash," I assured a grumpy Ellis.

"What's up?" Jen asked before I even made it back to the condiment bar.

"Grant showed up at the house last night with Heather in tow."

Jen said nothing for a couple of moments. "I have no words."

"I know. I was with Brian, and Ellis called me in a frenzy."

"Wait, you were with Brian? What was that about?"

"Later," I shushed her. "So, we got home, and Grant was there, and Heather was in the powder room. When she came out, I informed her, quite politely, I may add, that she wasn't welcome and to get out."

"Did you yell at her?" Jen was horrified. She knew that if someone was in my home, they were treated like an honored guest, but I hadn't invited her.

"No, but I think there are problems in paradise. She left in a huff, and Grant let her go. It was weird."

"Why did she make the trip?" Jen shook her head.

"Oh, oh!" I said with great animation. "I can't believe I almost forgot this! He may be relocating to Hartford!"

"Get out!" Jen pushed me lightly on the shoulder.

I didn't hold Jen's attention for long. She was looking over my shoulder. I wanted to look, knew I should look, but I couldn't. I had an idea of one of two people who had caught her attention.

I snuck a peak. What I didn't consider was that it would be both of them…at the same time. What were the chances they'd walk into Jen's shop together?

Or was Brian following Grant? I doubted that, but who knew?

There was a dance as to who would open and hold the door. Brian won and held the door for Grant. Grant huffed in but saw me and changed his facial expression to a pleasant one. What was his game? It was too much a change. He wanted something or did he not want Brian to have me? Grant seemed surprised to see me, or he acted like it. Brian was not. He knew my haunts and my friendship with Jen; Grant didn't.

"Well, look who the cat dragged in, and *both* of them," Jen smirked.

I rolled my eyes at her. Well, this was awkward. They both walked toward me, then veered off to get in line, nodding at me, but Grant smiled. He thought his smile was my kryptonite; it wasn't. They ordered, and I tried to return to my table where Ellis was seated, no longer bored but enjoying the show her father and Brian were putting on. Her smile at me was similar to Jen's.

"Uh, uh," Jen pulled me back next to her by my arm. "Spill."

"I shared everything. Now I'm on my way back to my table to have a most awkward breakfast with my daughter, ex, and high school ex. Fun times!" I said sarcastically.

Jen turned away. Gone was my bubbly friend. She looked troubled and well, sad. Something was up there. I'd have to get to the bottom of that. I added it to my "to-do list."

"Mom," Ellis hissed when I reached our table, somewhere between exasperation and delight at the drama. "Do you have a love triangle going on here?"

"Hardly," I rolled my eyes in a teenaged fashion. But I wondered if that was what was going on.

Grant sauntered over to our table and made himself right at home. "So, Ellis, is Monday's game home or away?"

Ellis tried to play it cool, but she was clearly pleased her father was interested and actually here for the game. "Home," she replied around bites of her scone.

"I'll be there."

Ellis beamed.

Brian chose that moment to pass by our table with a to-go cup and white paper baker's bag. "I'll be there too, Ellis. Have to support the home team."

I thought Ellis would give Brian the stink-eye, but she smiled at him too. This didn't earn Brian a smile from Grant, however. He scowled and seemed ready to say something, but I put my hand on his arm, and he stopped. Brian didn't miss the gesture, and it was my turn to get a frown from him.

"Have a good day, folks." Brian was once again the professional Eastbury Police Detective. He walked out, and I couldn't help but follow him with my gaze.

Grant was watching me with his. "That him?" he asked softly.

My face warmed. Ellis rolled her eyes. Her presence made me very uncomfortable.

"Him who?" I was fooling no one.

"Give me a break, Kate. Him, 'the guy,' the love of your life, the high school hero, *that* guy." Was his voice…bitter?

"Give *me* a break, Grant. Yes, I went to high school with Brian, and yes, we dated, but he's not 'the guy.'" My gaze slid to Ellis.

Yep, she was listening to our back-and-forth with glee. Was that a smile on her face? She seemed to be enjoying my discomfort. I was glad she didn't seem to resent Brian for her dad's thoughts.

Grant tossed his used paper napkin on the table in apparent disgust, shaking his head. I had always hated when he did that, and what right did he have anyway?

He got up and smiled at Ellis. "Nice having breakfast with you ladies. I'll be at the game, Ellis. Knock 'em dead, kid." He ruffled Ellis's hair as he walked by her to the door.

She allowed it, with a happy smile even. Boy…I'd never get away with that. But it made me realize how much she had missed her dad and his attention.

Ellis gave a wave and a smile to a girl in the coffee line similarly garbed in practice attire. "Hey, there's Gabby. I'm going to catch a ride to practice with her, ok, Mom?"

"Okay." I looked into my coffee. "I'll see you at home."

Surprisingly, she dropped a kiss on the top of my head. "Love ya, Mom."

She smiled softly.

Never knew what you were going to get with that kid, but I so loved her.

* * *

I sat another couple minutes, suddenly too tired to get up and start my day. I had a laundry room full of dirty clothes I really should attend to and a rare open Saturday to get it all done. I wished Jen would come over and give me an excuse to procrastinate further, but she was swamped. My phone pinged an incoming text. What *now*?

Please come to police station. Need to ask some questions.

It was Brian. Uuuuugggg. I didn't need this this morning.

Uuuuuggg, I typed back. **Can we meet at the fountain?**

Our sleepy berg of Eastbury, CT, had a most charming tradition. For the local high school's junior prom and senior ball, the whole town went down to the Town Center's fountain to take photos of the beautiful people and meet and greet their neighbors. Brian and I had our own history at the fountain. Yes, we had attended both junior prom and senior ball together and had our photos taken at the fountain like all our friends. I didn't suggest the fountain for old times' sake. I was just terrified of the police station.

Brian didn't respond right away. But then his text came in.

Fine 15 minutes.

Jen gave me a refill, and thirteen minutes later, I walked across Main Street to the town green. The water had been turned back on for the fountain April first. It, of course, had to be winterized and the water shut off for the season to avoid cracked and frozen pipes. It bubbled merrily, keeping safe all the secrets it had been witness to over the years. The tulips around its circular edge were rotating yellow and red; so beautiful. Brian was waiting for me, sitting precariously on the fountain's edge. He stood when I approached, always the gentleman.

I sat on one of the café chairs scattered around the green, and so did he. I offered him the extra coffee Jen had thrust at me when she heard I was meeting Brian. Couldn't hurt to butter him up.

"Thanks," he grinned sheepishly.

Uh, oh. What's up? "What's up, Brian? Did you find something? More questions? I imagine you want to read me the riot act about being at Ivy's," I babbled. Yes, I was nervous.

Brian pried the lid off his steaming coffee and blew on it. I knew that delaying tactic.

"Brian?" Crap. Was it bad news?

"Autopsy came back on Lori-Sue. Cause of death, anaphylaxis. Your clue about the granola wrapper and peanut butter allergy was spot-on. And even now, we know it was anaphylaxis that killed her; the medical examiner feels fairly confident the slit to her neck was done by a left-handed person."

"Wow! This clears me, yes? I'm a righty," I said hopefully.

"Katie, I never thought you were guilty. The thing is, all the evidence has always pointed to you, circumstantial as well as your interactions leading up to her murder. The dominant hand of the killer isn't going to make or break this case."

I hung my head.

Brian asked, "Why's he here, Katie?"

He momentarily surprised me. *What? He's asking about Grant, now?* What the heck! "What the heck, Brian?" I stood and started to walk away.

He was smart enough not to grab my arm and possibly make a scene for anyone driving by on Main Street. He instead said in a very soft silky voice, "Katie."

Brian knew I couldn't resist that voice. I sat back down and pouted.

"I know I don't have any right, as you so delicately pointed out, but you can't deny there is…there are…some remaining…feelings," he finally got out. "I thought he was totally out of the picture. Now he's weirdly back in. We're not kids. I'm not going to play this game again."

I shot him a look, one filled with anger and yes, hurt. I didn't respond as I should have to his question. He was right. There was something going on here, and it *was* weird Grant had shown up and might even be moving to Hartford. We weren't kids, so pretending there wasn't an electric charge every time we interacted was silly. But he'd made me mad.

I stood again and, this time, remained standing. "I don't know why he's here, Brian. But he *is* Ellis's dad and will always be part of both of our lives because of that. Grant and I are over, but you've got to realize he's not going away."

He looked hurt and confused at my outburst. I got a flash of the teen he had been. What a mess. Then a thought zinged in my mind, maybe my trying to find the Simpson ring, and then Mrs. Marion Rizzo's journal had stimulated a memory. We had never carved our initials in the Cotton Hollow "tree." I sat back down.

"Ya know what, Brian," I instantly changed the subject. "We never carved our initials in 'The Tree.'"

He frowned slightly. "No, we never did, did we, Katie? We were going to; then all hell broke loose between us."

I had another lightning flash, The Tree!" Could that possibly be Marion's hiding place? There was something in that journal, I just knew it. I stood again. I was going to Cotton Hollow.

"I've gotta go." I tossed my almost full coffee in the nearby bin.

"Wait. Hold on." This time Brian *did* take my arm, but slowly, and I let him. "I don't like the look in your eyes. I know when you've gotten a hair-brained idea. What's up?"

I should tell him, but he'd think I was crazy, but then...he did anyway. "You know I'm doing Marcy Simpson's wedding, right?"

He smiled and almost laughed and then checked himself. He got points for that. "Actually, no, I didn't. Congratulations." His attempt to look sincere was appreciated.

I shook him off in my frenzy. "It's not about that. The family asked me to find this old ring, and I think I did, but Tina from the bakery has it, and she's giving me fits about it, and there's a mystery involving this old lady who lives at Comfort Living, and she has a journal she doesn't want me to see, or anyone for that matter...."

"Whoa, Katie, wait. You're not making a whole lot of sense."

I turned to go. I knew I wasn't making sense, but I didn't have time to waste. I thought I had a lead, and I needed to see it through and then get home to do my oh-so-fun job of laundry. Seriously, how did two people generate so many dirty clothes? "I know. See you." I began my march away.

"Hold up, Katie." He touched my arm again as he came up beside me. "I'll go with you. Probably not a good idea, but why not?"

A car rolled by the green with its windows down. Aerosmith's "Don't Want to Miss A Thing" oozed out. *Are you kidding me? What are the odds?* My song with Brian was "Don't Want To Miss A Thing." Boy, did it bring back memories. I was right back in that high school gym at our last homecoming dance swaying to the song, which I would argue with *anyone*, was the most romantic song in the history of love songs. My head rested on his football player's chest, his arms held me lovingly but firmly. It was still new enough to get those butterflies in my stomach. I could feel the eyes of my enemies, Sarah and Lori-Sue, and whoever else fancied Brian that year, on me. But I didn't revel in it the way some girls might; I just reveled in his embrace. It seemed too good to be true. *He* seemed too good to be true.

And then he whispered in my ear. "I love you, Katie."

I was shocked. I couldn't believe he had said it. My gaze flew up to his, and he smiled a small smile. I returned it. "I love you too, Brian," I whispered, then shyly put my head back on his impressive chest.

I snapped myself back to the present day and shook off the memory, and we were off in search of a journal, a tree, and a ghost.

Chapter Twenty-Seven

Consider closing the bar at the end of the cocktail hour. You can reopen once dinner starts. You'll never get your guests into the dining area if you don't.

We jumped in Brian's car, which was parked on the street illegally, of course. That practice of cops annoyed me to no end unless I was benefitting from it, like today.

"So, where are we headed?" Brian didn't take his eyes from the road to look at me.

"Cotton Hollow." I could feel him smiling but refused to look and stared straight ahead.

He did laugh then. "Wow, Katie, I can't keep you away from there."

I looked at him. "Please, Brian." I quickly filled him in more coherently on the Simpson family connection to the ring, Tina, Marion, and the journal.

"So, how does Cotton Hollow fit into all of this? I'm not saying I have a problem going to our former make-out spot, but...*why* are we going there?"

"It's stupid, but you know how 'The Tree' has always been sort of a lovers' spot. Teenage couples carved their initials there; marriage proposals are made under it. Heck, I even had one wedding last spring under it. It *wasn't* great for the tree, although romantic. Let's just say getting guest chairs down there for the ceremony was a nightmare. When I visited Marion, I felt she remembered the ring but was hiding something. Then when I was leaving, she was screaming something about a *journal*. Then when I went back...."

"You went back?" Why did he sound incredulous?

"Well, yeah." I refrained from adding the duh.

"Not to throw water on your parade, but—"

"I think you're mixing clichés there, Brian."

"Well, sorry." He grinned. "But seriously, Katie, why would you make the massive jump from overhearing something in a retirement home to running off to 'The Tree' to look for some ancient journal?"

"Because it just makes sense. It's the perfect place for a romantic young girl to hide a missive of the heart." I didn't look up, but I could imagine Brian rolling his eyes. But he was still taking me there, so there was that.

It took all of six minutes to arrive at Cotton Hollow. No one was in the parking lot.

"How are your shoes?"

I looked at my canvas Keds, red, my favorite. I hated to get them all muddy, but it was nothing a spin in the washer wouldn't fix. "Eh, they'll do."

I looked over at Brian's pristine light-green Brooks and cringed. He'd have a mess from the mud the recent April showers had created. He wanted to come, I reminded myself. What was etiquette here? Did I offer to wash them for him? My thoughts were quickly interrupted.

"Let's get a move on. I have a lawn to mow."

I glanced at his back. *Hey, no one asked you to come.* The weather was mild. I wished we had time to enjoy it. I took a moment on our hike to admire the soft light-green budding leaves on the trees around us. How had I ever left this place?

In minutes and we were standing in front of "The Tree." How many stories could it tell? The oak's branches were thicker than the circumference of two men. It was a stoic, majestic landmark of our town. Yes, lovers' initials were carved into its trunk, but it wasn't done to disfigure it; it was done to mark a memory, to declare love. I thought "The Tree" understood and was honored.

Brian walked ahead of me and before I knew it, he had his pocketknife out. He began carving a heart. My face warmed like a girl's.

He looked back at me over his shoulder and grinned. "Should've been done a long time ago."

It actually took quite a while to carve into hardwood, and I thought he was getting tired by the time he was done. But it was worth it to both of us. BM +

KM. Was it nostalgia or a promise for the future? Our gazes met, but we had wasted enough time on the silliness of carving our initials on the tree. We had to complete the task that brought us here. I had chores to do at home, and Brian had, as he had so delicately reminded me, a lawn to mow.

"So now that that's done, what's the plan? Where are we looking?"

I ignored Brian's apparent apathy for the journal hunt. "Well, it would be perfect if 'The Tree' had a hollowed-out trunk, and we could find the journal inside wrapped in plastic," I joked.

Brian faced me. "So, you're convinced the journal is somewhere by 'The Tree?'"

I was beginning to realize the absurdity of my thought process. It *seemed* like a good idea when we were at the fountain.

"Ok, Katie, let's assume you're on to something." He looked up into the majestic tree limbs. "If I were going to hide something around here, I'd want it to be water-resistant." Brian was thinking out loud. He walked around the huge tree, all the while looking up. "Katie, how long ago was this?"

I had to do some quick math, not my strong suit. "Oh, about fifty years."

"So..." Brian continued. "The average oak grows between a foot or a foot and a half a year. Let's hope for a foot growth a year. Let's say, just to humor you, your suspect found a knothole at waist level, that's fifty feet up. Crap."

He looked up. We both did. We walked around "The Tree," and sure enough, there was a knothole about forty feet up. Hum... I couldn't ask him, could I?

"Bri..."

"Don't even, Katie."

I sighed, and he started rolling up his pant legs.

"It won't be that hard. There are a lot of low-hanging limbs." He turned and grinned at me.

I returned his smile. My hero. It was a long shot, but boy did I appreciate his vote of confidence. After a few slippery attempts, Brian made slow progress up "The Tree." He reached the knothole in question. I was holding my breath as he reached inside. He yelled down that it was actually a very small cavity. I realized it couldn't contain something as large as a journal. I was surprised at how disappointed I was. Really? It was a long shot. I sat down with a thunk on a nearby boulder.

"Hey!" Brian turned around so quickly, I was terrified he'd lose his precarious hold on his perch.

"Brian! Careful," I yelled up.

"Check this out!" He tossed down a dun-colored object, or I should say two objects, because a scrap of paper fluttered gracefully to the ground while the other thing landed a foot away.

I ran for the paper, then scooped up the piece of what appeared to be some sort of hide. Brian scrambled down, I wished I could say gracefully, but it was awkward. I enjoyed the view, though. He hustled over to me and looked at what captivated my attention. I had in my hand an old scrap of paper written in the most beautiful script, the perfect cursive in itself dating it to days gone by.

"What is it?" Brian asked as if I would know. Typical man.

"Well, I think it's a note or cryptic clue. It appears weathered but has withstood the test of time as it was wrapped in this piece of hide." I handed the buckskin over to Brian.

He reached for the note as well. "Bell's Turner, Horticulture."

"That's the library. Do you think it is even possible?" My words tripped over my tongue.

"Do I think the journal is hidden in the library's horticulture section?" Brian finished for me.

"Heck, I don't know. Let's go check." I had a thrill of anticipation. "Let's go." I took off at a jog, slipping on some wet leaves once. I wasn't even going to look at my soon-to-be-muddy Keds.

* * *

We arrived at our town's library, Bells-Turner, named after two patriots instrumental in the Revolutionary War effort. For a small town, our library was extraordinary. There were many town charity events for its benefit, and it showed. All our computers were new state-of-the-art jobs, and our books were plentiful.

I raced ahead of Brian through the doorway but had to stop at the front desk to ask where the horticulture section was. I was up the stairs to the second floor before Brian. I started looking randomly through the section, trying to find anything that looked out of place, worn and tattered; nothing was initially obvious. I slowed down. I had to. Nothing would be found with my frenzied search.

Brian, much to my irritation, was leaning against a stack, slightly frowning at me. Was this the same man that not twenty minutes ago had climbed a tree for me?

"Are you going to help, or what?" I couldn't keep the irritation out of my voice.

"I just wish you'd be as concerned about the potential murder charge hanging over your head, but OK, I'll help. Might as well." He actually started seriously searching for the elusive journal. Alas, nothing.

An idea struck me. "Remember when we were in high school, and they redid the library? They kept a historic section, I don't know, for the historical aspects of it, or whatnot. Do you think the journal could be somewhere there?"

Brian shrugged his shoulders with a disinterested look. His expression reminded me of the time we were on a scavenger hunt in high school. He participated to appease me, but his heart wasn't in it. He was acting much the same today. I didn't care. I wanted the support of another body, and it got my mind off my pressing problem, Lori-Sue's murder, and my supposed role in it, all the better.

I led the way to the "historic section" of the library. I thought the planning committee would have kept the whole building if they could have, but it wasn't a viable option. The structure was all but falling down when the remodel began. The cubby hole that was kept was reinforced and lovingly refurbished. Relics from bygone days adorned its walls. I looked around the room, seeing it as I hadn't before; it was beautiful. I scrutinized each and every item on the wall, on the shelves, on the mantle of the nonworking fireplace. Nothing stuck out. Then I saw it...a beautiful wooden boot bench.

The kind that looks like a low chest but has a flip lid where you could sit on it, remove your boots, then store them inside while they dried.

I removed a pot of dusty fake flowers and lifted the lid. It appeared someone had stored some random books and miscellaneous knickknack items inside…and forgotten about them. I rifled through them, then stopped. Was this it? I withdrew a slim volume. I hesitated. Yes, this was a library, but I had a weird feeling I was going to open something personal. But wasn't that what I was after? Wasn't I searching for an elderly lady's journal? I felt kind of dirty but then not too dirty, so I opened it. "Property of Marion Blackburn." Bingo. I couldn't believe it. I had actually found it by pure tenacity and a lot of luck.

"Brian," I whispered with urgency. We were in a library, after all. "I found it!"

"What?" Could he sound more incredulous? Oh, he of little faith.

I grinned at him. "Yep."

Chapter Twenty-Eight

Are there two women in your life that you'd like to honor? How about a "Maid of Honor" AND a "Matron of Honor"?

Brian had to get to mowing that lawn and, surprisingly, showed little interest in reading the journal. It was my thing, after all.

I was presently sitting in my kitchen, hunkered down with a fleece blanket and a small but robust fire in my fireplace. I had a steaming cup of Earl Grey tea at the ready. I was going to read Marion's journal; I couldn't wait. I had worked for this. It was no mean feat getting the journal out of the library. It wasn't as easy as you'd suspect. Was it the librarian who gave me grief? No. She didn't even know I had the journal. It was Brian. He didn't think I should abscond with the journal. He was right…I guess. Eventually, after some scrimmaging, I asked him to look the other way, literally, and we left. We each made our way to our respective cars, the library being on Main Street, where I had left my mine.

Now, I was ready to read. I had goosebumps of anticipation as I opened it.

Wednesday, June 27

He didn't come to me tonight. He said he would, especially as he didn't come last night. I'm worried. I heard the rumors like everyone else. Raymond was spending time at the Crawford Farm. Everyone fancies Eveline Crawford. But she is engaged, just like I am to Raymond. Why did she have to spark with him? I asked Raymond about her the last time he came to call, and he said they were simply friends; he had done some work for her father. He said she just happened to be at the house when he went to get paid, that she offered him a glass of lemonade. She sat on their porch with him as he drank it. She was "powerful kind," he said. I don't believe him. Raymond has been distant, and when I asked him when we should set the date, he suddenly had to get home. He has avoided me since.

Mama says not to worry. He has asked for my hand and won't go back on it. That would make him a scoundrel, and even though Raymond isn't her favorite person, (she by far preferred Joey Rizzo for my hand), he's no scoundrel. I wish I could believe her, but I can tell he's different. He didn't even kiss me goodbye when he left, and he has always been trying to push me in that regard. I'm always the one to tell him to stop. Maybe I made a mistake? Maybe if I had been more generous in that area...

Friday, June 29

I'm not proud of it, but when Raymond didn't come to call again tonight, I had a hunch. I thought he had most likely gone to call on Eveline. I wanted to see with my own eyes. I told Mama I had a powerful headache and was going to bed right after supper. I asked her not to disturb me, as I was taking some of her sleeping powder and hopefully, I could rest. Thank the Lord she didn't seem suspicious. I dressed in Wilber's trousers. They were so big I had to use a belt to keep them up and roll the bottoms, but they made it more modest to climb down a tree. And maybe if someone saw me, they'd think I was a boy. I also put my hair in a cap. I slid down the old apple tree, as I had seen Wilbur do. It is a huge old tree, and its branches lie outside both our bedroom windows. I won't fib and say it was easy making it to the ground. I have a few scrapes I'm going to have to find a fib to tell Mama about tomorrow. But that's tomorrow. Was I making a mistake?

I ran as long as I could then walked the rest of the way to the Crawford place. It wouldn't do to be gone too long. No matter what I said to Mama, she was likely to check in on me. I had put pillows in my bed, but Mama was a crafty one.

I slowed as I neared the Crawford place. It wouldn't do to alert the family or their dogs, I was close. I was friendly with their dogs, but it was night, and who knows. There are a lot of trees on the drive to the house, and I was able to hide behind them as I approached the porch. I heard him before I saw him. There was Raymond, sitting quite close to Eveline with his arm slung loosely over her shoulders, laughing. How I loved his laugh. It was scandalous, really. I was shocked at Raymond and Eveline's behavior. They were each engaged to others, after all. But, what about Eveline's parents? Where was their chaperone? I could hardly believe they would allow this to go on...unless her parents weren't home. Was that why they were sitting outside on a chilly evening? It was beyond that they were acting so, but if her parents weren't home and she had Raymond ***inside*** *the house, that would ruin her reputation. I could think of nothing else than Mr. and Mrs. Crawford were out. But I was worried about the wrong thing. I should be worrying about how my fiancé was carrying on with another girl.*

Maybe some would confront him right then and there. But I was here lurking among the trees, spying, dressed as a boy. There was nothing I could do then. I went home and snuck in the kitchen door. I had left it unlocked, well, we never locked our doors anyhow, but I made sure that was the case tonight. I crept to the second floor, knowing which steps to skip on the staircase so they didn't creak. I was almost safely to my room when Wilbur came out of his.

"Marion, what in tarnation are you doing in that getup?" My brother hissed at me.

"Wilbur, not tonight," I said softly. "I don't think I can bear to talk about it tonight."

His gaze softened. "Are you ok, Mar?"

"I'm ok," I whispered back. "I promise to talk to you about it tomorrow." I meant it too. I needed someone to confide in, to advise me.

He hesitated. "Okay, but we will talk tomorrow," he said this strongly, and not as a question.

"Yes." I stepped around him and closed my bedroom door. I cried myself to sleep.

Saturday, June 30

Wilbur found me when I was feeding the chickens before breakfast.

"Are you ready to tell me why you were dressed up in my clothes last night and were sneaking into the house at all hours? You're lucky Mamma and Daddy go to bed early."

I hung my head. Through all of my heartbreak, I was ashamed too. My fiancé would rather keep company with another girl. I quickly told Wilbur all about it. I can't bear to write it again, even here. Wilbur was so mad. I can't say I expected quite the anger. I loved him for it. At least someone thought I was worth something.

"You get a note to Raymond. Tell him I want to have a word. Tell him to meet me tonight here at our barn after supper."

I grabbed Wilbur's arm. "Wilbur, no. Nothing good will come of that." I didn't like the look on his face.

He took a breath. "Marion, it's not right that he drags it out. We need to get to the bottom of this. You can't be treated this way."

I knew he was right. "Okay."

I was able to get word to Raymond. I couldn't send a note, as he had trouble reading. Something about all the letters mixing up when he read. I'm not saying he isn't smart; he is, very. He could cipher like nobody's business. But he struggled to read. So, I sent a message by way of one of our farm workers.

I could tell by what our worker reported of how Raymond responded that he was hesitant to come by, which caused me more worry. Supper was finally finished, and Wilbur and I went out to the barn to do our evening chores. If Raymond was surprised, I had asked him to meet me in the barn instead of the parlor in the house, he didn't show it.

He entered the barn and saw me. "Marion, what's going on?"

I looked over to Wilbur, who joined us from one of the stalls.

"Nice of you to join us, Ray," Wilbur said in a menacing tone.

Raymond looked uneasy, as well he should. He looked to Wilbur, then back to me, "Marion?" I felt almost badly, but not much.

Wilbur kindly let me be the one to question Ray. "What's going on with you and Eveline?" I got right to the point.

Raymond had the grace to blush. "Mar, can we do this somewhere else?" His gaze shot to the menacing form of my brother.

"I think right here is just fine," Wilbur answered for me.

"Mar, please," he pleaded. "This is between us."

I remained silent.

"Ok." He sat on a bale of hay and exhaled deeply. "Marion, you know I love you, but you deserve to be loved deeply and wholly, and that person isn't me. You're such a wonderful girl. You deserve better than my sorry self."

"Cut the flimflam, Raymond." My brother's face was scarlet now, his brown eyes flashing, and he advanced. He was much taller than the rather short Raymond.

As for me, I was having a hard time taking it in. Raymond was truly breaking up with me.

"And Eveline?" I got out.

Raymond looked at the hay-covered barn floor. "I never meant it to happen, Mar. You have to believe me. One day she offered me some lemonade after work, and we just got on so well, and my feelings changed from there." He finally met my gaze.

What more was there to say? My heart was broken, yes, but no one could change someone else's feelings, just like I couldn't stop loving Raymond.

"What about Eveline's beau, Mr. Bellmont?" He was a local store owner to whom Eveline was engaged.

While Mr. Bellmont was quite a bit older than Eveline, her family, more prominent than ours, thought it a grand match. Ray didn't answer. I pulled off his ring and walked to stand in front of him and placed it in his palm. That's when I noticed the ring with the large diamond hanging on a gold chain 'round his neck; so odd to see that feminine babble on him.

"What's this?" I touched the gem and then let it fall back to bounce on his chest.

Wilbur had remained oddly silent.

And then Raymond really did color.

"And don't tell me nothing, cause it most certainly is."

"Don't make me say it, Mar," he pleaded.

"What is it, Raymond?" My voice had a steel edge to it now.

He sighed deeply and looked first at Wilbur, then at me. "It's Eveline's, well, her grandmother's. She wants me to sell it for her so we can get a fresh start...." Raymond wasn't evil. I knew what saying those words to me cost him. Probably as much as they cost me to hear them.

A lone tear rolled down my cheek.

And that was all it took for my brother, my life-long protector, to spring into action. He grabbed Raymond by the neck and, well, I can't write anymore. It's too heartbreaking. But, in the end...Raymond Wethersfield was dead. It truly was an accident. Yes, Wilbur was mad, but he never meant to kill him, of that I'm certain.

My in-charge brother, who always knew what to do, didn't know what to do. He sat on one of the hay bales, his face drained of all color. Then he started to shake. Wilbur had defended me. Now it was my time to help him. Yes, I was sad about poor Raymond, but he was a scoundrel. I was going to have no life with him after all. Cold, probably, but then I was numb too.

"We have to get him out of here," I told Wilbur.

He shook his head. "No, no, Marion. We have to call Daddy and then the sheriff. I have to own up to this."

"Don't be stupid, Wilbur," I snapped at him. Don't think harshly of me, Diary. No good would come from Wilbur going to prison. Daddy needed him here on the farm. I needed him.

I picked up Raymond's feet. "Grab his shoulders, Wil."

The hated ring slid onto the barn floor. The chain it had hung on round Ray's neck had broken in the scuffle. I kicked it into the corner.

I'd come back for it later. But maybe I wouldn't. I just couldn't stomach seeing it again. No one would find it, I felt certain. Let it rot for all I cared.

I won't tell you how we buried Raymond back behind the old barn we don't use anymore, how long it took us to dig his grave, or how Wilbur wept. I did not.

I put the journal down. Wow. No wonder Marion didn't want this journal to get out. There was no statute of limitations on murder. But I would imagine her brother was long gone. Marion's secrets were safe with me. Now that the great Simpson family ring mystery was solved, I wasn't going to allow myself to procrastinate any longer about my own situation. I grabbed a piece of computer paper and a pen and listed out my suspects again, using a *People* magazine to give the paper support.

Sarah Deloro, weird stuff with the Board of Realtors. And she had been at Joyce's bridge party and could have grabbed my contract and planted it in Lori-Sue's shop.

She was a leftie.

Addalee, she hated Lori-Sue. I knew she did, but she had asked her to do the flowers for her wedding. How strange was *that*? She, too, had been at the bridge party with her future mother-in-law.

Joyce, she looked like a possibility for the murderer. She, after all, was being blackmailed by Lori-Sue. But, after seeing Helen's Facebook page at her home, I realized she was right-handed. I doubted a woman would have the strength, and especially an older woman, to do thc damage with the knife with her non-dominant hand.

Ivy, she was very suspicious. And why would she send texts to Ellis if she didn't have something to hide? Was she at the bridge party? Was she a leftie?

And...Jen. Well, she ticked all the boxes. She was at the bridge party, hated Lori-Sue, and had been acting so unlike herself. I knew her better than almost anyone, and lately, I felt as if I didn't know her at all. She was right-handed, but very strong.

What now?

* * *

I opened my front door the next morning, not my friendly mudroom door that friends and family entered and exited from. There stood Brian with a look that was all serious. What a quick change from his attitude yesterday and our adventure.

"May I come in, Ms. Ludlow?"

Oh jeez.

I opened my door wider, silently inviting him to enter. "Come on, Detective. What's up? You seem so…serious."

I followed him into my family room. *Well, isn't he at home here?*

He sat down on my leather sofa, but on the edge, better not get too comfortable.

He still hadn't said a word, just fiddled with one of those cop's leather notebooks.

"Spit it out, Brian." I was starting to sweat. Was he here to arrest me? I had a bad feeling.

"Where were you last night, about nine p.m.?"

What? Not what I expected, not at all.

"Why?"

"I'm asking the questions here," he answered, none too friendly.

A shiver ran up my spine. Brian wasn't being the supportive cop/friend he had been yesterday.

"I was here at home with Ellis," I answered.

"Can anyone else verify that? Cause a woman's daughter isn't the most reliable alibi."

Alibi! What the heck? What was it I was supposed to have done? "What's this about?" My hands tugged at my skirt. It suddenly felt too short, the scar on my leg too exposed. Not a great help that the first time I had the nerve to wear a skirt, I was accused of *something*.

"What'd you do here at home last night, Kate?"

"Let's see. We watched a recorded episode of "*The Bachelor*" at about eight thirty, then went to bed. I think Ellis did some homework in her room, and

I read in bed. Brian…"

"Sarah Deloro was bludgeoned last night at one of the homes she has on the market. In fact, it was Lori-Sue's house. Lori-Sue's cousin, Ivy Jackman, has put it on the market. She's her heir."

"Well, it wasn't me. How can you think such a thing, Brian?" I stood abruptly. So abruptly, in fact, my bum leg almost didn't support me. I hoped he didn't notice. I thought he did as Brian's gaze went to my leg and then to my scar. My face burned hot.

He pulled my hand down, forcing me back into a sitting position. His voice softened. "I know that, Katie, but I had to ask. And all this isn't looking great for you. One more item to tick off in your guilty column. Did you really have words at a mutual client's?"

How did he know about that? "It wasn't words. It was a verbal sparring. Is she…is she ok?"

"She was admitted to the hospital last night and kept overnight for observation. But she's expected to be discharged today. She'll have one heck of a headache but is expected to make a full recovery."

"And she didn't see who hit her? Can't you get some sort of video footage through someone's camera doorbell or something?" I puckered my brow. Just what I needed, more problems, and more problems pointing directly at me.

"The camera doorbell at Lori-Sue's was dismantled, and the position of the driveway wasn't optimal for anything to be caught by the neighbors."

"But why me? Why am I getting the third degree?"

Brian leaned forward and rested his elbows on his knees. "Come on, Katie. Everyone knows you and Sarah hated each other, chiefly due to yours truly." He looked uncomfortable here, and I glared at him.

"Think a lot of yourself much?" I popped off and immediately regretted it. What was I trying to prove here?

"The perp used a softball bat." Brian rocked my world.

"You're not inferring Ellis had anything to do with this?" I unsuccessfully tried to keep the terror out of my voice.

"No, no, Katie. Providing you didn't crack Sarah-Grace's head with a softball bat, and I really don't think you did," he gave a hint of a smile here, "someone hates you as much as you hate Sarah. And that's pretty darn scary. Watch your back."

Brian left as quickly as he had arrived. Darn, double darn.

* * *

Was my plan ill-advised? Yes. But I was oh so tired of sitting around and doing nothing. I arrived at the hospital. Thankfully, the security sign-in kiosk didn't require photo ID. I wrote my maiden name in the log and put "maternity ward" as my destination. I smiled my Katie smile at the gray-haired, pink-coated volunteer and then made my way to the hospital gift shop. My flower trick of hiding behind a giant bouquet had worked so well at Comfort Living I thought it might work again. The tired, mid-fifties volunteer didn't bat an eye when I asked for the biggest bouquet she had in the gift shop walk-in flower fridge. I paid on my business credit card. Hey, if this wasn't a business expense, I didn't know what was. If I was taken in for Lori-Sue's murder, I could say bye-bye to all my clients, business busted. I was thankful the charge went through without a problem. My payment was due in five days, and I had put an extra strain on it this month.

I made my way to the elevator bank and, once inside the car, pushed the button for the second floor, where I knew the non-critical patients were housed. I was alone in the elevator, thank the Lord, as I wasn't confident my giant floral arrangement and I would ride comfortably with others.

After a brief ride, the elevator dinged, the doors opened slowly, and I made my exit hesitantly. I had to find Sarah's room without asking anyone. To ask would alert the staff to my presence. Although, I'd get a look or two with this ridiculous clump of flowers I was carrying.

A voice came over the intercom, "Code Blue, Code Blue, floor three, room 317. All personnel respond." I think I would have been questioned if that code hadn't just been called. Staff went running away from me. Yay! Then I caught myself. What was I thinking? Was I really cheering that some poor soul was struggling so? That sobered me up right quick.

My task proved to be ridiculously easy. There was a digital monitor mounted across from the nurses' station with the patient's name, room number, and status listed. Wow.

Deloro, Sarah was in room 217. The floor was like a ghost town. I guessed everyone was still in the room with the code. I refused to let my mind go there. I still felt guilty for my initial reaction to the code filling me with glee.

Her door was cracked open. I opened it, knocking on the doorframe, leading with the flowers. Sarah had been cracked on the head. She didn't need the initial shock of seeing me waltz into her hospital room.

"Come in," she said softly and politely.

That would change as soon as she saw my face. I gently lowered the flowers.

"Katie," she said slowly.

Ok, she was medicated. That made sense. This might be easier than I could have hoped.

"Sarah, I brought you something." I indicated the blooms with my head. I need both hands to balance this behemoth.

"You can put it on the windowsill with the others." She indicated the florist-shop amount of arrangements to her left. Wow! Maybe she was better-liked than I thought. I placed the arrangement on a side table. There wasn't room on the sill.

Sarah waved a hand to the chair next to her bed in a lackluster way to invite me to sit. She *must* be on some great meds. This wasn't the Sarah I knew.

I scooched my chair closer to her bed. I didn't have a lot of time. Someone would be checking on her soon. I was just glad there wasn't a police officer sitting outside her room, but that would be a much for a head bonk. Then again, I doubted it was just a random act.

"I'm so sorry this happened to you, Sarah. How are you feeling?" I went as far as to awkwardly pat her hand resting wanly on her blanket. Who *was* I?

She smiled at me benignly. "This whole hospital gig isn't so bad. I feel pretty happy."

I bet you do. "What happened?" My interrogation began.

"I don't know." Sarah winced slightly. "I was outside Lori-Sue's house; you know the green Tudor her parents owned when we were in high school?"

And then it came back to me. That was why the picture I'd seen in Sarah's club locker looked familiar. It was Lori-Sue's childhood home and was her home until her murder. Weird. Why would Sarah have a photo of Lori-Sue's house in her locker, which was purported to be her secret hiding place?

Sarah hated me, but she was drugged. Dare I...dare I ask? What did I have to lose? Well, a lot. She could call the police, and she could call a nurse who would summon the police. But times were dire.

"Sarah," I paused. There was still time to back out of my half-baked plan. "Did you know the police came to my house this morning to ask me about your attack?" I thought it prudent to leave out the fact the police was, in fact, Brian.

Sarah started to laugh. It wasn't a half-bad laugh. "Oh, Katie, I know you don't have it in you to whack me with a bat. Yeah, the police said it was a bat, and I know your kid is quite the softball star. No, it appears to be someone who is trying to make you look bad and conveniently doesn't like me much."

To say Sarah's statement surprised me was an understatement. Maybe it came down to the fact she wanted to ferret out who hit her as much as she wanted to put our past behind us.

"Can I do anything? I'm serious, Sarah." Somehow, I just knew she wasn't the killer, and I bet the killer was the one who conked her. No, we'd never be friends, but did she have any? She might need help. "Do you need a change of clothes or anything from the house?"

"God no, I really don't need help from you, Katie. I do have friends, you know, Jeez."

And... we were back.

* * *

I was on my way home from the hospital, my mind whirling. So, if I could cross Sarah off my list of suspects, who did that leave now? I decided a detour was in order as I didn't want to go home yet. My head wasn't in a positive place to be the dutiful mom to Ellis. She deserved more. Later I'd think about how I neglected her during this miserable time, but not now. I drove by the high school, and whom did I see but Ivy getting out of the biggest Chevy SUV I'd ever seen. Oh, right, her ex owned the Chevy dealership, didn't he? The school day had long been over, and so had all the after-school sports practices. Ivy didn't go into the school via the front doors. No, she went in a side door, but not before looking over her shoulder to make sure, I was guessing, that she was unobserved. And it seemed someone had let her in. Fishy, very fishy. Why was she going into the school at this hour, and why the side entrance? Because she was up to something. I decided to follow her. Boy, was I a super sleuth today. In for a penny, in for a pound.

I parked at the far end of the school lot and tried to keep to the shadows, away from the emerging parking lot lights. I got to the same *door* Ivy entered. I was sure it would be locked, and what would I do then? But surprise! The door was unlocked. Where would Ivy go? Actually, that was an easy guess. I wagered she was going to see the guidance counselor, Mr. Williams, the subject of Kelly's Snapchat photos. As I approached the guidance office, sneaking up on tiptoe, I heard voices, a male and a female. I found a pillar to hide behind. Could I be seen? I didn't know, but hey, I had a right to be in my daughter's school, didn't I? Granted, I was lurking around like a common thief, but...I didn't have an answer for that.

"I'm done, Ivy," the male voice said. "It's just too hot and frankly not worth the hassle."

"Hassle," Ivy's said with snark. "You have been well compensated for your hassle. You're in deep, Brad."

I knew this now to be the counselor, Mr. Williams.

"Well, I did what you asked, what I was paid for, and I'm done. And don't threaten me with exposure. If I'm exposed, so are you and your darling Kelly. Quit while you're ahead, Ivy." There was a finality to his voice that even Ivy seemed to recognize, as she didn't respond. Was she coming this way? Oh my gosh. I had to get out of there! I rounded the corner into hallway "A." The high school tried to make navigation easier for students and visitors alike by naming the hallways. Otherwise, making one's way through the hallways would be more of a nightmare than it already was, especially when crowded.

A door slammed. Probably it was an enraged Ivy leaving the guidance counseling center. I peeked around the corner and saw her retreating toward the side door she entered by.

I raced after her, getting to the exit door just before it closed. Ivy jerked around and said, "I knew you'd come to your..." then she saw me. Her eyes narrowed. "Kate?" She seemed truly puzzled.

What the heck? "Did you kill Lori-Sue?" Yes, she could lie, but I didn't think she would. But what I didn't count on was she would become enraged.

She ran toward me, bent her head, and butted into my midsection, knocking me flat on my behind. She knocked the wind right out of me. I rolled to my side, trying to get my breath, gasping frantically. Ivy took this opportunity to straddle me and slapped my face. Oww!

"I," slap, "did," slap, "not," slap, "kill...."

I finally got my breath and grabbed her hand, stopping the final slap. I hit her squarely on the nose.

"Oww!!" Ivy screamed as she toppled off me. "That hurt!"

Wow, what a jerk. Her nose was bleeding. I calmly reached for my pocketbook that had fallen not too far from me when Ivy attacked me. I grabbed some tissues and silently gave them to her.

"Thanks." She took them. She surprised me with her politeness. Hadn't she just been slapping me? If I were an emoji, I'd be one with my eyes wide open in surprise.

"What the heck, Ivy? Why'd you attack me?" I rubbed my sore; I beet red face gingerly.

She turned on me again. "Why'd you ask if I killed Lori-Sue? I loved her, Katie. *Loved* her. Without her in my life, I have very little family left, and, if you haven't noticed, I'm not the most popular girl around. Losing her has torn me up. People only like me when I'm making their wedding perfect. And I can do that well 'cause I boss everyone around." And then she began to cry.

Call me gullible or a softie, but I believed her. But I had to know what the heck she was doing with Mr. Williams. Would she tell me? Was it wise for her to do so? No, but she was emotional and vulnerable now. Best to strike while the iron was hot. I reaized sometimes I wasn't a very nice person.

But it still didn't stop me from asking, "What's the deal with Mr. Williams, Ivy?"

We were both standing now, each attending to our wounds. I hoped no one was driving by and saw our ridiculous scuffle. How in the world did it happen? I was mortified.

"Come on, Katie, you and your Ellis know what's going on."

I was confused. "No, Ivy, we don't." But boy, did I *want* to know.

"I guess it doesn't matter now, anyway. He's backed out." Ivy sat on the sparse grass with a thud.

I joined her. "Mr. Williams?"

"Yeah. He was going to pull some strings for my Kelly to get into a tier-one school, for a fee, of course." Ivy didn't seem at all embarrassed by this.

I was shocked. I had read about movie stars and uber-rich people paying for college admission advantages, but I never thought I'd see it in Eastbury, CT.

Ivy took my shocked silence for disapproval, and she was kind of right, but it was more disbelief than anything else. "It doesn't matter anymore 'cause he backed out. I bet that makes you happy, doesn't it, little Miss Goodie Two-Shoes." She was back to the nasty Ivy as she marched to her huge Chevy SUV.

Well, I felt comfortable crossing her off my list of suspects.

"Wait!" I yelled after her. "Why did you text Ellis all those nasty texts?"

Ivy stopped her march to her vehicle. "Because she was getting all up in my business and would have eventually figured out what Kelly and I were up to if she kept asking her stupid questions."

While I took exception at calling Ellis's questions stupid, I decided to let it go. There was no reasoning with this woman. Nothing additional to be gained here.

Chapter Twenty-Nine

Making a video of your wedding is a great lasting memento.

I was curious what Joyce knew about the family ring and what she didn't. I had a feeling she was privy to more information than she let on. She was also on my list of suspects for Lori-Sue's murder. The next morning, after a quick stop at the library, I was seated with Joyce and Marcy at the enormous Simpson family dining table.

We were having a celebration of sorts. For, on Marcy's right hand was the storied family ring. Tina had contacted Joyce, just as I knew she would, and held the ring hostage until Joyce agreed to her terms. I was too professional to ask the price, but boy did I want to. I so wanted to know. Joyce had confided that Marcy really shouldn't wear the ring until her wedding day, but she didn't have it in her to deny her daughter something she had longed for. I was a hero.

But my hero status didn't last long. To say we were all frustrated was an understatement.

"Urrarug!" Marcy screeched, her hands shooting into her hair and pulling both sides of it straight up.

"Marcy!" Joyce seemed horrified. "You're going to pull your hair out if you keep that up! Whatever is wrong?"

"Mom! This seating chart is impossible! There's no way we can make everyone happy. In fact, I think we may have a guest uprising!"

Joyce rose and padded softly on the moss-green oriental carpet over to where Marcy was having her breakdown. "It can't be that bad, darling." She sat on the chair next to Marcy's and winced. "Yikes, I see what you mean. You absolutely cannot seat Julianna with Troy and Rose."

"Well, they certainly can't come to the head table!" Marcy was displaying a rare show of independence.

Joyce's lips thinned, but she didn't say anything.

I was waiting for Joyce to push back and settle the matter of where the now very interesting Troy and Julianna would be seated, but instead, she said, "Marcy, love, I just got a UPS notification that a package was delivered. I'm fairly certain it's another wedding gift. Would you be a dear and go down to the gate and retrieve it?"

Marcy looked like she wanted to continue the battle over Troy and Julianna. In fact, she opened her mouth, then closed it. But the lure of a wedding gift persuaded her to let it go...for now.

"Sure, Mom," and once again, she was her sunny, docile self. Marcy put her pink highlighter we'd been using to mark friends and family of the Simpsons side and skipped off to the kitchen door–the one closest to the gate separating the rarified world of the Simpsons from the lesser mortals.

Joyce turned to me. "I have a bracelet I wish to give Marcy on her wedding day. I know it will seem like a bit of a let-down after the excitement of finding the family ring, but my mother gave it to me on my wedding day, in part to make up for the missing ring. I wondered if you had any ideas on presentation?"

I was inordinately flattered. "I think if I were presenting such a gift to my daughter, I'd want it to be intimate but still have it documented. How about if you gift her the bracelet during the getting ready photos. Maybe you can have your photographer capture some shots of you putting the bracelet on Marcy. Let me show you." I beckoned Joyce over to the gorgeous, gilded mirror hanging in her cavernous dining room. "So, the photo will be staged, but it's something you and your family can look back on and remember the moment." I held my wrist out to Joyce. "Just imagine I'm Marcy, and you're clasping the bracelet on my wrist."

Joyce smiled into the mirror. "I love this idea, Kate. But let's switch sides. I'm a leftie, so I have to be on your other side."

And then it hit me. Joyce was a leftie. That photo I had seen of her bridge group was a selfie, and everything was backward. I got a chill. How well did I really know her? Apparently, I didn't know anyone...

Chapter Thirty

Include your future mother-in-law in as many wedding planning items as you feel comfortable. She will appreciate it.

It had been a long day, and I was exhausted. I had my jammies on and was ready to turn in. I checked the front door lock, and that was when I saw it, a scrap of paper on the floor. I stooped to pick it up and found it was a note. I was guessing it had been pushed under my front door. I didn't know when the note could have been slipped in. And how could it have been done? I had motion detectors mounted on my garage, and I hadn't seen them go on. My dog hadn't barked. Who had dropped it off, and when? To say that my hackles were up would be an understatement. Should I roust Ellis? Should I have her read it with me? I knew something was suspicious about this, anyone would. But there was also a surreal element about it too. I almost didn't want to believe it.

With shaking hands, I opened the note. After I did, I thought I should have at least put on my dishwashing gloves to protect against possible fingerprints. But really? I shouldn't have even opened the note. I should have either called Brian or taken it tomorrow morning to the police station. But, of course, I was just too curious.

You're too close. We need to talk. I hope we can come to an arrangement. Meet me at Cotton Hollow-10:00 pm.

Was there any question about what I was going to do? I did know I wasn't going to wake my daughter, who was exhausted from a long day of school, and take her with me. It was too dangerous. I shouldn't go alone, but I was close. I had the real killer running scared. It *could* be a trap. Oh, I wished I had a gun. I was profoundly against them, but was I really? I was against them being in the wrong hands. Maybe when this was all over, I'd take a course and get my concealed-carry permit. Connecticut was surprisingly liberal in allowing that.

I put on what was becoming my standard sleuthing costume: black leggings, a black hoodie, and Ellis's black sneakers. I slipped my phone into my pocket. Even though the cell reception was weak, I planned to call Brian while I was talking to the person and leave the line open. I could deal with his wrath later at what I knew he would deem my "reckless behavior."

I pulled my Suburban into the moonlit parking lot of the Cotton Hollow complex and parked by the pool. It was a fun, inexpensive town pool during the summer months for those who either couldn't afford a private pool club in town, there were four in town if you counted the country club, or thought they were a waste of money. The most basic reason to join the private vs. pay the minor fee to the town pool was if your children had friends who belonged to one of the private clubs and wanted to go there all the time–ah, yes, peer pressure started young.

There was a delightful swimming hole not far from the parking lot. It wasn't supervised as the pool was, but it was a favorite of the teen set. Many a mother threatened her teen within an inch of their life about going there. Nary a one listened. There were not many accidents, however. And as I'd already confessed, year-round, it was the lovers' lane for couples, both teens and adults, who might just have cheating hearts. I tried not to think about my most recent visit with Brian.

There were no other cars when I pulled in. I wasn't surprised. I doubted the perp wanted me to see his/her car.

"Meet at the pool," the note had said.

This gave me pause. I wasn't the greatest swimmer. I already felt at a disadvantage meeting here. What if he/she threw me in? I wasn't a strong swimmer, and my phone, my lifeline to Brian, would be cut off.

I opened the gate to the pool, the padlock suspiciously cut and removed, and entered. I didn't close it, better to have an easy escape if needed. I reached my hand into my hoodie pocket. Brian's name was at the top of my recent phone log history. I had practiced touching the spot on my phone where his name was located and hoped it was right. If not, my dad would be getting an earful. No one was here. I knew the possibility of a wild goose chase was possible, or a trap. Maybe it was both. Then I saw it, a pale blue envelope tucked under the leg of one of the patio chairs. I had a little difficulty getting it out from under the chair leg, and that was all I remembered. Oh, and the blinding pain when someone hit me over the head with a blow that was probably harder than necessary. Whoever hit me didn't like me much, was my last thought as all went black.

I awoke to a blinding headache, and I meant blinding. I had suffered from headaches before I had Ellis–my doctor said they were hormone-related and very well might subside after pregnancy. They did. Another reason to love that kid. If possible, the pain in my head was even worse than a migraine; and those made me vomit. Uh oh...just the thought made me gag, and then I turned my head and vomited. Yuck, but I felt a bit better. That was always the way with headaches and me. If I threw up, I felt better. I was able to survey my surroundings some. I appeared to be in some sort of rustic shed. My guess was the supply shed for the Cotton Hollow pool. There were discarded lounge chairs and pool chlorine. But no one was with me. I moved away from my vomit. Just the smell made me sick again. I wasn't tied up, so I had that going for me. But I didn't yet feel well enough to stand. I had been a fool. I knew I was, but I thought somehow I was smarter than the other guy. Didn't we all?

I managed to get myself into a sitting position and felt for my phone. It was gone, and so was my lifeline to Brian. I had tried to fire off a call to Brian before I was conked on the head, but who knew if it went through? And then the door creaked open. A figure, and not a particularly large one, was silhouetted in the shed's opening. He/she came in and closed the door, careful to keep the flashlight carried low, not shining on me. *Thank you for that.* I don't think I could have taken any light coming my way with this headache. The figure walked to one of the loungers and took a seat. I watched warily.

"I thought you were smart, Kate."

So, a female. I was listening to the voice. It was a familiar one, but I couldn't place it in my befuddled state.

"Why would you come alone to this remote area and meet a dangerous stranger, much less without backup?"

Excellent question and one I had no answer for. It was beyond dumb. I held my tongue. Maybe she'd think I was still unconscious. No such luck.

"I know you're awake. You're sitting up. And FYI, your boyfriend came looking for you. Said he got a weird call from you. He must have you on that "Find My Friends" app. I had more than a little trouble explaining why I was here and you weren't, but I made it work. She shone the light on her smug face. Joyce!

"Joyce!" I had a knack for stating the obvious.

"Yes," she moved the flashlight down, no longer illuminating her face.

I had a bad feeling. It wasn't good she let me see her face. Dang.

"Why Joyce?" I whispered. The adrenaline rush was making my head pound again. Ouch.

"You know *why*, Kate."

"Actually, I don't." I looked around in the dim light from her flashlight, which she had pointed to the ground next to her, hoping to find some sort of weapon. None that I could see. And anyway, how effective would I be with the headache and my weakened state? I was in trouble.

Joyce tapped her flashlight against her left hand, almost as if she wanted to use it to bash something. Hopefully not my head. "You found out about my mother."

"What about your mother?" I was confused.

"She was pregnant with me when she married Johnny Belmont, and he wasn't even my birth father. But you know all this. Lori-Sue did."

Maybe I could reason with her? If I could convince her, I didn't know about her mother *or* Lori-Sue...

"I didn't know, Joyce, but what can it matter now?" I was trying to buy myself time by keeping her talking. Maybe someone would come looking for me. Yeah, right. I was on my own here, and I knew it.

"Was Lori-Sue blackmailing you about that?"

Joyce became agitated as I quizzed her.

"Yes, of course. But you know this." Joyce rubbed her head roughly with the large flashlight, messing her usually immaculate hair.

"Why would you think I know?" I was genuinely confused.

"You found the journal *and* the ring. I could tell you were taunting me when you were looking in the mirror with me last night."

Huh, well, who knew what went on in the mind of a murderess? And that was exactly what I was sure Joyce was now. It all fell into place. The fear of discovery of her mother's secret was why Joyce wasn't fully on board with my hunt for the ring.

"Why are you trying to keep all this a secret, Joyce?" I was truly interested and slightly confused by her compulsion to bury the truth. "Marcy doesn't know? Seems silly to me. She's a grown woman, and really? It was so long ago and not a big thing anymore."

Joyce's response was quiet but harsh. "Not a big thing? Silly? Her beloved grandfather wasn't her grandfather at all."

Well…when she put it *that* way.

"Not only that," Joyce hissed, "she adored Eveline's memory and worshiped the ground she walked on. She wishes she could have met her."

I understood, didn't I?

"Do you still have the journal?"

"No," I lied. But maybe I should have said "yes." Maybe she would keep me alive a while longer if she thought I had something to offer. But I never would have given Joyce the journal of her grandmother's rival, Marion. Wilber's secrets would also remain buried. Was it *my* call to make? Well, probably not, but I had to make it. But, in all reality, I thought that ship had sailed. I was in deep trouble.

She slid over and leaned well into my personal space. "Did you at least read it?"

"I read it, and let's just say there was a terrible accident. Raymond *couldn't* make it back to Eveline, but I think he truly loved her. Why kill me over this? And, by the way, I didn't know. I had no idea who sent the note setting up the meeting, just that whoever did had something to hide and might be Lori-Sue's killer. How did you even know about the journal?"

Joyce ignored my question, just waved the flashlight around, and I was able to see her confused and haggard face. "You really didn't know about my mother, about my birthfather?"

"No. And I don't think anyone would care. Come on, Joyce. This is extreme, all the cloak and dagger stuff, hitting me on the head."

Joyce paced back and forth in the confined area. The agitation showed in her jerky movements. I was sure she was contemplating how her actions tonight would play out with local law enforcement. Would she be accused of kidnapping? Assault?

But I was to be surprised yet again.

"So, you didn't know I killed Lori-Sue?" She rubbed the flashlight against her cheek in a distracted manner.

My eyes had adjusted to the gloomy ambient light, and I could see there was blood on the torch, my own, I presumed.

Crap. I was incapacitated in a tiny place with a psycho, and no one knew where I was. How stupid was I?

"You?" was all I could think to say. Surely there was something better.

Joyce smiled at this. "Yes, little 'ole me. Didn't think I had it in me, did you? You're a mom. Isn't it amazing what we'll do to protect our young?" Her eyes were still not on me but focusing on something only she could see.

While I would kill to defend Ellis in a life-or-death situation, I didn't think I'd kill to prevent her from hearing family history.

Joyce jerked her gaze to me. "But you knew about my mother, you found the journal."

"Yeah," I agreed. "How did you know I found it? How did you even know there *was* a journal?"

I didn't know you found the journal," Joyce confessed. "I guessed, and you admitted it. And you're not the only one who can snoop on an old lady." Joyce grinned wickedly here. "You should have seen old Marion's face when I went to see her. She thought my mother was visiting from the dead." Joyce cackled. "And, of course, I had to kill Lori-Sue because she was blackmailing me. She made some lame excuse that she had fallen on hard times and simultaneously wanted to grow her business. Boohoo. Imagine! I took pity on her and didn't make her suffer much." I didn't think Joyce was really even talking to me. I had to get her back.

"You poisoned her with the granola bar, didn't you? Was that before or after you stabbed her?"

"Not as dumb as you look." Her smile wasn't a kind one. "Lori-Sue was a frequent vendor in my home. I have at least one flower delivery a week. We got to know each other well. As it turns out, too well. Somehow, she found out my greatest secret, which my mother confided to me on her deathbed. My father wasn't my father at all, but some random man." Joyce's face crumbled.

"Very few knew Lori-Sue had decided she was tired of living in fear of dying via peanut. But she confided in me." Joyce continued. "She was terrified she'd accidentally eat something containing peanuts or peanut oil or just eat something made in a factory that manufactured products made with peanuts, so she was seeing an allergist who was desensitizing her. She could eat up to a peanut and a half. She had started allowing products in her shop made in a factory that also used peanuts. I found a granola bar chock full of peanuts, and put it in a wrapper that said, 'peanut-free product' with the disclaimer it could have traces of peanuts due to the factory. I suggested a snack at her shop during a decorating session for one of my parties and opened it for her. Lori-Sue thought it was so liberating that she could now eat those products. I knew she would. She gobbled it up. And, within a matter of minutes, she was gone. It was gruesome, and I have to admit I felt bad, but someone had to stay with her in case she tried to get help or call nine-one-one. My big slip-up was I didn't grab the wrapper. I thought I was so flawless. But the whole process unnerved me. No one's perfect."

"But why did you stab her?" Seemed like overkill to me, pun intended. I knew she was unsure what to do with me. I was trying to buy myself some time, and I was scared to death.

"If it looked like a peanut allergy death, the police would mainly look at people who knew her well. I may have been a suspect as we worked together frequently. I couldn't risk that…So, I gave her a poke with my kitchen knife right after she passed. She still bled like a pig, even though she was dead." Her callousness shocked me. "Let's go," she pulled on my arm.

"Wait," I said desperately, trying to delay her until, until what? Who was going to save me? "How did Lori-Sue's blood get on my contract you planted in her shop?"

"Think, Kate, think." Joyce jabbed at her head with her finger. "It wasn't Lori-Sue's blood; it was mine. I just lucked out we had the same blood type. The police just typed it. They didn't confirm it was Lori-Sue's. By the time they do that, you'll no longer be a problem for me."

I had to get out of here. "Well, Joyce, this has been nice, but I really have to get back." Maybe if I acted as if all was normal, she would too, and she would let me go…not.

She laughed with genuine mirth. "You're not going anywhere, my friend. Now you know all, I can't have any loose ends. But I can't get rid of you here as your creepy boyfriend, Brian, saw me here." She looked off, thinking about my demise, I bet.

Chapter Thirty-One

Some brides are opting to have their mothers walk them down the aisle along with their fathers. But think long and hard about this. A great joy for a woman is to watch her daughter walk down the aisle on her wedding day.

Well…here we are. Add another to the books. If you had told me I would be in a damp, cold, musty basement tied up with Sarah Deloro, I'd have laughed and run for my life from the crazy person telling me such a tale. Sarah had informed me that Joyce had picked this house to stash us as Marcy and her soon-to-be-husband had it under contract. Guess who the listing agent was? You got it, Sarah Deloro; karma was a witch. Sarah, recently released from the hospital, had made an unplanned visit to the house where Joyce had just arrived with yours truly. Joyce got the jump on a frail Sarah, and now we were both trussed up like pigs and left in the basement. Did this mean we were to live? I wasn't counting on it.

Our gazes met, mine and Sarah's. For the first time ever, there was no animosity. We were afraid. Joyce couldn't let us go. We both knew that. Why she hadn't gagged us, I didn't know, too much trouble?

"You okay?" I asked Sarah.

Joyce had whacked her on the head when she was tying Sarah up. Obviously dangerous to have two head injuries so close together.

"Headache. I'm not going to let her take us down, though. "Scoot over here and try to undo my hands." Our hands were tied up behind our backs.

I basically hated Sarah, but I did like how she didn't give up on something she wanted, ever. This had made my life hell in high school but just may save it today.

I started scooting over to her and then had a thought. "Hey, I saw this girl in a Facebook video a year or so back. She showed how someone could use their shoestring to break zip ties. Did you see it?"

Sarah rolled her eyes, and it must have hurt because she grimaced. "Ouch. No, little Miss social media, I did not. And, brain-trust, neither one of us has shoelaces."

I looked at her shoes and mine–flats, no shoestrings. Yes, I felt like an idiot. But the idea was sound. Where were my trusty Keds when I needed them?

"Yes, I know, Sarah, but we're in a basement packed full of junk. We might not find a shoestring, but maybe something of value." I looked around at all the boxes.

"Yeah, true, but how are we going to get into the boxes? We're not exactly mobile and don't have the use of our hands." She looked defeated.

It was my turn to be the strong one. "Sarah Deloro, when have you *ever* given up on anything? Who's the top-selling Realtor in New England? Who stole my boyfriend right out from under me?" The last part was said with a bit of a snark.

Sarah laughed. "You were a worthy adversary, Katie. I never would have gotten Brian if you two hadn't had that big blow-up. We both know that. Whatever happened?"

I was too tired and scared to respond.

"Let's DO THIS!"

"Ok. Let's each take a box and try to open it."

"How are we going to stand up?" Sarah asked.

I finished scooting over to her. "Turn around."

For once, she didn't argue but turned her back to me. I leaned my back to hers. "Now, let's see if your personal trainer has been doing his job. Try to stand pressing your back to mine, and I'll do the same."

We struggled, both trying to be the alpha, but, in no time flat, we were standing. Our hands were still bound behind us, but I felt confident we could rummage through some boxes in an attempt to find something of value to free ourselves.

"Hey, Katie, do you have a knife to slit these boxes open?"

Anger surged through me as I tried to blindly rip a box top off with my hands behind me. "If I had knife, you idiot, I'd use it to cut us free!" My face burned. I glared at her.

She was grinning ear to ear. A joke…from Sarah Deloro? And I had to laugh. It was just so, so stupid; then she started giggling. We sounded like a couple of lunatics.

"A sense of humor, Sarah, who knew?"

But she smiled. "So," she began as we made our way to the storage boxes in our prison. "We weren't exactly tight back in the day, back in high school. I heard loads but never got the real story."

"What are you talking about?" I turned and frowned at her, rubbing my sore wrist.

She smiled a mean smile. At least she must be feeling better. "Oh, you know, that 'thing' in high school everyone was always talking about."

My face burned again. I was so, so embarrassed by that. It was completely out of character. Almost like I was a different person, at least a possessed person.

"Come on," Sarah goaded. "We may never get out of here. You might as well provide some entertainment." She playfully bumped my shoulder with hers.

Seriously? We could *die,* and she wanted to hear about one of the most embarrassing days of my life? What the heck? Maybe it would take our minds off our dire situation as we looked in these disgusting storage boxes. I hobbled over to another promising prospect of a box and fumbled as I peeled back the drying packing tape. Dust flew up and caught in my nose–gross.

"I never liked Lori-Sue, not in elementary school or middle school, and definitely not in high school. She was a royal 'witch.' She cheated off my tests when she could and spread nasty rumors about me, mainly that I stuffed my bra with toilet paper–I did not!"

Here I got an actual giggle from Sarah, a giggle! She, too, was ripping open gross boxes, rooting for something, anything to aid in our escape; then she sneezed a mighty sneeze.

"Go on." She wiped her nose on her shoulder, gross again.

"I put up with it all, but one day, I was in a cranky mood to begin with. Lori-Sue pushed me too far."

Sarah rolled her head in a come-on motion.

"She said my younger sister, Vivian, was putting out for the senior class. I know it was to get at me, and she finally hit gold."

Sarah was listening wide-eyed.

"I cornered her outside the café and asked her if she, in fact, had been spreading the rumors. My sister, by the way, was the sweetest, shyest girl you'd ever want to meet back then."

Lori-Sue just smirked at me. "Yep."

"I put my head down and ran for her belly. I headbutted her right in the gut. Knocked her down and knocked the wind out of her. It really wasn't much of a fight. She was down for the count after just one headbutt from me."

At this point, Sarah started laughing and, irritatingly enough, didn't stop. She actually bent over and belly laughed. Tears ran down her face. "I heard that was how it went down but didn't believe it," she said with difficulty around her gales of laughter. "What did they do to you?"

I narrowed my eyes at Sarah. Just when I was beginning to not hate her, she laughed at me. But then I realized it really was funny, *very* funny. And I began to laugh too, so hard it was silent at times, and I had trouble catching my breath. Then I sobered. "The vice-principal suspended me. I thought my parents would kill me, but they were actually kinda cool about it."

"Don't take it so hard, Katie. Kids got in fights all the time, not girls so much, but they did. What was so epic was that perfect Miss Prim and Proper got into a *fight*." And she cackled.

Sarah whooped. "I hit gold!"

"What is it?" I hustled over.

"Give me a minute!" The snark was back. "Oh, my God!" Jubilance. "One guess what's in this box?"

Really? She wanted to play twenty questions NOW? "I give, Sarah. What have you found?"

"The idiot who packed these boxes, a moving company, I'd wager, decided to leave the empty roll of tape in one of the boxes and then proceeded to tape up said box."

Was she irritating or what? What help was an empty roll of tape going to do us? "And this helps us…how?"

She grabbed the tape and hopped around so her back was to me, and I could see what she was holding in her hands. Yes, it was an empty roll of tape, but in a tape *dispenser*. It had serrated edges where one was to cut the tape. We were saved. But the question that begged to be answered was, who was going to do the cutting? One of us would be doing it blindly, cutting the other to bits. Was there a winner? Well, hopefully, both of us, if we were going to get out of this alive.

Our gazes met. We were thinking the same thing.

"I'm thinking one person holds it, and the bound person does the cutting of their own zip ties." Sarah made sense.

"Makes sense." I decided to take one for the team. "You found it, and you came up with the strategy. Keep it steady, and I'll saw these bad boys right off." I sounded, even to myself, more optimistic than I felt.

But you know what? Except for some nicks, it worked fairly well. In under five minutes, I was free, and then I worked on Sarah's ties.

"So, Sarah," maybe now would be a good time to quiz her about the rumors I had been hearing. She was vulnerable and couldn't go anywhere. "Was Lori-Sue blackmailing you about some real estate transaction?"

She froze and became even more still than she had been. I kept sawing.

"You heard about that, huh."

"Just rumblings."

"Randall Howard was hiding some property from his wife during the financial phase of their divorce. He wanted me to help him. I'll do a lot of gray stuff but draw the line there. I'm not going to help some jerk cheat his wife out of her fair share of their marital assets. Lori-Sue caught wind of it and tried to spin it. She claimed that just because he had approached me, I was in on it. I think she was trying to expand her business and needed cash."

"Wow, Sarah. I'm sorry. Quick question. Why did you have a photo of Lori-Sue's house in your locker?"

Sarah was quiet. "Would you hate me if I told you I was planning to sell her house for a rock-bottom price to get back at her for all the trouble she was trying to cause me, so I kept a photo of her house to remind me?"

"No, Sarah, I don't think I'd hate you more." I laughed so hard I snorted.

After I cut her loose, I didn't feel like such a sitting duck. We weren't helpless. Bad news? The basement door to the upper level was locked, probably with a deadbolt, and there were bars on the basement windows. The windows were also boarded over, I guess the homeowner had moved out and had no intention of being robbed. Now, we needed a weapon; and a tape dispenser wasn't going to cut it—no pun intended.

"We need a weapon," I said.

"Duh."

We again began rummaging through boxes; it was so much easier with two untied hands. I was finding mostly old, musty clothes. Were they musty to begin with, or was the basement odor responsible? My bet was on the basement. Then I was the winner. I found a trophy box. If a trophy didn't scream weapon, I didn't know what did. Sarah came over to me, and we both dug madly through the box, rooting for the biggest, heaviest trophy we could find. I chose "Men's Bowling League, 1998," Sarah, "First Place Varsity Cheer Competition," of course.

"Ok. We have these." She set her trophy down. "Now we need to keep looking for something better."

"Like what, a gun?"

"Yes, like a gun. You forget I'm a licensed real estate agent. You wouldn't believe what some people put in their basements to store!"

She's right, I wouldn't. Who would store a gun in a box down in one's basement?

I wasn't a fan of guns, but what help could they do you down here? "What if a child found one?"

"Quit being such a mom, Katie, but you're right."

And then we heard it. Footsteps. Oh…my…stars.

"Shush," my former mortal enemy quieted me.

I didn't need any help. I was scared silent.

"Do we hide?" Sarah asked.

I nodded. We stealthily made our way behind some boxes. Sarah signaled we should split up; made sense. If our captor found one of us, perhaps the other could sneak up behind her and bash her head in with our trusty trophy. If she didn't come down here now, we really better look around for something deadly. What moments before had seemed ideal now seemed flawed.

But the footsteps receded, and we heard a slight clicking of an outside door.

We both breathed a sigh of relief.

"Oh, my, God," Sarah wheezed, collapsing against a grimy rocking chair. "Now, let's get down to business and find something to get us out of here!"

This proved to be more difficult than it should have been. We found no guns, knives, or power tools. We did find a couple pairs of old ice skates. This brought to mind the Tom Hanks movie, *Castaway*. Didn't he use an ice skate which he found among the floating FED EX packages in the wreckage of his aircraft?

"Hey, Sarah, let's use these skates as a weapon, like Tom Hanks in that movie." I held up a pair.

She stopped. "Brilliant."

Why did the approval of Sarah Deloro mean so much to me? But it did. Maybe because I knew she wouldn't give it unless she thought it was deserved.

She stopped rummaging. "Hand me a pair." She held her hands out.

I handed a clunky pair of yellowed white ice skates to her. She began stripping them of their crusty laces.

"Why are you taking the laces out?"

"Don't know, but I'm hopeful we can use them in another capacity."

Huh, always thinking, that Sarah. She turned one of the skates over and looked at the blade. Not a whole lot of damage was going to be done with them, but I imagined one could crack someone's head nicely with the tip.

Then we heard it again. A door was opened, sounded like the front door.

Now there were two sets of footfalls. Hard to tell, but I was guessing women. The steps weren't heavy. Had Joyce brought a friend?

Sarah motioned for me to hide behind a group of boxes to the right of the basement door. She hid behind the water heater, located against the left side of the room. The door opened. A tan pair of shapely legs began their descent down the basement stairs, followed by another slim set. Excellent two women. Zip ties removed, trusty ice skates at the ready, element of surprise; we could take them. I *hoped* we could take them. What if they had a gun? I could just see Sarah. She held up three fingers. Okay…I thought that meant on the count of three, we'd pounce. Yep, she was counting down with her fingers. This would work, as long as the women proceeded into the room far enough. I wanted to get behind them, not grapple with them face-to-face. *Marcy* was with Joyce and seemed unperturbed.

"Mom, why are we down here? What are we looking for? This makes no sense." Marcy was relentless in her questioning.

Joyce must have thought she was annoying as well, as she shushed her daughter somewhat rudely. But then I would have done the same if I had two women held hostage in a basement.

Sarah's third finger dropped, and we each grabbed the woman closest to us and held the blade against her throat. I still thought a bonk to the head with the tip of the skate's blade would have been more effective. But that was just me. We had decided, by some sort of unspoken agreement, to do it this way.

Both struggled, and neither knew what we were holding against her throat, so slowly, they stopped.

"Okay. No one has to get hurt here," Sarah said as if she were in a movie.

I chanced a look at her and rolled my eyes. *Really?*

She had Joyce, and Joyce squeaked. "Sarah, let's take a moment here. This has gotten out of hand. No need to get all worked up."

"Ya think?" Sarah chortled.

Marcy seemed to be in shock and bounced from foot to foot, moaning. "Mom!"

"Stop her from moving around, Katie!" Sarah ordered.

Well, this was awkward. Could I really continue to restrain a client? But I looked at Marcy. She wasn't taller than me, and she potentially might pose a threat to Sarah and me.

Wow...when did Sarah and I become a team? I did as she said and grabbed Marcy tightly. She didn't resist.

"Now what?" I questioned Sarah.

And then it happened. Joyce must have decided she wasn't going down without a fight. Marcy squealed as her mother, and Sarah went down on the grungy basement floor. I held Marcy back from aiding her mother, which was no easy task, as we watched the two women scuffle. It was nothing like TV. There was a lot of slapping and hair-pulling. It was obvious neither had ever taken a self-defense course, at least, I hoped not. If they had, they had both wasted their money. But my bet was on Sarah. But no...Joyce appeared to be getting the upper hand. She had Sarah down and was sitting on top of her. Enough. I shoved Marcy behind me and conked Joyce on the head with the flat side of my skate. Down she went with a big thunk. Marcy squealed, covering her mouth with both hands.

I turned and glared at her. "Shut...up...Marcy. Do you want some of this?" I waved my skate at her.

Marcy cowered and moved away from me, shaking her head.

"Now pull your phone out from whichever pocket it's in." I knew from experience her cell wouldn't be far from her side. "And call nine-one-one."

On the floor, a heavy-breathing Sarah-Grace grinned at me. We both looked at the fallen Joyce.

"Nice work, Kate."

* * *

Our story was so bizarre, I was glad we had a friend at the Eastbury Police Department, i.e., Brian. They took our statements separately, of course. It took what seemed like hours, but when I checked my watch, it was only 1:00 a.m.

"I need to get home to my daughter." I had called Ellis from Marcy's phone to tell her I was ok, but the call seemed to agitate and worry her more than help.

Ellis didn't need any additional stress. Brian had kindly sent a policewoman over to our house to sit with her until I could make it home. Was this nightmare over?

Joyce wasn't playing it smart but was all but foaming at the mouth, yelling at anyone within reach, proclaiming her innocence. Marcy just cried. I wanted to hug her, but it didn't seem appropriate. Hadn't I just threatened to bop her in the head with an ice skate? My God! I shocked even myself.

Marcy's dad was on his way, and she was going to be released to him. I hoped he was a decent guy; she was going to need a lot of support. And then it hit me as I watched her being led away…I remembered the journal and Marian mentioning that her ex-fiancé had trouble reading, just like Marcy. Did she suffer from the same learning disability as her biological grandfather? For surly, Raymond was Joyce's father.

And Joyce, well, Joyce continued to make a scene. So much for my gauge of people. I couldn't have been more off with Joyce. She was cuffed and placed roughly in the back of a squad car. She would be booked and held over for arraignment. The full charges I didn't know. Murder would be enough, but they could certainly tack on the kidnapping of Sarah and me. I imagined her family would get a top-notch legal guru to avoid embarrassment as much as possible.

Brian loaded Sarah and me into the back of his unmarked, both of us wrapped in blankets. The irony of our situation wasn't lost on any of us, and Sarah and I stole looks at each other and grinned. Then we began to giggle. No, we'd never be friends, but, gosh darn, she had earned my respect. There was an old question, "If you have to be stuck in a foxhole with someone, who would it be?" Well, I'd been in that foxhole with Sarah Deloro, and she was darn good to be partnered with. There was a ruthlessness about her that served her well in her personal life and life-and-death situations. I'd been on both sides of that ruthlessness. I'd take it for life and death but didn't like it much for personal issues—like in high school. Maybe she had grown up since then, but maybe not… I'd keep her at arm's length but didn't want her for an enemy either. Been there, done that.

Chapter Thirty-Two

If you choose a cutting cake instead of a full wedding cake, the cake should be for you and your groom. All other guests should partake of a different delicious dessert. If you don't have enough to serve ALL your guests, you serve none.

I must admit, the aftermath of the fiasco with Joyce was overwhelming and wonderful at the same time. I had never been so fussed over or felt so loved in all my life. Brian and Grant even seemed to have formed a truce, for the short term anyway.

I still had a wicked headache. My mother, holding down the fort at my house, chased *almost* everyone off; and then Brian chased her off. I was glad he stuck around for a while longer. We were sitting in my family room, nestled in my down duvet. Even though it was a balmy 68, warm for a New England spring, we had a wonderful fire going in the fireplace. Ellis had made herself scarce, and Brian was enjoying a Sam Adams. The doctor, who Brian *and* Grant had insisted I see after my run-in with Joyce, had prescribed some mild pain pills for my minor injuries, so I wasn't drinking. Brian helped me eat some of the soup my considerate neighbor brought over. I didn't need any help with the apple pie she also left; to heck with my diet. There was always tomorrow.

"So, I'm the last man standing tonight," Brian said softly. "Does that mean I'm top man in your heart? I was kind of surprised Grant took being nudged home so easily."

I didn't agree with Brian's theory that Grant was hoping for a reconciliation.

"Brian, really. Heather came here with Grant. She's probably at the hotel waiting for him to patch up their lover's quarrel. And besides," a steely quality took over my voice, "I will never, ever, e-v-e-r go back to Grant. He left me, Brian, for another woman, my former friend and neighbor. Give me a break. I do have *some* pride."

And he kissed me. Chastely at first, and then like he meant it.

Chapter Thirty-Three

Assign a responsible person to make sure your wedding gifts and cards are gathered at the end of the evening and safely transported home. Same goes for personal/sentimental items, such as toasting glasses, family photos, and cake cutting knives.

Three days later, Brian and I were at the beach, and we'd had a lovely day. I had always loved the ocean and sorely missed my view of the Pacific when we left our home in California. While the Long Island Sound, which made up Connecticut's beaches, not the Atlantic, wasn't the Pacific Ocean, it had its own special charm. And I was again here with Brian. Once we had gotten our driver's licenses junior year of high school, we had come here plenty in the summer. But this was one of the few times we had come in the early spring. And early spring in New England was very different from spring in California.

Brian and I both had on hoodies, and the wind was chilly. But we were holding hands, and I was warm from the inside. I was looking forward to dinner; Brian was making his famous meatballs and sauce.

I had a failing. I couldn't let things alone. Not happy things, not bad things. I had to get them out there. Usually, not much came from it, and I regretted opening my mouth. But it was…a compulsion, so I spoke. Was it going to be one of those times I hated myself for opening my big mouth?

I stopped walking the beach. I turned to Brian, looked at his tall loveliness, and jumped in. "Brian…" I paused. Did I really want to do this? I looked over his shoulder at the perfect blueness of the ocean. Did I really want to ruin today? Apparently, I did.

"Yeah?" He cocked his head inquisitively at me.

"Why didn't you come that day? At least to talk. I thought we would both benefit from getting it all out."

He grinned. He knew from our short time together in high school that I didn't let anything go. "Come on, Katie. How long ago was that?"

I started walking away from him. Fine. We didn't have to talk about it. We had gone all this time without talking about it.

"Whoa, whoa," he said, gently tugging my arm and stopping my retreat. "Where is all this coming from?"

I didn't want to look at him, but I did. I covered his hand on my arm. All or nothing. I might never have the guts to do this again. "It's always bothered me, Brian. But we went our separate ways. I got married, had Ellis, but now…."

He finished for me. "Now you're back here, we're seeing each other again…"

"Yes. So, why didn't you come that day?" I had to get it out before I lost my nerve. What if he said something I didn't like? Suddenly, I couldn't meet his gaze.

Brian lifted my chin with one finger and forced me to look at him. "When, Katie? What are you talking about?"

"You know, after we broke up, over a stupid fight. I don't even remember what it was about now. But I do remember how I felt when we were broken up, and I had Jen give you a note asking you to meet me after school to…talk."

"What are you talking about? I got a note from Jen soon after we broke up, but you didn't ask me to meet. The note said something like I still care, Brian, I always will, but I need time now. Please respect that, and don't try to contact me…"

I didn't say anything at first. What? Brian looked at me questioningly.

"That's not what my note said. It said, 'I'm sorry for our stupid fight. I don't know what's going on, but we can figure it out together. Meet me today after practice at the tables outside the café,' or something like that." Yeah, something like that, as if I couldn't remember every word of that ill-fated note.

"Katie, I would have been there. I felt awful about how we fought. I wanted to make things right. But, after that note Jen delivered... Well, I just thought I'd better let it alone for a while, and I hoped I'd get another chance. But, as you know, it didn't work out that way."

I knew now why people didn't revisit issues like this. I was mad. All the same emotions I felt so many years ago came flooding back. How was that possible? *It's because you never resolved this,* an internal voice said. I pulled my arm away from Brian more aggressively than I intended. It was so long ago, why did he have to lie to me? I *shouldn't* have brought it up. I never could leave well enough alone. Never. But what...what if he was telling the truth? And really, what reason would he have to lie now? But if Brian wasn't lying, that would have to mean that Jen... No! NO! Jen was my oldest friend in the world. She'd never betray me. Would she do such a thing? But *why* would she?

I could tell Brian was thinking what I was thinking.

"She wouldn't have done that to you, to us, would she?"

I didn't know how to answer. To even put my thoughts into words seemed like a betrayal of Jen. A little voice reminded me I was ready to accuse her of murder mere days ago. But if our suspicions were right... I couldn't even imagine it. Put simply, it floored me; but I had to know.

"I can't fathom it, but now I have to know." I raised my gaze to his.

He opened his arms and held me.

* * *

"Kate! How was the beach?" Jen was all sunshine and light when I called her cell later that day.

I almost hung up. How could I ask her? If I was wrong, would she ever forgive me? If I was right, could I ever forgive her?

"Hi, Jen," was all I could get out. I said nothing else.

"Hi, Kate. What's up?"

I just couldn't say it. I just couldn't.

CHAPTER THIRTY-THREE

"Kate?"

I cleared my throat. "Hey, Jen, can we talk?"

Jen giggled. "Ah, isn't that what we're doing right now?"

I didn't respond.

"What's going on?" The concern was apparent in her voice.

"Can we meet at your shop now?"

She didn't respond right away. "Kate, you're scaring me. You know we're closed. Want to come over here?"

"No, Jen. I think it's better if we meet somewhere alone."

"Thirty minutes?" Jen asked with resolve. Almost as if she *knew*. Almost as if she had been waiting for twenty years.

When I got to Jen's shop, she was already there. Low lights were on behind the coffee bar. I took a moment to stop and look at my friend. Was it really possible? Could Jen have betrayed me all those years ago? If she had, how would I react? My mind was blank.

I walked in, and Jen met me with a steaming cup of my favorite coffee. The shop, always my safe place, felt darker today. It wasn't just the lack of light. It felt unfamiliar. My coffee was already doused with a heavy dose of cream. I took the mug and sat at the nearest table. Jen joined me.

I couldn't wait. If I didn't say it right off, I never would. I'd just let it go. And

I had to know. I had to.

"Jen..." I stopped.

Her face was so worried and so...dear.

But I powered on. "All those years ago, when I gave you that note to give to Brian," I paused here. I knew she would know what note I was referring to. I could stop right now and let it go. I didn't have to ask.

"All those years ago," I started again.

"No, I didn't give it to Brian, Katie." Jen covered her face with her hands. And then she tore my heart out as she sobbed. Deep anguished sobs. "I'm forever sorry and ashamed. I can't explain the motive of that girl of long ago. And yes, I know my actions may have changed the course of your history. I never meant for it to be permanent," she gasped between sobs. "I've wanted to tell you for so long I can't tell you how it has weighed on my heart, how my guilt has worsened since you've been home." In her distress, she wiped her dripping nose on the sleeve of her black t-shirt.

"But, Jen," my soft heart was coming to grips with her betrayal, and I wasn't as mad as I had imagined I'd be. "Brian said he did get a note, but it wasn't what I wrote and gave you."

She said nothing at first but looked somewhere over my left shoulder. I gave her time.

Jen met my gaze. Softy, she said, "I wrote another note and substituted it." There was great shame in her eyes. "Remember that stationary we bought at CVS together?" She didn't wait for my nod. "I used that. I could imitate your handwriting well enough. All of us high school girls basically wrote the same–all hearts and curly q's." She almost smiled.

Was it being a mother that allowed me to view Jen less harshly than I most assuredly would have as the girl back then? Or was it the certainty that I wouldn't have my beloved Ellis had my life included Brian then?

I took her cold hands. "Jen," I started, and then I surprised myself by breaking down too; so much emotion, hard to contain it.

"It wasn't very nice," Wow...how was that for making light of it? "But it was so long ago."

Jen just sobbed louder. Her hands returned to cover her red face. Was it embarrassment or the tears coloring it?

"But why, Jen? Why did you do it? I thought we were the best of friends."

Jen stopped sobbing for a small moment, hiccupping. "We *were* the best of friends, Katie. That's why I did it. I had just broken up with Jack and was so lonely. And then you broke up with Brian, and it was like old times before we got boyfriends. We did everything together. I just couldn't lose someone else I loved again."

"But you wouldn't have lost me! You had to know that."

Jen almost laughed. "I was a teenage girl." And yes, that did say it all.

"Hey," I said softly, pulling her shaking hands away from her face again. "I wouldn't have Ellis." And *that*...was all *I* had to say.

Chapter Thirty-Four

Want to wear flowers in your hair? Consider silk instead of fresh. They will last all night, and if you plan a summer wedding, they won't be affected by the heat.

I was emotionally drained after speaking with Jen. I was surprised at my reaction to her. I thought I would be livid; well, I *was* livid until she started talking. I realized the girl who was so selfish and had wronged me wasn't the woman of today. I loved today's Jen, and I loved the teen. We would get through this.

What I wasn't able to cope with was Grant sitting on my front porch when I got home. I felt violated somehow to see him sitting on my prized porch swing. This was my home, the home I had worked hard to afford, to shelter my daughter, to cherish. He had left me; he had no right to infringe this way.

I parked my Suburban in the drive and walked wearily to the front porch. "What's up, Grant?"

"Nice to see you too, Kate." Grant smiled the "Grant smile."

"Not now, Grant. I'm exhausted." If he only knew how close I had been to never being his. If Jen hadn't pulled her stunt…

"Kate, it won't take long, but we have to talk." He walked toward the front door as if he owned the place. Well, he didn't.

"Not tonight, Grant. I mean it." I stood firm in my words and body.

Just then, Ellis decided to walk out to meet us. "Dad! I didn't know you were going to come over tonight." She truly seemed delighted.

Ellis opened the door wider with a welcome flourish. Golden light spilled onto the porch. And yes, the scene was inviting. Warm air greeted us as we crossed the threshold. It had been a pleasant spring day, but the night had turned chilly as a New England spring night could. Ellis had built a fire. The popping and crackling of the fire met us, along with the smell of baking cookies. Ellis loved to bake. It was almost as if she was setting the scene for a big family reconciliation. I didn't think she had missed her dad much; maybe I had been wrong. Or…was she just being hospitable?

Grant smugly looked around the cozy room. He had wormed his way in. The face he showed me said it. I gave him a sour look in return.

"Hey, kiddo, Mom and I need to talk. Can you please give us a minute? Check the fridge, 'cause after, I'll grill us some burgers if you have the fixin's!"

Really? "Really, Grant?" I hissed as Ellis all but skipped away. I sat on the sofa.

He'd have his way, might as well get it over with.

"Ok, what?" I was unsettled at my rudeness, but why did I have to be polite to the man who cheated on me and was now unwelcome in my home?

"Kate, it's over with Heather. She's headed to New York for shopping and sightseeing before returning to the OC." Grant knew I hated when he called Orange County "The OC." It sounded so pretentious, or like a teen soap opera.

"And I've accepted the job in Hartford. I'll be finding a place in West Hartford. The city planners have done a great job of revitalizing that area. I'll most likely get a condo in Blue Back Square. And then, oh, Kate, I'm so sorry. It was a momentary lack of judgment. It never meant anything with Heather." He tried to hold my hand.

I snatched it out of his reach. "Really, Grant? I bet it meant something to her. Why the sudden turnaround? It doesn't make sense."

"Does it have to make sense?" This time he captured my hand.

I didn't resist. I was too tired.

If I had to make a guess, I'd guess ole Heather was becoming a bit of a nag. Her husband had always said she was. Heather always had a huge "honey-do" list for him. And I'd bet she was putting the pressure on to have a baby. Grant was *not* that guy. He wasn't a terrible father. I bet he really did miss Ellis and softball. They had spent a lot of time in pursuit of the big yellow ball. But a baby? I don't think he'd want to go down that road again. As for me, I had always thought he loved me until he didn't anymore. I bet Ellis had shared tales about Brian, either with intent or not. Grant always wanted what he couldn't have. And he couldn't have me. I didn't care if Ellis wanted her parents together. It was more important she saw that if a man cheated on his spouse, they were done. Expectations. Her husband better know hers. I wished I had made it clear what mine were.

"Yeah, Grant, it kinda does." I stood. "You left me, you left our home, and you left our daughter for another woman. I'm going to make it very clear to our daughter I have more self-respect than to take you back. Now, I think it's great, really, that you'll be close. It will be positive for your relationship with Ellis. But as for you and me, well, there is no 'you and me.' I'm not going to be swayed or courted. We can co-parent and be friends. In fact, I hope we can be friends. One can never have too many friends. But never, ever, EVER, Grant, will we be a couple again. You threw all that away. And no, this is not sour grapes or get-even time." I breathed a sigh of relief. Boy, that felt empowering. I had been waiting a long time to say that. It was therapeutic.

And then I saw Ellis. Her face was unreadable. I wasn't sure if she was crestfallen, surprised, or angry. I held my breath.

Grant saw her too. He smiled his Grant smile, then looked at Ellis and then at me. "Ellis may just have something to say about your feelings, Kate."

Ellis sat next to me, put her arm around my waist, and smiled at her dad. "You know I love ya, Dad. But when you left Mom, you left me." And her smile fell.

I hurt for her. I'd do anything to take her pain away. I thought, at the time, I had been too focused on myself and not on her feelings.

"I'm psyched you're moving here. I miss you, Dad. But Mom's right. You can't leave *us* and come back–well not the way it was. But different can be okay too."

To say I was floored wouldn't do my emotions justice. Wow…just…wow. I didn't think I had ever been prouder of my daughter. I looked at Grant and our daughter.

Grant looked like a deflated balloon. He wasn't used to not getting his way. But Ellis's words were completely defining. I wasn't saying he'd give up, but for now, he was silent.

And, of course, the doorbell rang. What now? My heart flooded with dread. I opened the door, the golden light once again spilling onto the darkened porch. Standing there was Brian–my past and, I hoped, my future.

Chapter Thirty-Five

Make sure a reliable person has instructions to take your wedding gown to a certified wedding gown cleaner and preserver. (Your local dry cleaner may send it out for you to a specialist). Do your research at least a month before your wedding so all is in place. You may think there are no stains, but it's those hidden ones that can do permanent damage over the years.

Eastbury High Girls' softball had made it to the State Finals. It was a well-attended event. The Little League Hot Dog Cart was out. Even the cheerleaders were putting in an appearance. The girls' parents and friends were in the stands, as well as much of the student body. The game was held at the neutral softball field of Southington High School, Southington, Connecticut. Perhaps it wasn't the most politically correct choice as Southington was beaten handily by Eastbury in the semis. Eastbury was playing Fairfield Prep. They had one heck of a team, and the Eastbury girls were in for a fight. But fight they would.

I was in the stands with Brian. Grant was a couple of seats down the bleachers. He tried to keep his eyes and focus on the game and his daughter, but it appeared he was considerably distracted by me above him with my high school boyfriend. I knew my appeal to Grant had gone up when he figured out he was second to Brian. Grant, plain and simple, didn't like to lose. He wasn't going to go quietly. Brian was annoyed by what he called "Grant's crush," but I laughed it off. In private, I didn't think it was so funny. I knew Grant.

The score was 2-1 Fairfield, bottom of the 6th. Only seven innings were played in girls' softball. Eastbury had scored their single run this inning. Top of the 7th, Ellis closed the inning with three strikeouts in a row. Bottom of the 7th, Roxanne, a cute freshman strong enough to make varsity, was at the plate and popped one up—out. Sandra, the third baseman, hit a line drive in the gap between third and the shortstop—solid hit, man on first. Rosemarie, the catcher and the strongest hitter on the team, hit one to the fence. It looked like it was going to go over, but the brilliant center fielder made a miraculous catch—a second out.

Ellis was up. Ellis loved having the game in her hands. I, however, didn't like it. It was the last out of the State Championship. Ellis would either be a hero or regret the swings she took or didn't take forever. I covered my eyes with my hands. Brian pulled them away.

"Katie," he whispered. "You have to watch. You don't want to miss this."

Maybe I do. And then it happened. The most beautiful thing I had ever seen. Ellis, who batted left but pitched and threw right, hit a honey of a ball well over the third baseman's head. It, by no means, was out of the park, but Ellis was fast. I hoped she'd make it to third. Sandra ran home and scored; 2-2. Ellis rounded second, making her way to third. The Fairfield girls were still chasing the ball down in the outfield, but the left fielder had one heck of an arm.

Please let her make it to third without getting out. She'd never forgive herself if she made the last out and lost her team the State Championship. Never mind, she had pitched the game of her life. But it was a team sport, neither won nor lost by any one person. Then Ellis did something no one saw coming. She made it to third with time to spare and continued going. She was headed home. She couldn't make it...could she? If she did, the game was over, a walk-off home run...of sorts. *But she can't make it.*

Ellis ran. She ran hard and fast. The third baseman had received the ball from the left fielder. She caught it as Ellis was on her way home. She threw the ball to the catcher. Ellis started her slide. One thing Grant had done well, he had taught Ellis how to slide like a champ. She slid to the side of the bag to avoid the catcher and the tag. It was close, but all could see Ellis had arrived home well before the catcher could reach her to tag. The cheer that went up in our stands was crazy. It was deafening. I almost felt sorry for the Fairfield Prep fans, and I absolutely did for the team. But not enough to miss out on the joy of this moment. I jumped up and screamed. Brian grabbed me and lifted me off my feet, not easy in bleachers. Grant whooped from his seat below me. He reached over people and hugged me. I hugged him back. Logic said Ellis shouldn't have made a clean slide into home, but then she had tried. Sometimes, if one tried, they would succeed even if logic said they shouldn't. Oh, my, next year was Ellis's senior year. How was the team going to top this?

Chapter Thirty-Six

Your DJ can be your wedding's best friend. He will announce when dinner starts, when the cake is cut, and when the guests' transportation will arrive. He will need a timeline of the important events.

Strawberry Moon –

- When: June 21st (rain date June 28th)
- Where: Main Street and Lebonon Avenue around Fountain Green (roads closed)
- Time: 6:00 – 10:00 p.m.

*New this year ERCI will have a beverage/identification ticket station for the ERCI beverage tents (21 and older). Tickets are $5.00 for wine, beer, and Mike's products, and ID band is $1.00. Ticket tent will be located on the Fountain Green; ERCI beverage tents are located at each end of the venue and will accept tickets only. Restaurant tents are pay as you go as each restaurant keeps 100% of what they sell.

Volunteers: Be part of this great Eastbury tradition—one hour pouring shifts and ticket sales are available and venues set up and take down. High School students will earn community service hours for their time.

Sponsors—information packages will be furnished upon request. To reserve a table is $150.00
Inquire for availability at: erri@mail.yahoo.com

Every June, the sweet burg of Eastbury held an event called "Strawberry Moon." According to an article by *CNN*, a full "Strawberry Moon" in North America was derived from the Native American Algonquin tribe and was their sign to harvest their wild strawberry crop. A huge full moon hung low in the sky and so seemed bigger than your average full moon.

Eastbury closed Main Street and invited all local restaurants to erect a booth and sell their favorite menu items. Beer and wine were also sold, and a band played. Dancing was encouraged, and the street was filled with young and old. It was the one event where middle schoolers partied with their grandparents. In a region where it rained almost as frequently as Seattle, "Strawberry Moon" was almost never rained out. This year was another perfect mild, low-humidity evening.

I wasn't at all surprised to see Ellis and her friends at the event. It brought back happy memories for me of my own "Strawberry Moon" nights. And who was that boy Ellis was dancing with? It looked like one of the Westfield boys, my friend Rainey, the librarian's son. Not sure which one it was. I'd have to ask Ellis later. He was a handsome kid. He looked a lot like his dad had in high school.

It was lovely to see some familiar faces. Addalee went sailing past on her fiancé, Cory's arm. He whipped her around on the dance floor with great enthusiasm. I knew, as their wedding planner, they were taking ballroom dance lessons in preparation for their wedding in the fall.

The last time we had a planning meeting in my Main Street office, *without* Cory, she had opened up about Lori-Sue.

"Lori-Sue found out about some less-than-pure photos I allowed to be taken of me when I was living in New York when Cory and I were broken up. I couldn't make rent, Katie." Addalee hung her head. "I'm so ashamed."

I shushed her. "Addalee, we all do things we regret."

"It was stupid, and somehow, Lori-Sue found out about it. She called me one day and hinted she knew something and that she really wanted to do my wedding flowers. I didn't want to use her. I wanted The Rose Petal but thought I'd better at least hear her out. She wrote up a beautiful PowerPoint presentation for our flowers, from the bouquets to the centerpieces. I was so excited. It was exactly what I wanted. I had made a couple of suggestions, but it was like she was in my mind and put my mental vision in a presentation. I was excited. I didn't care about how she got me to attend this presentation. I wanted her to be our florist. Then, at the end of the presentation, was the price… seventy-five thousand dollars for about eight thousand dollars' worth of flowers. Cory and I weren't going over the top. I thought it must have been a typo. You know, should have been seventy-five *hundred,* not thousand." She paused here. She looked into her lap; a single tear rolled down her cheek. "I'm so ashamed, Katie."

"Addalee, I'm so sorry you had to go through that." I handed her a tissue when she began to sniffle. "It was long ago. You were young. You were alone."

She met my gaze and tried to smile through her tears. "Thanks, Katie. I was uncomfortable but had to point out Lori-Sue's error. And she laughed. It wasn't a nice laugh, Katie. It was harsh and mean. 'It's no mistake, Addalee,' Lori-Sue said. 'It's for my floral artwork and for keeping quiet about your side job in New York back in the day.' I truly didn't know what to do, but then when she was dead, I was safe. I felt such relief. I still feel guilty about being almost happy she was dead. I never did find out what she wanted the money for."

"I think she was hoping to open multiple shops and needed the capital."

"Isn't that what banks are for?" Addalee smiled wryly. She seemed to be feeling better.

"One would hope," I answered.

It was all water under the bridge, but I appreciated Addalee sharing her story about Lori-Sue with me. I never would have asked, but she satisfied my curiosity.

April Summers had also put in an appearance at Strawberry Moon. Barbara had finished the changes on her dress, and wonder of all wonders, she was happy. The dress looked slightly different from the original, but then it had to. I didn't care what kind of seamstress you were; if you were making a dress three sizes bigger than it originally was, something had to give. In all honesty, April wore her fuller figure well. She was too thin when I first met her. Her wedding was quickly approaching. Was I nervous whether I'd have Sweet April or Bridezilla April on her wedding day? Ah, yeah! But that was the nature of the job. That was why I made the big bucks. As for Barbara, I shared with her as much as I was comfortable with about the ring, and she seemed satisfied.

Brian swung me around the Main Street dance floor as well. I couldn't remember the last time I had so much fun. I imagine there were people in the crowd who were surprised to see us together, and there was talk. Yes...Katie and Brian were together again.

I wondered if I'd see Sarah Deloro here tonight. I hadn't so far, but the night was young. I didn't know how I felt about her. Did I still hate her? Would we ever be friends? 'Maybe, it was a small town.

I looked over Brian's shoulder and saw Grant. I felt oddly unsettled. Maybe I wasn't as ready to settle down as I had thought. My attorney, Charlie Wentworth, caught my eye. He had been my knight in shining armor, the handsome devil.

The song ended, and my mutual agreement Brian and I walked toward the bar. A silence came over the crowd, and the band stopped playing. What the...? And then I saw him, Jen's Jack, her high school boyfriend, and now MLB star. He grinned at the crowd, encircling the tiny waist of the woman accompanying him. My eyes flew to Jen. Her face went white.

Wedding Tip #1

Bridesmaids' Duties

Bridesmaid duties...real or ceremonial? Have you heard about the Bride who "fired" one of her bridesmaids via email? The rejected bridesmaid then shared the email on Twitter. I just glanced at a couple of tweets, and the bride was ***crucified by other tweeters!*** What do you think about it?

I bet I am one of the few who was on the side of the bride. Fact is, the "Twitter Bridesmaid" wasn't doing her job. Based on the bride's email to the bridesmaid, which the bridesmaid shared on Twitter, (how's that for a friend?), even though she blacked out the bride's last name, everyone in their social circle knew who she was. The "fired" bridesmaid did absolutely nothing for the bride in her role as honor attendant. When asked to be an attendant, the young lady should have thanked the bride and declined the honor if she couldn't manage the duties. If you don't have the time or money to be a bridesmaid, gracefully decline. Being a wedding attendant is expensive and time-consuming. You are expected to buy your own dress, shoes, gifts, (shower, bachelorette, and wedding), and travel. The bride should spring for your housing the night before the wedding and the night of the wedding, however. You should do your best to attend ALL pre-wedding events–but the rehearsal, rehearsal dinner, wedding...UNTIL THE END, are non-negotiable. If you can't be at those events, you shouldn't be a bridesmaid. Period.

According to the brief email the "fired" bridesmaid shared on Twitter, it appeared she attended no pre-wedding events, (I took it to include the rehearsal and rehearsal dinner but could be wrong), and wanted to fly back before the reception was over. If the bride were my daughter or client, I'd encourage her to suck it up and deal with the lack-luster bridesmaid; but the Twitter bride was well within her scope of expectations to "fire" her friend. As for the email, she probably thought things would be less heated via the written word, and she offered to speak if the bridesmaid desired.

Perhaps "Bridesmaidzillas" are why some brides are opting to have just family members as honor attendants or have no bridesmaids. Perhaps that's why the English use children? Less temperamental than grown women. I think brides today are trying to make it easier on their attendants.

Moral...brides, be sensitive to the costs, both monetary and time, of your attendants; and bridesmaids, say "No, but thank you," if you can't do the job.

Wedding Tip #2

How to Be a Good Wedding Guest

1. Respect whatever the bride and groom choose to do regarding photos during the ceremony and reception. Today, when everyone has a camera on their phone, photos can get out of hand. Some brides today are choosing a "social media blackout" until she can select what to showcase on the internet. Respect that.

2. Don't wear white, cream, ivory, or even blush. That's for the bride. Black used to be a taboo color, but no longer. It's acceptable now.

3. DON'T HIGHJACK THE PHOTOGRAPHER. I think of all the items in this post, this is the most important. I was a guest at a wedding last year. The beautiful wedding ceremony was over. The guests were kindly asked to proceed into the reception tent and enjoy "the cocktail hour" while the bridal party and family members took pictures. Dinner would commence after. What did a group of grown women do? They rounded up their daughters, a couple were bridesmaids, some were not, and grabbed the photographer and strongly asked he photograph them. Now, I do blame the photographer. He could have told them "No." Perhaps the mother of the bride could have stepped in. And as this wedding didn't have a Wedding Coordinator, she wasn't an option. This delayed the photo session by 15 minutes or so, said the Mother of the Groom, when she told me about it. Doesn't sound like a lot of time...but it is.

4. Be a happy guest and don't complain, especially to the mothers of the

bride and groom. A friend related an incident to me recently. She had been the guest at a wedding and a fellow guest had a complaint. She informed the mother of the bride about it, and it was resolved. The guest herself easily could have fixed it. But the guest kept talking about it, to all who would listen. Not very thoughtful.

5. Don't steal others' seats. Three years ago, I attended the wedding of a friend's son. My husband and I claimed our escort cards and went to our table. We were allowed to choose our own seats at our assigned table. We were the first to arrive, and I chose what I thought were GREAT seats. Another guest we were seated with thought so too. I went to greet a friend, and when I returned to our table, she had moved my purse and shawl from our saved seats and put her items there. "I hope you don't mind," she said. "We have a better view here." Normally, I would have said, "Yes, I do mind." But I didn't want to make a scene. I think she counted on that...

6. Don't take a gift to the wedding. A card with your monetary gift, or gift card enclosed, is great to take to the wedding, but a big bulky gift, no. If you'd like to send a gift instead of giving cash, a gift card, or a check, please use the couple's gift registry and have it shipped to the bride's home. Remember, someone at the end of the evening has to get all those gifts home.

Wedding Tip # 3

How to Be a Good Wedding Host

Hopefully, we all know how to be good wedding guests. But do you know how to be a good wedding host? It's not hard. I don't think I've worked with a bride yet who hasn't been thoughtful and considerate of her guests' comfort. But sometimes it's helpful to check-in with some online resources, and you may run across something you haven't thought of yet.

Serving ice cold drinks in the late summer heat? How about a "cozy" to keep that beverage cold and your hands comfortable? You can also consider flip-flops for the ladies to dance in. While high heels are killer for one's fashion sense, they can also be "killer" on the feet.

With an outside wedding, you might encounter a pesky mosquito or two. Never fear, bug spray conveniently located for guests can fix that issue. I love the novelty of hanging a basket of bug spray in trees if there are convenient ones around.

What about a signature cocktail to keep the guests cool as they wait for your wedding to begin? This can be a risk, however, as it's never a benefit to get your guests intoxicated before the wedding begins. You can make everyone happy. Make the beverages quite mild and limit the number to one each. How to do this? Only have a limited number pre-made.

And lastly… you may not always have this option, but if you anticipate a hot day for your outdoor wedding, try to choose a time of day when it won't be as hot and place your guests' chairs in the shade if available.

Wedding Tip # 4

Would You Buy Your Wedding Dress Online?

In the age of online shopping, you can truly buy anything online. As a bride, this makes wedding planning a lot easier. But…would you ever consider buying your wedding dress online? Today, if you Google "trusted online wedding dress site" you get 35,600,000 results, right at your fingertips. You could find any dress you could ever imagine online, but is it worth it? Years ago, I would say no. But now, I think it's a real option to consider.

What I like about the idea of shopping online for a wedding dress is the amount of time you can save, as well as all of the color and design options that are available. Almost anything you can think of can be found online! Not to mention, it's very likely you'll pay a fraction of what you would at a boutique–who wouldn't love that? If you're planning a wedding with a limited amount of time, or you're trying to maximize your efforts, online stores could be your best friend. Some websites even have an option where you can put in your exact measurements, and they'll make your dress custom for you with no extra charge.

If you're having trouble finding a truly unique design, you can find sellers who will make a custom gown for you. Remember, you will need to find a seamstress who will do the final alterations for you, however. Plan this service well in advance. Many seamstresses have long waitlists.

If you've ever seen TLC's show, "Say Yes to the Dress," you'll often see many brides who have traveled to NYC in desperate hope of finding that perfect wedding dress, after numerous failed shopping trips and an approaching deadline. To the bride who is looking for her dream dress and can't seem to find it in person: ditch the boutiques and open up your Internet browser.

Wedding Tip # 5

Whom and How to Invite Guests

If you send a "Save the Date" card to guests, you must send a wedding invitation. If you're unsure about whether or not to invite someone, skip the "Save the Date." You can always invite them later. Likewise, if you invite a lady to your bridal shower, you must invite her to the wedding. This is just being a gracious bride.

Ah...the "Plus Ones." This can be a minefield for you when planning your budget and seating chart. It can also be a source of anxiety for your guests. Be very clear on your wedding invitations. If you're only inviting a single person, his/her name, "Mr. John Doe" goes on the outside envelope with "John" on the inner envelope. I highly recommend the two-envelope invitation option as it helps clarify exactly who is invited. Sometimes people won't keep the outer envelope and then don't know whether they have a plus one or not. If you're giving a guest a "Plus One," the outer envelope says, "Mr. John Doe" and "Ms. Jane Smith." The inner envelope will say, "John and Jane." There is no confusion this way. Not sure of your guest's date's name? Outer envelope, "Mr. John Doe," inner envelope, "John and Guest."

Tip for Further Down the Line

First Comes Love...

What DOES a mother give to her daughter upon the occasion of her first child's birth? I think gifts from the heart are by far the dearest gifts of all. Here are some ideas.

"Mother/Daughter" outfits you wore with your little one when she was a child are sure to be a hit. Before presenting these treasures to your daughter, get them dry-cleaned, if they require that process, or freshly laundered if they are washable. I suggest using Dreft baby soap and stain remover. Babies' skin is so delicate. You must use nothing else than baby soap.

If you have a photo of you and your daughter wearing the matching outfits, make a copy and wrap it up in the package.

What about a handmade gift? If you knit or crochet, a baby blanket is always welcome. Can you ever have too many of those?

Some people like to give religious or personalized jewelry. A tiny enamel St. Christopher metal is a popular choice. St. Christopher is the patron saint of travelers. They are so beautiful, especially when enameled. They make them in varying sizes and colors. You can also get them engraved with a personal message.

The gift of diapers is always a welcome one. I know expectant mothers who purchase a package of diapers, in varying sizes, every time they go to the market or houseware retail store. Baby shower guests will sometimes get into the spirit of the diaper collection and bring a package along with their shower gift. Often the party hostess will suggest this on her invitation. Sometimes the hostess will purchase a bunch herself and create a "diaper cake." This requires opening the packages, though, which I don't recommend.

BRIAN'S SPICY MEATBALLS

Ingredients:

½ lb. spicy Italian sausage
½ lb. ground beef
2 cloves chopped garlic
½ cup chopped parsley
1 egg, beaten
1-cup breadcrumbs
½ cup Parmesan cheese
½ tsp. salt
¼ tsp. pepper
½ cup milk
1 small onion
1 tsp. cayenne pepper

Instructions:

- Crumble sausage and combine with ground beef.
- Combine garlic, parsley, egg, breadcrumbs, parmesan cheese, salt and pepper in large bowl. Pour milk over the mixture. Mix thoroughly but don't pack too tightly.
- Form meatballs. Some people like bite-size meatballs, other prefer larger, both are good choices.
- Place each on a baking tray and bake at 375° degrees for 30-45 minutes or less for smaller meatballs.
- Remove and add to sauce (see next recipe) and simmer for one hour.

BRIAN'S SAUCE

Ingredients:

1 can of 14 or 16 oz. diced tomatoes
1 can 14 or 16 oz. canned tomatoes
1 small onion, diced
I bell pepper, diced
1 can 6 oz. tomato paste
2 cloves chopped garlic
1 tsp. cayenne pepper
2 Tbsp. olive oil
½ tsp. sugar
2 tsp. basil
1 tsp. salt

Instructions:

- Add tomatoes to a large pot and simmer over low heat then add onion and bell pepper to the mixture.
- Add all remaining ingredients and simmer for a minimum of one hour.
- Remove from heat. Use hand blender to make sauce smooth (be careful, it's hot).
- Return to stove and simmer as long as desired.
- Add meatballs (from the previous recipe) to warm.

MOON ROCK MUFFINS

These are dense muffins but quite moist. A tasty way to get fiber and extra fruit into your diet!

Ingredients:

Cooking Spray
1-1/4 cup whole-wheat flour
1/2 cup ground flax seed
1/2 cup oat bran
2 tsp. baking powder
1/2 tsp. baking soda
1/2 tsp. salt
1/2 cup vegetable or canola oil
3/4 cup sugar
2 eggs
1 tsp. vanilla
2 ripe bananas
Fifteen pitted prunes*
1 apple, peeled, cored, and roughly chopped (or 1/2-cup applesauce)
3/4 cup semi-sweet mini-chocolate chips
1 cup Craisins or raisins (or a combination)

Instructions:

- Preheat oven to 350°.
- Line two 12-cup muffin tins with cupcake wrappers and spritz wrappers with cooking spray.

- Whisk flour, flax seed, oat bran, baking powder, baking soda and salt together in a medium bowl. Set aside.
- Place oil, sugar, eggs, vanilla, bananas, prunes, and apple into a large mixing bowl. Using a hand-held immersion blender, puree until mixture is blended and apples and prunes are very tiny pieces. Alternately, you can use a food processor to puree the ingredients together.
- Add dry ingredients to the fruit mixture and stir by hand until moistened.
- Add chocolate chips and Craisins/raisins and stir until incorporated.
- Fill cupcake liners 3/4 of the way full of the batter. I like a spring-loaded 2-Tbsp. cookie scoop for this.
- Bake at 350° for 18-20 minutes, rotating the pans halfway through the baking period. Remove from pan and cool on wire rack.
- Makes 22-24 muffins.

These will keep for five days stored in an airtight container. If you live in a very hot and humid place, you may want to store in the refrigerator. Alternately, wrap individual muffins in plastic wrap or foil and place in a freezer-safe Ziploc bag. Freeze for up to four months. Remove muffins from the freezer as needed, leave the plastic wrap on and thaw until room temperature. Reheat in the microwave for fifteen seconds and enjoy!

*If you don't have an immersion blender or food processor, place prunes in a heatproof dish with 2 Tbsp. of water and cover with plastic wrap. Microwave on high for 1-1/2 minutes. Remove and let cool slightly, then finely mince before adding to recipe.

KATE'S CREAM CHEESE BROWNIES

Ingredients:

1 4 oz. package Baker's sweet chocolate
5 Tbsp. butter
1 3 oz. package cream cheese
1 cup sugar
3 Eggs
1 Tbsp. flour
½ cup sifted flour
1½ tsp. vanilla
½ tsp. baking powder
¼ tsp. almond extract
½ cup chopped nuts (optional)

Instructions:

- Melt one package Baker's sweet chocolate and 3 Tbsp. butter over very low heat (or use double boiler or microwave). Stir then cool.
- To make cheese layer, cream the cream cheese with 2 Tbsp. butter. Gradually add 1/3 cup sugar, creaming until fluffy. Blend in one egg, flour and ½ tsp. vanilla. Set aside.
- To make chocolate layer, beat 2 eggs until light colored. Slowly add ¾ cup sugar and beat until thickened. Add baking powder, almond extract, and chopped nuts (optional).
- Preheat oven to 350°. To bake, spread half the chocolate batter in greased and floured 8- or 9-inch square pan. Top with cheese mixture. Spoon remaining chocolate batter over top. Zigzag knife through batter to

marble. Bake at 350° for 35-40 minutes. When inserted toothpick comes out clean, it's ready! Enjoy! These are one of Ellis's favorites.

Acknowledgements

I must first start with my husband, Ken. You have made it possible for this work to be. As a writer, I should be able to put into words what your strength and love has meant. Alas, some things are too great to put pen to paper.

To my children and grandchildren, Tyler, Kathleen, Maggie, Rob, Tess, Julia, Lily, Teddy, Bill, and Charlotte, I don't think anyone has had better cheerleaders. Thank you, I love you all.

Charles Salzberg – wow – thank you for being my friend and guide. You started me on my way.

To my darling cousin, Kim Davis, more sister than cousin, you have been my support and inspiration my entire life, including my writing life. Thank you.

To my agent, Dawn Dowdle, you believed in me, you made this happen. You are not only my agent, but my friend. There is no one better.

Shawn Simmons and Level Best Books…how can I thank you for giving me this opportunity? Well,…thank you, thank you! You have been a joy to work with and I look forward to many more years of happy collaboration.

To Stephanie Perkins, my first writer-friend and now friend-friend. Thank you for your unconditional availability and friendship. What a delight to have met how and when we did.

Susan Furlong, thank you for investing your time and energy in me. I'm so grateful. I appreciate your friendship so.

Thank you to Hank Ryan for being supportive and an inspiration.

To Kate Young and Dana King-Esquer, thank you for your social media love, it takes a village. This includes all my writer friends, virtual and live who have so kindly taken me under their wing.

To Korina Moss, Shari Randall and Jane Willan, my Connecticut writer buddies, I love the lunches and coffee dates with our lively industry talk. It has kept me happy and sharp. Thank you for being resources and my friends.

Mom and Dad…I wish you were here to see this publication, but know you are nudging each other and saying, "She did it."

This has been extensive, thank you for reading. I'm blessed to have such a long list of thanks and I know it.

About the Author

Mary Karnes, a college English major and former teacher, is the mother of four who raised her family though six corporate moves. She always dreamed of being an author and dabbled with writing throughout the years. Once the children were grown and out of the house, she started a wedding planning business, while simultaneously chasing her dream of being a traditionally published author. Her 'Wedding Planner Mystery Series' was born, with her business providing delicious subject matter for her books.

Mary resides in New England with her husband, Ken, and her mini-dachshund, Lucky. Her door is a revolving one with her children and grandchildren visiting frequently.

SOCIAL MEDIA HANDLES:

@marypkarnesauthor – Instagram
@marypkarnesweddings – Instagram
MaryKarnesauthor- Facebook

AUTHOR WEBSITE:

marykarnesauthor.com

Printed in the USA
CPSIA information can be obtained
at www.ICGtesting.com
JSHW021949130823
46470JS00003B/6

9 781685 12403